THE FLEECING OF
FORT GRIFFIN

THE FLEECING OF FORT GRIFFIN

A WESTERN CAPER

PRESTON LEWIS

THORNDIKE PRESS
A part of Gale, a Cengage Company

Copyright © 2016 by Preston Lewis.
Thorndike Press, a part of Gale, a Cengage Company.

ALL RIGHTS RESERVED
Thorndike Press® Large Print Hardcover Western.
The text of this Large Print edition is unabridged.
Other aspects of the book may vary from the original edition.
Set in 16 pt. Plantin.

**LIBRARY OF CONGRESS CIP DATA ON FILE.
CATALOGUING IN PUBLICATION FOR THIS BOOK
IS AVAILABLE FROM THE LIBRARY OF CONGRESS.**

ISBN-13: 979-8-8857-8563-1 (hardcover alk. paper)

Published in 2023 by arrangement with Preston Lewis.

Printed in Mexico
Print Number: 1   Print Year: 2023

For John Kemp,
with admiration

CHAPTER 1

A battered feed pail in one hand and a fractured wooden shingle in the other, orphan Sammy Collins was collecting horse droppings off the dusty street the day royalty arrived in the West Texas town of Fort Griffin. Local folks had seen plenty of red blood on the town's haphazard streets, but never a blue blood like Jerome Manchester Paget, Baron Jerome Manchester Paget, to be precise. No Fort Griffin visitor had ever created such a stir as the Baron Paget.

Nor had any man ever arrived in Fort Griffin with $25,000 in an English club bag and the look of a dupe on his royal face. And Sammy Collins was there to greet the esteemed baron as perhaps the only guileless resident of Fort Griffin, in spite of the bad breaks that had befallen him in his young life. Young Collins was as hopeful about his future as any young person could

7

be in Fort Griffin in the spring of 1878.

The town of Fort Griffin clung to the banks of the Clear Fork of the Brazos like a scab to a wound, the farthest outpost of civilization in West Texas, excepting El Paso. At least the buffalo hunters thought it civilization, but then they had been out on the High Plains all winter, sleeping on the hard, cold ground or under some canvas tarp that passed for flimsy, wind-whipped shelter.

Of course, the itinerant Baptist preacher who had once ventured into town to singe sin in its many local variations considered Fort Griffin uncivilized and counted as proof its eight saloons, four dance halls, three gambling dens and, most especially, its many cribs where women entertained men. The preacher, however, had conceded the town to Satan and moved back East where ministers were respected instead of ridiculed and where iniquity had lost its rough edges.

The winter kill was over and the buffalo hunters had returned, grizzly and itchy. They camped on the outskirts of town, their piles of flinty buffalo hides splotching the open land like festering, black sores. Acres of hides were baled or staked on the open land that stretched between the Clear Fork's tree-lined bank and the limestone outcroppings at the slope of Government Hill, a plateau topped by the military post which shared its name with the town below. By some estimates a million hides fermented in the early May sun, bits and pieces of flesh turning to death's rot, the stench attracting flies by the millions and rats by the thousands until the earth around the hides seemed to writhe with vermin. Occasionally, the stench had been known to gag an army bugler when the wind carried the pungent odor up Government Hill. The hunters, though, were long accustomed to the smell and the townspeople accepted it as the aroma of money since the hides this May were said to be bringing three dollars apiece at markets in Kansas. The buffalo trade dominated the look and smell of Fort Griffin such that some people called the place "Hide Town" to differentiate it from the army post on the hill.

The army payroll, the hide trade, and the emerging cattle operations gave local merchants a swaggering cockiness that this town was the city of the future in West Texas. Merchants like Zach Fenster would stand outside their mercantile emporiums, rocking on their heels, their thumbs hooked in their suspenders, their noses held high as they inhaled the aroma of money, secure in Hide Town's economic survival. While a few lesser West Texas communities like Albany to the south were scrambling to get a railroad extension out of Fort Worth, the Fort Griffin town fathers were confident that no railroad worth having would bypass a town as important as Fort Griffin.

After all, why would royalty, especially royalty with a satchel containing $25,000 ever have come to Fort Griffin were it not such a consequential community, soon-to-be consequential city?

As he prospected for fresh horse droppings along dusty Griffin Avenue, fourteen-year-old Sammy Collins didn't consider Hide Town to be of any import, nor the afternoon stage to be any different from the dozens of others he had met the last three years, ever since his parents had died of smallpox and he had been taken in by the Millers, who ran the Planter's House. Moses Miller and his wife were so beloved by the folks of Hide Town that everyone called them Uncle Moses and Aunt Moses. They were a fine couple, Sammy Collins figured, if you didn't work for them in their hotel. They had taken him in, for sure, but their benevolence was tempered by the idea of cheap labor to do the hard and irksome work that was a part of running a hotel. They put him up in a lean-to shed abutting the back of the hotel so as not to remove a room from paid public use. And, they set him to work washing dishes, sweeping floors, emptying slop jars, chopping wood, fetching supplies, doing laundry and cleaning the one spittoon Aunt Moses permitted in the hotel.

Sammy's duties included meeting each stage and convincing new arrivals to patronize the Planter's House. That would have been his favorite job were it not for Alonzo Giddings, his sixteen-year-old rival from the competing Southern Hotel. Because of Alonzo, Sammy was scooping horse droppings into the feed pail and drawing the stares of passing men and women. A horse trotted by, lifted its tail, and added to the mother lode of manure that was typical on a dusty Fort Griffin street. Collins ambled over to the scattered deposit, a trace of steam rising from its moist warmth, and scooped it up with the shingle fragment. Dumping the steaming chunks into his pail, Sammy felt his face redden at the laugh of saloonkeeper Burley Sims, who was sweeping the boardwalk in front of the Bee Hive saloon.

"Aunt Moses baking a horse apple pie or

11

has she finally run out of things for you to do?" Sims called out.

Sammy skulked toward the Bee Hive. "I lost a bet to Alonzo."

Sims clucked his tongue and leaned on his broom. "Tell me more."

"Whoever registered the fewest passengers off the last stage had to collect horse apples and toss them at the feet of passengers on the next stage." Sammy shoved the shingle in the pail.

Sims shook his head. "You won't get many customers off today's stage, then. Sounds like a foolish bet."

"He said he'd whip me if I didn't."

"Just don't dump the droppings."

Sammy shrugged. "He's bigger than me."

"And a bully," Sims responded. "Just punch him in the nose."

Sammy cocked his jaw at Sims. "I'd get whipped. You ever been whipped?"

Sims shook his head slowly, deliberately. "I haven't always won, Sammy, but I've never been whipped."

"Huh?" Sammy scratched the cowlick in his muddy brown hair.

"If you stand up for yourself, you may not win but you'll never get whipped. If you don't make a stand, you'll always be gathering horse apples."

12

Sammy lifted the shingle from the pail and stared at it. "Uncle Moses says to turn the other cheek."

"You can only turn your cheek so far before you break your neck, Sammy." Sims pointed to the Clear Fork crossing at street's end. "Stage's coming."

Sammy spun around, seeing the Bain and Company coach a half mile beyond the river crossing. "Thanks, Burley," he called, then darted back up the street toward the stage office.

Like vultures awaiting a fresh carcass, three dozen men and women gathered outside the sun-bleached office. Elbowing his way through the spectators, the stage agent strode out into the middle of the street, megaphone in hand. A bulldog of a man with sagging jowls, the agent scowled at the passing riders and jerked the megaphone to his lips. "Afternoon stage," he yelled. "Women and children clear the street. Bain and Company is not responsible for any injuries to those who fail to heed this warning."

The admonition reminded Sammy that today's was Shorty DeLong's stage run. Sammy angled for the stage office a little faster than before. Shorty, a bantam rooster with red hair and eyes squinty from hours

13

of driving into the sun, had never been and vowed never to be late at the reins of a Bain and Company stage. Rumor said his impetuous driving had trampled one old woman, not to mention dozens of slow dogs and cats and an occasional pig that wandered around Hide Town. From beyond the Clear Fork, the pounding of hooves, the rumbling of wheels and the rattling of wood and metal in motion sounded like distant thunder.

When he reached the plank walk in front of the stage office, Sammy realized Alonzo Giddings was standing beside him, his smile as crooked as his teeth and his intent. Planting his balled fists on his hips, Alonzo spat at the pail. "That all you got?"

Sammy lifted the pail to Alonzo's face.

The bully scrunched his nose and pushed Sammy's hand away. "We bet a bucket full."

"This'll do."

Alonzo waved his fist at Sammy's nose. "Don't forget to dump it or . . ."

"Or, you'll whip me," Sammy mocked. "I remember." He strode away from Alonzo, several spectators wrinkling their noses as he passed. He looked around, nodding at Marshal Gil Hanson, who stared suspiciously at his bucket. Hanson generally met the stage to keep up with troublemakers arriving in town.

14

"Women and children clear the street," growled the Bain and Company agent as the stage splashed through the water crossing. "Danger's approaching." The agent lifted the megaphone above his head and — like the Biblical Moses parting the Red Sea — watched a wide path open up down the middle of Griffin Avenue. Then, the agent joined the stampede, taking a place beside the marshal on the plank walk.

Behind the spectators lurked the Tonkawa Indian everyone called "Cat Tails," a sobriquet bestowed upon him for his stealthy habit of slipping up behind stray cats and whacking off their tails. Unlike the arriving stage, Cat Tails was as silent as the approaching dawn. The necklace he wore was made not of prized bear claws, but of cat tails, maybe three dozen. His muscled chest siphoned down into a narrow waist where a sheathed knife hung over a loin cloth. His greasy leather leggings lapped over equally greasy moccasins. His black hair, shining from animal tallow and hanging in thick strands down his back, was circled by a beaded leather band punctured by three drooping turkey feathers. His eyes and disposition were dark, his nose wide, his hands nimble.

Cat Tails fidgeted nervously as his dark

eyes studied Colonel John Paul Jenkins, commander of the military outpost just up the hill. The colonel's father had named him for the great naval commander John Paul Jones and had expected his son to become a third-generation Navy man. John Paul Jenkins had nothing against the Navy, except for two things — ships and water. Ships were unsteady and water was never still. The combination left his knees mushy and his stomach turbulent. If seasickness were a sin, John Paul Jenkins was bound for hell in the Navy. He went into the Army, thinking that service — even land-based service — to his country would mollify his father's naval ambitions for him. The son had been wrong. The father had seen West Point not as a compromise between father and son but rather as outright rejection of all his paternal and naval values.

As his father had been hard on him, John Paul Jenkins had been hard on soldiers under his command. He hated shirkers, malingerers and, most of all, deserters, men like Private Burns, the fort's appropriately named cook and baker. The private took criticism of his cooking as poorly as the soldiers of Fort Griffin took to his meals. Consequently, he deserted regularly, his brief absences making the troops, if not

16

fonder of his meals, at least more reluctant to criticize them. After three desertions and three re-captures the previous month, John Paul Jenkins had had enough of Private Burns' fickle devotion to his country. If Private Burns failed to execute his assigned duties, the colonel would simply execute him. And, he did!

Bad as Burns' cooking had been, it was better than anything the troops had eaten since his burial. Private Burns had carried to the grave all the recipes for the fort. It was one thing to make a single loaf of bread and another to make enough to feed a troop of cavalry. With his men on the verge of mutiny because of poor meals, Colonel Jenkins realized he might have made a mistake in executing Private Burns, especially since he hadn't notified his superiors of his plans. Perhaps some man with cooking skills would step off that stage to save his Army career.

From down the street, the stage rumbled toward them like a coach from hell, churning up dust and apprehension. The six horses pulling the stage were mismatched except for their wide eyes, their flaring nostrils, their bared teeth, their sweat-flecked hides, their heaving chests, and their pounding hooves. The stage swayed from side-to-side as if out of control and on the verge of toppling over and flinging passengers and baggage and mail all the way to the Rio Grande. Bouncing in the driver's box, Shorty DeLong surveyed the street through the cloud of dust, his gaze as nonchalant as his greasy boot calmly tapping on the footboard. His left hand held the reins and his right hand snapped the whip that kept the horses plunging ahead. Shorty DeLong appeared too small, too insignificant to control the 2,500-pound stage and the six galloping animals.

Folks up and down the street trembled as Shorty DeLong aimed the coach for the stage office. "Whoa, damn you, whoa!" he finally yelled, his rough voice hoarse and deep from years of road dust lodged in his throat. His right hand joined his left on the reins, and he jerked back on the leather strands, his foot shoving the brake lever forward, the horses' heads rearing up as he tugged. The back wheels locked, giving off wisps of smoke as the stage slid toward the walk and retreating spectators. By instinct, DeLong released the brake a moment, the wheels spinning long enough for the jehu to compensate for the slide before he shoved his foot against the brake lever again. The stage came to a sudden halt precisely in front of the stage office, but the cloud of dust kept moving down the street as if it were hitched to the souls of the horses. As the dust cleared the coach, Shorty DeLong tied the reins around the brake handle.

"Fort Griffin, on time like always," De-Long announced as he climbed out of the driver's box onto the front wheel, then jumped to the street.

The crowd breathed again and stepped forward, Alonzo Giddings pushing Sammy Collins and his bucket to the front. "Dump it," Giddings demanded.

Collins hesitated.

"Now!" screamed Giddings.

Taking a deep breath, Sammy lifted the bottom of the bucket and flung its contents at Shorty DeLong's boots as he approached the door to the coach.

"What the hell?" Shorty spun around, his boots wading into the droppings. He looked from his boots to Sammy. "Boy, you been eatin' loco weed?"

Sammy shrugged and motioned with his thumb toward Alonzo.

Alonzo Giddings laughed. "Sammy just threw out a Planter's House welcome mat. I happen to represent the Southern Hotel, the best in town."

Feeling his cheeks burn with embarrassment, Sammy Collins flung the pail under the stage. "Best rooms in town at the Planter's House. Only hotel with feather mattresses," he called by rote. "Good food and good rates for room and board."

Shorty DeLong unfolded the metal step at the foot of the coach door, but before he could finish, the door swung open, knocking his hat off. "Hold your horses," Shorty DeLong said gruffly as he grabbed his hat and brushed off a smudge of manure.

A man, a gambler by his dress, poked his head out the door. "Why should I? You didn't hold your horses," he answered, then emerged from the coach, planting his foot confidently on the step and looking at the swath of horse manure strewn before him. He jumped from the step toward the walk, landing with the graceful balance of a cat just beyond the trail of horse droppings. He swatted at the lapels of his black broadcloth coat drawing little puffs of dust, then tugged at his string tie. His eyes, dark and narrow like the mustache above his slender lips, studied the crowd, then came to rest on Gil Hanson and the marshal's badge on his chest. The man pursed his lips and brushed his coat away from his hip, revealing an oiled .45-caliber Colt Revolver, then started toward the marshal.

Before the man could take two steps, Colonel John Paul Jenkins slid into his path. "Pardon me, sir," said the officer, "you wouldn't happen to be a cook or baker would you?"

His mouth curling into a snarl, the man studied the colonel. "If you're looking for someone to do your cooking, you need a wife. For that, I'd suggest a woman." The gambler brushed by the officer and headed straight for the marshal.

Gil Hanson's hands turned clammy for this man had the look of a gambler or a gunfighter, two species Hanson despised but seldom challenged. Hanson felt his back stiffen.

Cat quick, the stranger lifted his hand, extending it cordially to the lawman. "Marshal, Joe Loper's my name. I'm a gambler who runs a straight game. I'll be in Fort Griffin a while and I plan to stay on the straight. I want you to know that up front."

Slowly, Gil Hanson took Joe Loper's soft hand, the hand of someone who had done little manual labor, someone like a gambler. Gil Hanson studied Joe Loper a moment. Should a gambler who called himself honest actually be trusted? Before acknowledging Loper, Hanson looked past him to the stage. "Any more passengers, Shorty?"

"One," DeLong said, "a prissy Englishman, royalty, so he says."

Loper's grip tightened around the marshal's hand. "That's what I wanted to talk to you about, Marshal. You need to keep a close watch on this Englishman."

Hanson pulled his hand from the gambler. "How's that, Loper?"

"That damn fool is carrying a satchel full of money, and he's not bashful about letting folks know," Loper said, glancing back over his shoulder. "In a town rough as this, he could get killed quick."

Hanson studied Loper a moment, thinking maybe he had misjudged the gambler. "Worried about him, are you? That's mighty ..."

"Sure am, Marshal," Loper replied. "I don't want anyone taking him or his money before I get him in a card game."

Hanson coughed. He hadn't misjudged Loper after all.

"What's the best saloon in town, Marshal?"

Hanson shrugged. "Most folks say the Bee Hive. Me, I say they're all trouble."

Loper tipped his hat. "Good day, Marshal." Loper turned to the stage driver. "I need my bag," he demanded of DeLong.

"Just a minute," DeLong said, never even

gazing Loper's direction. With balled fists planted on his hips, DeLong faced the stage. "You ever coming out, your royal highn-ass?"

"The damn Englishman can wait a minute," Loper said. "I'm a Texan and royalty don't mean beans to me. Now get my bag."

DeLong withered under Loper's scowl. Moving to the back of the coach, he untied the leather thongs holding the tarp over the rear boot. He grabbed a carpetbag and tossed it at Loper.

The gambler caught it chest high. "I've got a couple bottles of good liquor in here. If you broke either, I'll be back to settle damages."

Marshal Hanson watched Loper stride away. By nightfall, thanks to Loper, every thief, swindler, and murderer in Fort Griffin would know about the Englishman and his satchel full of money. The marshal's job would grow more complicated with each re-telling of the Englishman's arrival. The Englishman hadn't even gotten off the stage and already the marshal was anxious for him to leave.

"Your royal highn-ass," DeLong called again, "I don't want to spend the rest of my life in Fort Griffin."

Slowly, the Englishman poked his head

out of the stage, like a turtle emerging from its shell. "Lacking my valet," he commenced, his English enunciation drawing smiles from all the faces except the Indian Cat Tails, "I require more time, governor, to get my effects in order."

DeLong thrust his chest forward, announcing to the crowd, "He calls me 'governor' and I call him 'his royal highn-ass.' " DeLong moved to take the man's satchel or cane, but the Englishman waved him off, eased down the two steps, then hopped to the ground, his polished shoes landing in clumps of horse manure.

Alonzo Giddings laughed. "You can have that dude, Sammy. He'd stink up the Southern Hotel, but you'll never know the difference at Planter's House."

From the back of the crowd a terrifying scream pierced the air, followed by a commotion as Cat Tails shoved his way up front, brandishing his knife and a wild look upon his face. He sprang off the wooden walk and landed in front of the Englishman, his legs astride the swath of horse droppings.

Startled for a moment, the Englishman smiled at the crowd, especially as the Tonkawa waved his knife over his head. Cat Tails took up a chant of gibberish, then pointed to the Englishman's shoes.

24

"Bravo," the Englishman called, dropping his satchel atop a clump of horse apples at his feet and shoving his cane under his arm. He held up his left hand at his chest and patted it with his right, his effeminate applause drawing snickers from several. "Excellent theatrical," he pronounced. "Now, allow me to announce myself. I am Jerome Manchester Paget, Baron Jerome Manchester Paget, late of London and now of Texas, where I have come to enlarge my fortune so that I may continue to live in the splendor that has been known in the Paget family for almost two centuries."

Cat Tails kept chanting and gesticulating with the knife.

The baron seemed amused by the spectacle. "Fascinating aboriginal display," Paget intoned, studying the Indian while all around folks gawked at him, his maroon cutaway coat, his gray and maroon-plaid trousers, his white shirt yellowed from road dust, the lion's head cane under his arm and the black bowler hat atop a neatly combed nest of brown hair. He stood just under six feet tall with piercing gray eyes, a hawk-like nose, and a close-cropped brown beard and mustache in the style of the Prince of Wales. The beard made him appear older than his years. His jutting jaw, his direct gaze, and his stolid stance reaffirmed his claim of royalty. His occasional effeminate mannerisms like his delicate manner of applauding or the toss of his head were gestures drawn from a gentler society of fancy balls, audiences with the queen, sailing boats, afternoon teas, and fine meals served with sterling silver on imported bone china.

A broad smile creasing his face, Shorty DeLong jumped beside the baron and pushed Cat Tails aside. Ever mindful of the Army colonel to one side and the city marshal to the other, Cat Tails made a playful feint at the driver with his knife. Shorty DeLong ignored the Indian, turning to the baron and then to the crowd. "Tell them, your royal highn-ass, how you plan to make your fortune here."

"Ranching, governor," Paget said, with a wave of his gold-headed cane and a lift of his regal chin. "I'll start the first buffalo ranch in Texas."

Laughter rippled through the crowd, then ended suddenly with the realization that here was a man who could be taken. Marshal Gil Hanson shook his head and pinched the bridge of his nose. Keeping an eye on the baron would be a full-time job. As much as he hated gamblers, he much preferred to keep watch over them than over fools.

"That's not a cod, a howler," Paget responded, looking over the crowd of puzzled faces. "How do you say it, you Yankees? A joke? That's not a joke. The hide market will survive long after you have decimated the beasts. I propose to extend my fortune by raising buffalo for that market."

Sammy Collins groaned. This Englishman had less sense than a tortoise had feathers. Even so, Sammy at least owed him the courtesy of wiping the manure off his satchel. Sammy picked up the bag and began to scrape off the sticky droppings with his pocket knife.

"Thank you, lad. Can you show me a flat?" Paget asked.

Sammy shook his head. "A flat?"

"A kip or a room, lad, a room."

Sammy smiled. This Englishman spoke funny. "I can, sir."

"Bravo, lad, bravo. There'll be a drop in it for you."

"A drop, sir?"

"A gratuity, lad, a gratuity, what you may call a tip." Sammy smiled again.

Shorty DeLong shook his head. "A tip? Why his royal highn-ass has more than a tip on him. Tell the fellows what you've got in your carpetbag there."

"Five thousand pounds, governor," Paget answered. "That's all."

The spectators groaned, one pointing at Sammy Collins holding the carpet bag. "Not a man in Fort Griffin could pick up 5,000 pounds, much less a boy," challenged a surly aproned merchant who had just joined the crowd.

"It's not weight," Paget explained, "but money. British money." The baron took the carpetbag from Sammy Collins, unhooking its catch, then spreading its mouth like he would the jaws of a trophy lion. He offered a glance to the skeptics of bundles of money tied with twine and stacked inside. He smiled at their gaping mouths and jerked two one-pound notes from the bundles. He offered one to Sammy and the second to the Indian.

Sammy had never seen such odd paper money.

"That note's worth about five dollars American specie," Paget announced.

Turning to Alonzo Giddings, Sammy Collins loosed a wide smile.

Cat Tails stared at his note a minute. Paper like this always made him thirsty. Cat Tails didn't understand all the white man's ways, especially since funny inked paper was usually worth a few drinks. He whooped and dashed away for the back door of the Bee Hive saloon.

Colonel John Paul Jenkins stared contemptuously at Cat Tails, then turned and marched to his Army mount hitched down the street.

"Okay, fellows," called Marshal Hanson, "you need to do like the Colonel and get back to your business. No other passengers."

"The Englishman's enough," one man called, drawing the laughter of several and the hard stare of the marshal. Shortly, the crowd melted away, several men looking back over their shoulders at the baron, burning his profile into their brains should they meet him in the night or alone when they might relieve him of his 5,000-pound satchel.

"My trunk, please," the Englishman commanded Shorty DeLong, who motioned for the stage agent to help pull it from the back boot.

Marshal Hanson sidled up to Baron Jerome Manchester Paget, extending his hand. "Baron, I'm Marshal Hanson."

"Ah," Paget said, "the local constable. I am distinctly honored that you would meet my carriage upon its arrival. This is a singular honor that no other Texas community has extended me."

"I meet all the stages," Hanson replied.

"Ah, you Yankees, always so democratic in your traditions. I commend you for honoring the common man as well as royalty."

Hanson shook his head. "Mostly what we get here are common murderers and thieves. That's what I want to talk to you about, Baron." He motioned for the Englishman to join him on the walk.

Nodding, the baron shut his English club bag and offered it to Sammy Collins. Paget moved to the lawman, then used the tip of his cane to scrape the manure off his glossy shoes.

Hanson whispered, "It's not a good idea to show your money so freely. Many hard men in these parts would kill you for it."

The baron stroked his close-cropped beard, pursed his lips, and nodded. "Constable, sir, I am indeed gratified by your concern for my well-being, but let me assure you I am prepared to defend myself and my belongings." As he spoke, the baron unbuttoned his coat and lifted his lapel. There, beneath his left armpit, rested a tiny holster and a tinier revolver.

From what he could see of the weapon, Marshal Hanson suspected it was a .22-caliber Colt New Line Revolver. With a barrel two-and-a-quarter inches long, the Colt

New Line was accurate at ranges adequate for suicide but not for defense. "That's a peashooter in Fort Griffin. Some of these men have rifles that'll shoot more than a thousand yards."

"Ah, but constable, sir, they do not have my intellect? Intellect is as important as weapons in defense."

The arrogant ass, Hanson thought. "It'd be a shame to get killed by an inferior intellect, Baron, but there are plenty men around here who'd give it a try for the kind of money you're carrying."

"Highly unlikely they would succeed, constable," Paget intoned, "especially not when I get a guard animal."

"It may take a while for you to find a dog, Baron."

"Dog? Why, constable, sir, I have another creature in mind."

Hanson shook his head. He didn't know if there was an animal mean enough to protect this Englishman in all his royal arrogance.

"A rooster, constable, is all I need for protection."

"A rooster?" The marshal jerked his hat off in disbelief. The baron had to be dumber than a brick. Hanson shook his hatless head. "You're joshing?"

"Joshing, constable?"

31

Hanson pulled his hat back on his head. "Yeah, you know, codding or howling or whatever it is you English fellows call a joke."

"Indeed not. Roosters make excellent guard animals."

"Fighting cocks, you mean?" the sheriff asked.

"No, sir, just a regular rooster. You may take me for a fool, constable, but I am not. Good day. Now, come along, lad," Paget said with a wave of his cane at Sammy Collins. "Take me to my flat. It has been a long day in the carriage. Now I am ready for a bath."

CHAPTER 2

With his free hand Sammy Collins pointed to a single-story, whitewashed building at the next corner. "That's the Planter's House. It's off the main street and away from the saloon noise."

The baron took in the hotel, its shaded porch and its tall windows. "Satisfactory, lad, nothing more," the baron said, his cane tucked under his arm. Wriggling his patrician nose, he studied the neighboring buildings, a warehouse fronting the hotel and a livery stable across a side street. Beyond the hotel toward Government Hill, a giant pecan tree reached for the clouds. Paget pointed his cane down the street. "Huge tree, that is, lad."

"Pecan tree, some say the biggest in Texas," Sammy replied.

The baron stopped and turned around, taking in the weathered buildings and adobe huts of Fort Griffin. "Pitiful town, lad, save for your parents' hotel."

Sammy sighed. "My folks died three years back. Uncle Moses and Aunt Moses took me in, made me work for them."

"My sympathy, lad. This uncle and aunt, they treat you well?"

Sammy shrugged. "They ain't my kin. Uncle Moses and Aunt Moses is just what folks around here call them. I get a lean-to out back for a room and leftovers for board but nothing more."

"Lad, perhaps I can retain your services. I need a valet, someone who can lay out my clothes, draw my bath water, see to my laundry, those types of duties. Those chores can be so taxing. I couldn't pay you much, perhaps a dollar a day in American currency."

Sammy's jaw dropped. "A dollar a day?"

"An embarrassing amount, I know," the baron apologized, "but if you agree, lad, you must relate to no one how poorly I'm paying you."

"It's a deal, sir, and I'll not tell a soul." Sammy bounded up the plank steps onto the hotel porch, then flung open the door for the baron, who removed his bowler and strolled inside, swinging his cane. Sammy followed.

The room was small, but clean, and lit

34

only by shafts of afternoon light diffused by lace curtains hanging over the open windows. The furniture — two benches and a half dozen chairs around a cold pot-bellied stove — was wooden and plain. Off to the side, the Englishman saw a dining room with a long table and a dozen mismatched chairs.

At the registration desk, a tall, husky man with a bewildered black beard towered over the guest register, glaring at a smaller, older man. "That's Uncle Moses," Sammy Collins said, pointing at the slender reed of a man with thinning white hair, emaciated frame, gaunt cheeks, and eyes afire with determination.

"I've told you a dozen times, Ike Mann, that I'm not letting rooms to no buffalo hunters. You've all got lice that'll ruin my sheets, get in my mattresses, and give the hotel a bad name. I've a hard enough time keeping the Southern from taking all my business."

The buffalo hunter took off his greasy hat and slapped the guest register, drawing a puff of dust. "Now, Uncle Moses, all I want is one night on a feather mattress. I could stay at the Southern if I just wanted a room, but I want a feather mattress."

Uncle Moses folded his arms across his

35

puny chest. "Nothing against you, Ike Mann, because I know you're honest, but your types leave lice and odors in my rooms."

Mann growled, then straightened to his full six feet, four inches, his muscled arms well capable of picking up Uncle Moses and snapping him in half like a matchstick. Instead, Mann grumbled and spun around, marching angrily toward the door.

Sammy Collins jumped aside, but the Englishman stood transfixed, his eyes wide at this specimen of manhood with muscled arms leading to broad, oxen-like shoulders. Mann's eyes were black and wild like his full, untrimmed beard, and his clothes reeked of wood smoke, buffalo tallow, spent gunpowder, and uncured buffalo hides.

"You're in my way," Mann scowled and the Englishman stepped aside, just in time for the buffalo hunter to pass through the door without breaking stride.

"Good day, governor," the Englishman called after him.

Sammy approached the registration desk, dropping the carpetbag atop it. "One from the stage, Uncle Moses."

Uncle Moses frowned. "Did the Southern get any?"

"Nope." Sammy smiled, awaiting congrat-

36

ulations.

"Run along to your chores, then," Uncle Moses ordered.

The Englishman stepped to the desk. "One moment, governor, please. I've some tasks for him to attend."

Uncle Moses stroked his wrinkled chin as he studied Paget.

"He's royalty, Uncle Moses," Sammy interjected.

Paget placed his hat over his heart. "Baron Jerome Manchester Paget, cousin five times removed to Queen Victoria herself and longtime companion to the Prince of Wales."

"Then what are you doing in Hide Town?"

"Acquiring land for a buffalo ranch, governor."

Uncle Moses rubbed his lips to disguise his chuckle. "A buffalo ranch?" he managed. "How long you staying?"

Tapping his cane on the floor, Paget shrugged. "Two, maybe three weeks."

Uncle Moses turned the guest register around. "Sign your name. Room is two dollars a day, twelve dollars a week. With board, it's twenty dollars a week. If you object to anyone sleeping in your room when we're full, it's an extra five dollars a week."

Paget picked up a pen from the desk and

dipped it in the ink well. "Charge me twenty-five dollars a week. Do your rooms have locks? I carry considerable funds with me."

Slowly, Uncle Moses shook his head. "Men around here would just kick in a locked door."

With a flourish, Paget signed his name and returned the pen as Uncle Moses rocked a blotter over his signature. Paget opened his satchel. "I can pay you now in British pounds or later in American dollars."

Uncle Moses' eyes widened when he saw the bundles of bills in the baron's satchel. "American money later. You're in number five, middle of the hall," Uncle Moses said, pointing down a dim hallway. "Sammy will see you to your room."

The baron shook his head. "And then, I need the lad to find me a poulterer," Paget commanded.

"A poulterer?" Uncle Moses asked.

"A chicken dealer," Paget answered. "A poulterer is a chicken dealer."

"No chicken dealers around here," Uncle Moses answered.

Paget waved his cane like a sword. "Then find someone with chickens and buy me a fine rooster."

"But what if they won't sell?" Sammy asked.

Paget grinned. "Acquire it at whatever price because I need a guard animal."

Sammy Collins shook his head. "A guard rooster?"

Uncle Moses turned around and snickered.

Joe Loper strode up to the bar in the Bee Hive saloon and motioned to Burley Sims, who sauntered over, drying a beer mug with a clean towel. His arms were muscled from waltzing beer kegs around the saloon, but his waist was narrow because Sims was temperate in all matters. He avoided sampling drink from his backbar or victuals from his food table because every sip he drank and every bite he took cut into his profit margin. There were floors to sweep, dishes to wash, spittoons to polish and those were pleasures compared to keeping an eye on gamblers who might be taking too much from regular customers. Sims eyed Loper suspiciously.

"You run the place?" Loper asked.

Sims nodded, lifting the dry beer mug up to the window light and wiping away a final smudge. Placing the mug on a pyramid of others on the backbar, Sims tossed the towel over his meaty shoulder.

The stranger placed a carpetbag atop the bar's polished wood. "I'm Joe Loper. I'm a gambler," he announced.

Sims nodded. "I figured. I'm Burley Sims. I run the Bee Hive."

"I'm looking for a place to deal cards. I play a square game."

"All of the time?" Sims asked, pulling the white towel from his shoulder and wiping the sweat from his mustache.

Loper grinned. "Most of the time."

Sims studied Loper. He liked his directness, even if he didn't trust him. But what gambler could you trust? "You any good, Loper?"

"Among the best!"

"If that's so," Sims quizzed, "how come I ain't heard of you?"

"I haven't killed a man or been caught cheating."

Sims stroked his chin and eyed Loper, wondering if he could be trusted, knowing no gambler was trustworthy.

"I'm not after your regulars," Loper offered. "Their pokes don't match my ambition."

"Whose does?"

Loper's voice fell to a whisper. "Sims, I'm after a damn fool Englishman who rode in

40

on the stage today. He's bragging about a satchel full of money he carries around."

Sims shook his head. "He won't be long for this earth, if he stays in Hide Town."

Loper's lips curled sinisterly. "I'll take care of any man that threatens the Englishman before I can get him in a card game. Even if I cheat him out of all his money, he'll come out ahead because he'll still have his life. Not every man in these parts would be so sporting."

Sims snapped his towel at a couple flies on the bar, then brushed them onto the floor. "You can deal here as long as you don't cheat my regulars, Loper, and you pay me for using my table."

"You want a cut of my winnings or a straight fee?"

"Straight fee," Sims answered. "Two dollars a day for every day you use my table."

Loper nodded. "As long as the Englishman is mine and you don't change your mind, it's a deal."

Sims agreed. "I can live with that."

"Now, Sims, let me give you a couple decks of cards and a couple bottles of whiskey. Both decks are stacked. When I call for one of them, you'll know I'm about to fleece the Englishman."

"You're an odd one, Loper," Sims replied.

Loper shrugged and dug deeper into his satchel, removing two brown bottles of S.O.B. Bourbon and placing them side by side on the bar.

Sims shook his head. "Never heard of such a brand."

"It's fair liquor, but hard to find. The name distracts some men, giving me an edge. If I'm in a game and I call for something special to drink, bring out the S.O.B., first this bottle with the notched cork, the other bottle next."

Sims cocked his head. "This ain't poison, is it?"

"Nope," Loper replied. "If it was, you'd likely heard of Joe Loper before now."

Loper closed his carpetbag and lifted it from the counter as Sims stashed the two decks and two bottles behind a sliding door in the backbar.

Sims started to offer Loper a drink until he heard a pounding on the back door. Suspecting it must be Cat Tails, who had likely found whiskey money, Sims retreated to the door, unbarred it and swung it open. The door stopped with a clunk, then Cat Tails emerged from behind it, rubbing his head.

Cat Tails gestured for firewater, then shoved paper currency in Sims' hand.

The saloon owner unwadded the bill and shook his head. This was a new one on him, an odd sized bill with the likeness of a be-crowned and bejeweled woman atop it. "Wait," he said, closing the door so the Tonkawa wouldn't follow.

Sims strode to the bar, holding the piece of paper to the window light. Uncertain of its worth, Sims figured he would give Cat Tails a jigger of whiskey. "Never seen anything like this," Sims said to Loper.

"That's an English one-pound note, worth about five American dollars," Loper said.

"Who says?" Sims asked.

"I do," Loper responded, digging into his pocket and pulling out a roll of American currency. He counted out five greenbacks. "Even trade," he said, putting his bills on the counter.

"Fair enough," Sims replied without hesitation. He exchanged the British note for the American currency, thinking he could now give Cat Tails a full bottle of whiskey. Cheap whiskey, of course.

"The Englishman's got a full satchel of those," Loper said.

Burley Sims groaned. Why hadn't he insisted on a share of Loper's game with the Englishman? A man just couldn't trust a gambler, Burley Sims thought.

■ ■ ■ ■

Colonel John Paul Jenkins dismounted in front of the post's military telegraph office and strode inside, his boots pounding the warped wooden floor. Jenkins enjoyed surprising his men like this, the terror in their eyes salve to his military soul.

The sergeant in charge jumped up from the table and saluted. He was a lean soldier, made leaner by the absence of the cook and the lack of a filling meal for days. The sergeant stood straight as a flagpole. "Any messages, Sergeant?"

"No, sir," he called back.

"At ease, then," the colonel replied, relieved that headquarters had not yet inquired about the demise of Private Burns. The colonel pulled off his riding gloves and licked his dry lips, thinking about the satchel of money he had seen the Englishman open. "Oddest thing, sergeant. The stage brought in an Englishman with a satchel of money, $25,000 worth."

The sergeant whistled. "I don't suppose the stage brought us a replacement cook, did it?"

"No," snarled the colonel, spinning about and leaving the telegraph office. He marched toward headquarters, ordering a soldier to tend his horse that he had tied outside the telegraph office.

As he strode across the parade ground for headquarters, black soldiers with scowls on their faces stopped their chores and saluted Jenkins, then invariably mumbled something under their breath before resuming the petty work the Army thought necessary to maintain proper military decorum. Jenkins had to admit that part of the men's morale problem was the fort itself. It was an outpost built on good intentions and budget cutbacks. Instead of barracks, the men lived in wooden huts. The green lumber used in building the huts had warped and buckled as it dried, making maintenance a constant problem and thunderstorms and blue northers seasonal challenges. What the fourteen-foot-by-eight-foot huts lacked in dryness and warmth, they made up for with ventilation. And, each hut was home to six enlisted men. Bad as the huts were on the men, the wooden stables were even worse on the horses. Fort Griffin lost more horses to pneumonia and other diseases than any other Texas outpost, another black mark on Jenkins' Army record.

And while the War Department had not found the money to build more substantial barracks and stables, it had seen fit, to Colonel Jenkins' profound pleasure, to provide quarters of local limestone for the camp commandant. Besides the hospital, the commissary, the powder house, and the bakery, which had necessarily been out of use since the untimely demise of Private Burns, Colonel Jenkins' home was the only stone structure at the outpost.

Across the parade ground, Jenkins spied a couple of officers and ordered them to find constructive activities for a clump of soldiers gathering around the flagpole, smoking their pipes and cursing their diet. Entering the headquarters building, Jenkins removed his hat and blasphemed a spot of bird droppings on the blue wool and yellow braiding. He tossed the hat on the table of his adjutant and demanded he clean the spot immediately.

The adjutant disappeared into an adjacent room, leaving Jenkins alone in the plain outer office filled with plain unpadded chairs, a plain desk covered with plain Army reports and plain whitewashed walls decorated with lithographs of Presidents George Washington, Abraham Lincoln and U.S. Grant. The colonel waited impatiently, running his hands through his thinning hair, scratching the mustache beneath his petite nose, and tugging his big ears. When the adjutant returned, Jenkins snatched his hat and studied the damp spot on the brim where the bird's missive had landed. Looking up from the brim, Jenkins issued a command. "Find the bird that did this and shoot him."

The lieutenant stiffened to attention, though his face was slack with bewilderment. "What if the bird can cook, sir?" the lieutenant managed.

Jenkins jerked his head at the adjutant. "Mine was a funny, Lieutenant, a joke."

"Mine, too, sir," the lieutenant responded.

"Yours wasn't funny," Jenkins growled.

"Yes, sir," the lieutenant answered.

The colonel spun around and marched past the adjutant. "I'll not be needing you the rest of the afternoon. You are dismissed."

"Thank you, sir," the adjutant responded. Before the colonel could change his mind, the lieutenant grabbed his own hat and strode out the door, closing it gently behind him.

Glad to be rid of the adjutant, Jenkins entered his office, ignored the papers stacked on his desk for review or signature, and went immediately to a locked cabinet. Pulling a key from his pocket, he slipped it in the lock and twisted it until it clicked.

He opened the door on a treasure of food: jerked meat, jellies, hard biscuits, candies, and other delicacies provided by the post trader. A little food on his stomach would make his evening meal with the enlisted men more tolerable.

After an hour of nibbling on the perks of a commandant's position, Jenkins gathered up his unused food and locked it in the cabinet. He brushed biscuit crumbs from his uniform, missing a spot of blackberry jelly on the placket of his Army blouse, as he made his way to the door. Emerging from headquarters, he marched quickly across the parade ground for the mess hall.

Approaching the cookhouse, he heard the chatter of men and the clatter of spoon and fork against tin plates and bowls. He convinced himself it was the sound of happiness. He snapped the door open and stepped inside to be greeted by an impulsive groan, then momentary silence. In the dim lantern light, he stared into a surly sea of black faces and white teeth.

"Attention!" yelled the sergeant and the men shoved back their benches and stood up, stiff and belligerent.

"Sir," they said in unison, their elbows folding into salutes.

"As you were men," Jenkins called. "Just

came to share supper."

The troopers' groans were muffled by the sound of shuffling boots and rattling utensils as Jenkins moved to the food line and picked up a tin plate and bowl. A black trooper with a sweat-soaked face and a food-stained apron pulled a ladle from a tall black pot and poured hot water into the colonel's bowl. "I like a thin soup," Jenkins offered, then wiped his face. The trooper scowled. The trooper then moved step for step with the colonel down the food line, stopping over a stack of moldy hardtack biscuits. Taking a square of hardtack, the trooper dropped it in the colonel's bowl of water.

"Hardtack stew, sir," the trooper said, then advanced past a pile of burnt biscuits to a blackened coffee pot. "Take all the biscuits you want, sir," he said, then picked up the coffee pot and a tin cup, filling it to the brim so it would spill out and burn the colonel's fingers when he carried it to the table.

The three biscuits Jenkins dropped on his plate rattled the tin when they landed. "I ate a lot of hardtack stew when I fought for the Union to free you boys," the colonel said loud enough for everyone to hear. "Soldier, bring my coffee to the table for me."

The trooper followed the colonel to a table, biting his lip as the coffee scorched his fingers. The colonel placed his plate on the plank table and crawled over the bench to take his seat, then realized he had forgotten fork, knife, and spoon. Before he could get out of his seat, the aproned trooper returned with the utensils. Jenkins grabbed them, using the fork to attack the hardtack in the hot water, but the hardtack was stubborn enough to withstand assault by any liquid short of acid or any implement short of a pickax. The colonel picked up a blackened biscuit and weighed the damage it could do to his teeth. It felt like a lava rock. He opened his mouth and bit into it. The outside crunched with char, but the biscuit's innards were uncooked and doughy. "I've had worse," he said.

About the room, the chatter had been replaced by hushed whispers and then belligerence. "Pass more of them creamed taters," one soldier in the back called out. Several laughed and others took up the cry. "Is any more roast beef left?" asked one. "What about them apricot pies?" cried another.

Jenkins just shook his head, allowing his lips to break into a grin. That was what he liked about these black troops, their indomitable spirit. Here rations were bad and yet they could play games with it. Jenkins wondered if other commanders were as beloved by their troops. Giving up on ever dissolving his hardtack into gruel, the colonel finally stood, waving an uneaten biscuit in each hand. "I'll save these for later, boys."

"Use 'em with some of that jelly on your shirt!" called an unseen trooper.

Jenkins glanced down at the spot of black-berry jelly then looked around the room for the wiseacre. Insubordination like that was grounds for a court martial. He stormed away.

"So long, Colonel Jelly Belly," he heard one trooper call, followed by an explosion of laughter.

Jenkins cursed the black men and their indomitable spirit.

Sammy Collins had seen that the baron's trunk was delivered to the Planter's House and then had found a feisty rooster for the Englishman. Sammy had even talked Zach Fenster, the town's most prosperous mer-chant, into the loan of a brass cage for the chicken. Of course, Sammy could always turn to Zach Fenster for a favor ever since he had seen the merchant slipping out of

"Lop-Eared" Annie Lea's place one afternoon. "Lop-Eared" Annie Lea was known throughout West Texas for her mismatched bosoms. Unlike other women of shady reputation, she refused to sleep with men. Instead, she allowed them to unbutton her blouse, remove her chemise and view her lopsided top.

Sammy didn't blame Fenster for his rendezvous with Annie Lea because Beulah Fenster was as ugly and mean as gangrene. As wife of the town's most prosperous merchant, Beulah Fenster was too proud to cook her own meals and too sour to grant conjugal favors to her husband. Consequently, Beulah Fenster, with husband in tow, took her meals at the Planter's House and Zach Fenster took his carnal urgings to "Lop-Eared" Annie Lea's. After all, Annie Lea's lopsided bust was, on average, bigger than Beulah Fenster's modest figure. Behind her back, the young boys called her "Pencil Fenster" while the adults about town had named her "Spinster Fenster."

After slipping the rooster through the entry parlor and then into the Englishman's room, Sammy scurried to the kitchen to help Aunt Moses prepare supper. Aunt Moses was a pudgy woman with wide hips, wide shoulders, wide smiles, and wide eyes behind narrow spectacles.

Sammy carried dishes to the dining table, then the utensils, and gradually the food as Aunt Moses emptied pots and pans into platters and bowls. The regulars gathered in the dining room, nodding their approval as more food arrived. Zach and Beulah Fenster had taken their places, sitting stiffly across the table from one another and eyeing the food, the dishes, the walls, the ceiling, the door, but seldom each other. The chairs on either side of Beulah Fenster were never occupied except by first-timers.

Jake Ellis was a buyer from Kansas City and always spent the spring and early summer at the Planter's House making deals with buffalo hunters for their winter kills, then hiring freighters to carry the hides back to Kansas. A lanky man with a surprising eye and appetite for making money, Ellis was the principal buyer in Fort Griffin and his price established what hunters could expect to get for their hides. From experience, the hiders always expected to be short-changed.

The Fensters, Jake Ellis, and Uncle Moses were seated, waiting for Aunt Moses to bring a pitcher of lemonade to the table when Baron Jerome Manchester Paget appeared in the door. "Good evening, ladies and gentlemen," Paget intoned, then bowed crisply. "I pray I haven't delayed your dinner."

"Oh, no," cried Beulah Fenster, patting the chair beside her. "Not at all. Why, I've saved this chair just for you."

"The pleasure would be mine to dine beside such a lovely lady."

Zach Fenster rolled his eyes.

Paget wore a ruffled shirt beneath a black cutaway coat and matching pants and carried his English club bag in his hand. As he marched around the table, the men grimaced at the aroma of his perfumed hair. He stopped by the chair Beulah Fenster had pulled back from the table and lowered his satchel to the floor. He glanced from Uncle Moses to Aunt Moses just entering with the lemonade and waited a moment for introductions. Then after no response, he spoke. "I shall announce myself. I am Baron Jerome Manchester Paget, late of London, and now of Fort Griffin, Texas."

Realizing he had made a blunder on introductions, Uncle Moses sputtered out the names of all those seated around the table.

"Baron, do you know the queen?" gushed Beulah Fenster, patting his chair for him to sit down.

54

"Indeed, madam, met with her not three days before I set sail for America."

Envious, Beulah sighed while her husband rolled his eyes again.

Sammy Collins stood at the kitchen door, his post during dinner. He would help keep glasses full and food on the table, then eat the leftovers in the kitchen.

Paget turned to Aunt Moses. "Doesn't the lad join us? He's been such a help to me."

Aunt Moses blushed and nodded. "Sure, sure, just an oversight," she lied. "Sammy, get a plate and utensils for yourself."

Once Sammy had seated himself, Paget slid elegantly into his chair, his back ever straight, as Uncle Moses said grace. Then Aunt Moses began to pass bowls of stewed prunes, succotash, and boiled potatoes and platters of roast beef and fresh bread. "We've mincemeat pie for sweets," Aunt Moses announced.

"You are really royalty, Baron?" asked Beulah Fenster. "It's proper to call you baron, is it not?"

"To be proper, you should address me as 'Your Lordship,' but that sounds so pompous among the philistines. Baron is fine," Paget replied, taking a petite piece of beef from the platter. "And, yes, I am royalty, a cousin five times removed from Queen

55

Victoria herself. And by the law of primo-geniture, I have inherited the title."

"Primo-genitals?" Zach Fenster said, scratching his head.

"No, no, governor, prim-o-gen-i-ture," Paget said slowly. "It's the tradition that the royal titles and everything in the estate — the land, the mansions, the paintings, the jewels — go to the first-born son. By the good fortune of my birth, I am the heir and my brother, the spare."

Ever the businessman, Jake Ellis spoke up as he forked a couple boiled potatoes. "Now pardon me for asking, Baron, but if you inherited all that, what are you doing this far from London eating supper with us plain folk?"

Paget lowered his head a moment and touched a corner of his napkin to his lips. "Much as I loved my father, he left many debts that threaten the style of life that the Pagets have enjoyed over the centuries. I came to America to rebuild the Paget fortune. First, I must start a buffalo ranch . . . ."

The men around the table laughed, even after Beulah Fenster telegraphed them an ugly look.

Paget smiled. "It's visionary, but someone must look to supplying the leather markets once the wild buffalo are decimated. And, this may shock you Yankees with your romantic notions of love, but fortunes are being made in this country by industrialists with eligible daughters."

Beulah Fenster's face turned white with shock. He husband tossed her a smug look.

"Should I encounter such a woman of suitable means," Paget continued, "I would not be averse to a marriage of convenience. I would share my royal title in exchange for a share of her father's fortune."

"That's scandalous," sputtered Beulah Fenster.

Paget reached to her and patted her hand. "Isn't it," he said with a soothing voice, "and isn't it a shame you're already spoken for or I might reconsider my notions about love."

Beulah Fenster fluttered her eyelashes and thrust her chest out to its fullest, if still shallow, extension. Across the table, Zach Fenster choked on a bite of food until Jake Ellis hit him on the back. Enthralled by his charm, Beulah Fenster threw question after question at the baron. And, the baron, with a seeming endless fount of patience, answered every one until the mincemeat pie was completed and the men were about to adjourn to the porch for cigars.

"Care for a smoke?" Jake Ellis offered, opening the lid of a cigar box for Paget.

"Thank you, no, governor. A gentleman shouldn't smoke in the presence of a lady."

Ellis snapped the cigar lid shut. "Suit yourself, but nobody here's the queen of anything."

Paget smiled sweetly at Beulah. "I'm not so sure about that." Turning from Beulah, he addressed Aunt Moses. "Delightful meal, most pleasing to the palate. Now if you would excuse me, I should like to retire, the carriage ride being so exhausting."

Everyone nodded, except Beulah Fenster, because they were anxious for the baron to leave so they could talk about his strange manners and his preposterous idea of starting a buffalo ranch.

"As one last favor, might I borrow the lad," Paget said, nodding toward Sammy Collins, "to help turn back my bed?"

"Why, yes," replied Aunt Moses.

"Thank you, madam, and good evening all," Paget answered, picking up his satchel and departing, Collins trailing him down the hall.

At his room, Paget pushed open the door and gave Collins a moment to light the lamp. Then he pointed to the window, which was cracked a couple inches. "Open it, lad," he instructed, then moved to the corner where he jerked a quilt from over a rectangular container. A rooster with mottled feathers crowed in surprise. As Paget picked up the cage, the rooster strutted furiously around as the Englishman carried the rooster to the window. Placing the container astride the sill, Paget pulled down the window until it wedged the cage in place.

"The rooster," he explained, "will alert me should any man try to slip in my window tonight." His hand slid under his coat and returned with a small revolver. "I shall be ready for him."

CHAPTER 3

The Reverend G.W. "God Willing" Tuck looked to the bright San Angelo sky and gave silent thanks for this glorious Sunday and the glorious crowd gathering on the grassy banks of the Concho River. As he wandered among the people, Bible in hand, he judged it a stingy crowd that would tithe little more than meal money for himself and his two shills, Monk Partain and Surry Nettles. And then, as Tuck strolled by a clump of rowdy soldiers from nearby Fort Concho, he stopped and bowed his head as if praying instead of eavesdropping.

Tuck listened as an Army telegrapher told his fellow soldiers about a practice telegram he had received after midnight from Fort Griffin some hundred miles to the northeast. Yesterday afternoon, related the soldier, an English nobleman had arrived in Fort Griffin with a fortune in his hand. When the telegrapher mentioned $25,000, Tuck caught his breath. Suddenly, the Reverend Tuck felt God calling him to Fort Griffin, where he could enrich souls. And, his pocket!

The Reverend Tuck, a self-anointed Baptist preacher, cleared his throat and turned toward the murky river. It was time to get on with the baptism of Zadocks Crawley and his cork leg.

The soldiers pointed and snickered as Tuck approached Crawley. The town folk craned their necks or moved in groups up the sloping river banks for a better view. Zadocks Crawley stood at water's edge, arms crossed at his chest, bloodshot eyes rimmed with tears, the cork of his artificial leg visible beneath the frayed hem of his britches.

During the War Between the States, Crawley had lost his leg, not to a cannon ball as he told folks, but rather to a whiskey barrel, which crushed it during some unauthorized foraging. By the time Crawley hobbled back to Texas on crutches, he had fashioned a heroic tale of losing his leg while saving the regimental colors from a horde of Yankee locusts.

"I'm scared, Reverend," he said.

Reverend Tuck laid his hand upon Crawley. "Your baptism will wash away your fears and replenish you with heavenly courage."

"I can't swim, Reverend."

"You have professed your belief before Gawd and your fellow man. Now, Gawd will take care of you until death."

Crawley spat into the Concho. "I don't want to die, just to get this over with."

"It would go easier if you unstrapped your leg."

Crawley's tearful eyes suddenly boiled. "You said God'd make us whole again in heaven, that he'd restore body and soul as long as we're saved and immersed in the waters of the Concho."

Crawley had a point, Tuck admitted with a nod.

"Well, Reverend, I don't want to get to heaven and find I can't have my real leg back because I didn't dunk this 'un."

Theologically, it was a hard point for Reverend Tuck to argue. "Let us proceed." Lifting his soothing hand from Zadocks Crawley's shoulder, the Reverend G.W. Tuck turned to face the assembled worshipers and skeptical soldiers. He raised his eyes and head to the heavens. With his left hand he removed his hat and with his right hand lifted his Bible to the sky.

"Hallelujah!" he shouted and the crowd's chatter dissolved into whispers. "Praise the

Lord and let us pray silently, each man, each woman and each child to Gawd Almighty." The crowd noise evaporated.

Tuck glanced about the crowd. He loved these moments of control, when the worshipers were at the mercy of his voice, when he could scorch their emotions with fire and brimstone or soothe their consciences with the salve of compassion. But most of all, he loved to preach the money out of their pockets and into his own. At the first brush arbor sermon he ever heard as a boy, he was stunned that a man could pick his neighbor's pocket simply by preaching a sermon. On top of that, after the larceny the fleeced flock would shake the preacher's hand, congratulate him on giving the devil his due, and then invite him to a Sunday dinner of fried chicken. It sure beat chopping cotton or following a balky mule and plow up and down a field all day. Before he turned twelve, George Washington Tuck had seen the light and his life's profession.

"Amen!" Tuck shouted and every eye turned from God to him. This was the biggest crowd Tuck had ever attracted to a baptism and he had dunked hundreds over the years, but never one with a cork leg. If baptizing Zadocks Crawley proved harder than finding a horse thief in heaven, Tuck had stationed Monk Partain and Surry Nettles with shotguns just beyond the bend in the river to fire off their weapons and yell "Injuns!" The commotion would distract folks long enough for Tuck to claim he had indeed baptized Crawley whether anyone had seen it or not. Tuck just prayed the crowd had tithe money.

Tuck tossed his hat on the ground, his thick mane of hair, prematurely gray, tumbling free as he thumbed open his Bible. His eyes, the green of freshly printed money, scanned the spectators. The people were anxious. And, so was he as he looked at Crawley's cork leg. Taking a deep breath, he flashed teeth, as white as new gravestones, and began to speak, low at first so everyone would strain to catch his words, then louder until he was in a full yell that could be heard all the way to Fort Concho.

"This is a glorious day for the Lord Gawd Almighty, glorious indeed because he is adding another soldier to the army of the righteous, another man to His glorious roll of heavenly honor," he began, his voice rising with each word. Before him, people nodded, their eyes widening at his mellifluous baritone voice, which he played like a musical instrument. "Hallelujah, friends and neighbors," he called, lifting his arms and the good book to the crowd, imploring everyone to share his joy.

"Hallelujah," they repeated half-heartedly.

"Hallelujah!" he screamed.

"Hallelujah!" they shouted.

He dropped his arms and his gaze, looking at the new convert. "When I lift Zadocks Crawley from the waters, he will no longer be just Zadocks Crawley. He will be Brother Crawley, a fellow Baptist to those of us who have shared in Gawd's glory through the purification of baptism. Now there are other religions and other preachers, well-meaning creatures I am sure, who profess you can be cleansed by the sprinkling of waters, but they are mistaken. I mean no offense to my Methodist friends, but they are wrong. When you bathe, do you use a spoonful or a tub full of water? A tub full, of course. Our sins are like dirt, there's more of them than a spoonful of water can wash away. There's greed and lechery and drunkenness and pride and envy and more. Yes, many more sins than I can name."

Tuck paused a moment, thumbing the pages in his Bible and studying the crowd. Most were solemn-faced, save the soldiers, who stood grinning, mocking God and him.

"Turning in the New Testament, we find that Jesus, Gawd's own Son, was baptized and this, friends and neighbors, is the biblical proof that Baptists are the one true religion. Who did Gawd have immerse his Holy Son? Why, John the Baptist, of course. It wasn't John the Methodist or John the Episcopalian or John the Jew and especially not John the Catholic, but John the Baptist, friends and neighbors." Tuck paused and turned the pages for all to see. "This is the Bible and there's the proof." He slapped the pages.

"And now, Zadocks Crawley is about to join Gawd's Baptist army," Tuck shouted, placing his hand upon Crawley's shoulder. Tuck felt a tremor of fear. "Are you ready to join Gawd's army?"

"Yep," Crawley answered softly.

"Louder," Tuck implored.

"Yep," Crawley cried out, "if we can just do it, dammit."

"Amen!" Tuck shouted, "Amen! Now, friends and neighbors and brothers and sisters in the Baptist Lord, please join in singing 'Shall We Gather at the River.'"

With a wave of his arms, Tuck started the singing, his rich baritone voice carrying over everyone else's. As he sang, he placed his Bible on the ground beside his hat, kicked off his shoes, and pulled off his socks. He took off his coat, then glanced casually toward the river bend, confirming that Monk Partain and Surry Nettles were slipping toward the crowd. After placing his coat on the grass, he retrieved a folded bed sheet that he used as a baptismal gown. The bed sheet, a hole cut out of the center for his head and slits in the side for his arms, was dingy and splotched from baptisms in dozens of muddy Texas rivers. He slipped the gown on and resumed singing as he slipped off his trousers.

At the end of the chorus, Tuck motioned for the singing to stop. He stepped to the river and waded in up to his knees, the slick silt squishing between his toes. Tuck grimaced at the cold water, then turned around motioning for Zadocks Crawley to approach. "Step forward!" he shouted for all to hear. "Leave your old life, your sinful life behind. Come to me as you come to Gawd, a sinner."

Crawley advanced, his good foot entering water to the ankle. Then followed the cork leg. Man and leg stood steady.

So far, so good, Tuck thought. "In these waters, you'll be reborn."

"In these waters, I'll freeze," Crawley shivered.

Tuck gritted his teeth. "Come to Jesus, Zadocks Crawley."

Crawley took a tentative step with each leg.

"Hallelujah!" Tuck shouted, thankful Crawley's cork leg had held steady. Maybe this wouldn't be so bad after all.

Shivering intensely, Crawley stepped forward with his good leg, then fought against his cork leg stuck in the mud. Crawley reached for the reverend and Tuck grabbed his outstretched arms. Reassured, Crawley jerked his cork leg free of the river bottom. His leg swung forward for a moment, then rose to the surface. Crawley shook his hand free from Tuck's grip and pushed the leg beneath the water, but it popped back up. He hopped toward Tuck and together, like a clumsy couple at a dance, they backed deeper into the river, the water reaching their thighs.

The moment of truth was nearing Tuck as the water reached his waist. "Hallelujah, for the miracles of Gawd!" he yelled at the slap of the cold water rising past his navel.

As the water reached Crawley's waist, he screamed at the cold shock. "Damnation!"

"Satan's final hold on Zadocks Crawley's soul," Tuck shouted.

The hold of gravity, not Satan, frightened Crawley. With the water at his waist, his cork leg floated to the water's surface, pushing him backward and off balance. Women and children gasped as Crawley tilted like a tree about to fall.

With one hand the Reverend Tuck submerged the cork leg for an instant and with the other hand grabbed Crawley's shirt to hold him upright. Neither hand succeeded for long, not with Crawley's windmilling arms and bobbing cork leg. Tuck heard the Fort Concho soldiers whooping and hollering. Had they no respect for God? Tuck knew he must act quickly.

"Pinch your nose and cover your mouth," Tuck gasped at Crawley.

The sinner nodded vigorously, then closed his eyes and grabbed at his face.

"In the name of the Father, the Son, and the Holy Ghost," Tuck shouted as he struggled to keep Crawley upright; "I hereby baptize you . . . ;" Crawley was starting to fall backward; "in the blood of Jesus . . . ;" Crawley broke the water with a splash; "to wash your sins away . . . ;" Crawley had forgotten to take a deep breath; "and to give you everlasting life."

Crawley thrashed at the water.

Reverend Tuck wrestled him, fighting his flailing arms, his mad lunges for breath. Crawley's head broke the surface, coughing, sputtering, gasping. Tuck shoved him back under, then pushed the cork leg with his left hand. The leg slid briefly beneath the waves created by the commotion, but not before Crawley's head broke the surface, spitting water and heaving for a breath.

Still, Tuck had not immersed all of Crawley at one time. Satan and the cork leg were winning. Taking a deep breath, Tuck shoved Crawley's head as far beneath the water as he could, then hopped over Crawley, straddling his chest. With both arms free and Crawley's head and torso pinned between his legs beneath the water, Tuck lunged for the cork leg, strangling it like some stubby serpent as he threw all his weight into it. The cork leg and Tuck went under together. For an instant, the cork leg and Zadocks Crawley were both submerged. Tuck could tell because of the thrashing between his legs. Then the cork leg shot to the surface. Tuck rolled off Crawley and tried to stand, but his feet snagged in his baptismal robe. Finally getting his feet on the slick river bottom, Tuck stood, spitting water and rubbing at his eyes.

Beside him the water was a fury of thrashing arms and legs. Every time Crawley's head surfaced, the waves from the flailing arms drenched his mouth and nose, intensifying his terror. Every time he managed to stand up, his cork leg floated to the surface, destroying his equilibrium and pushing him back into the water. Tuck lunged for Crawley, but the man was horrified and fought help. Finally, Tuck managed to grab Crawley's collar and to tug him toward the bank. Tuck maneuvered his horrified convert to the shallows where a couple men jumped in and jerked Crawley to his feet. Crawley shook his head, slinging water from his mouth, his nose, his ears, his hair, his clothes. Finally, he seemed to regain his senses. When he did, he shoved his two rescuers aside and stumbled for the bank, collapsing on the grass, taking deep breaths and mumbling.

The Reverend Tuck emerged from the river, dripping water like fresh laundry, and moved over to the prostrate convert. "Brother Crawley, welcome to the army of Gawd."

"It looks more like the navy to me," yelled a soldier. The assembled crowd broke into laughter. Damn him, Tuck thought. That remark likely would cost the Reverend whatever meager tithe this stingy crowd would offer.

"You have witnessed the miracle of Gawd," Tuck shouted as the grinning crowd began to disperse. "And now Gawd is waiting for you to stand by Him in supporting the work of this lone preacher against sin. I'll pass my hat. Dig into your hearts and your pockets. Support Gawd's work in West Texas." He fairly shoved his hat into the hands of the nearest man, who passed it to another and another, as if it were contagious.

Tuck shivered in his clothes, knowing there would be little in his hat to warm his spirit or fill his wallet when this was done.

Beside him, Crawley pushed himself to his hands and knees. "I should'a been a Methodist," he said as he stood, then limped away as fast as his water-soaked cork leg would allow.

Tuck looked upriver at Monk Partain and Surry Nettles, who were holding their sides from laughter. Tuck just shook his head. Some help they had been.

The crowd moved to their horses and buggies, the soldiers marching back toward the fort, windmilling their arms in imitation of Crawley. A passing man tossed Tuck's hat at his feet. Tuck saw a few coins but nothing more. He'd be lucky to make a dollar.

As the crowd thinned, Partain and Nettles sauntered toward Tuck, shotguns in hand. Partain had a full beard of hair that hid his ugly features and a thick head of hair that

72

cushioned the blow whenever they had to cold-cock him in the name of the Lord. He was slow of foot and slow of mind, possibly because of all the times he had been knocked unconscious by the Reverend Tuck or Nettles.

Nettles had hair the color of fresh cut straw, eyes as blue as the sky, and a smile that could charm man or beast. He had the skills and the looks to make a good preacher or an excellent swindler, but lacked the ambition or drive to try either. He was content to make a few dollars shilling for Tuck.

Tuck scowled as they approached. "Why didn't you shoot?"

Nettles lifted the double-barreled shotgun for Tuck's stomach, cocked the hammers and pulled the twin triggers. Tuck yelped and dodged as the hammers clicked onto empty chambers.

"We forgot to buy shells." Nettles shrugged, then smiled.

"Do I have to think of everything?" Tuck planted his hands on his hips.

Partain nodded. "Yep."

Nettles' smile bloated. "You're the one with God's ear, Reverend." He laughed.

Tuck spat. "We're ruined in San Angelo

73

for a while. Gawd's calling me to Fort Griffin."

"Ain't been there," Partain said.

Tuck nodded. "Some Englishman's brought a fortune to Fort Griffin, plenty of money to do Gawd's work."

"What's the plan this time, boss?" asked Nettles.

Tuck looked at the sparse coins in his hat. "Sell your shotguns and steal the fastest horses you can find. Get to Griffin quick."

"Yeah, yeah," Nettles said, "but what's the plan?"

Tuck scratched his chin. "Griffin needs a miracle worker. Try the cripple and the stutterer."

Partain groaned and rubbed the side of his head. "Not again."

The reverend scowled. "This time, Monk, think you can remember to keep stuttering until I heal you?"

Partain kicked at the ground. "I made a mistake, won't you forget it?"

"Sure he will, Monk," Nettles interjected, "because forgiveness is what the Reverend Tuck is all about."

Wallace Sikes sat in the overstuffed sofa by the lobby window in the Mansion Hotel, scanning the latest edition of the *Fort Worth*

Democrat. Occasionally, he patted the revolver tucked in his belt beneath his coat. He bit his lip and glanced outside impatiently awaiting Gregory Patterson's return from the bank. A successful South Texas cattleman, Gregory Patterson had come to Fort Worth to take payment on a herd of cattle. Patterson was big in ranching, big in banking, big in investing, and big on his wife and five children back home.

Wallace Sikes fumed downstairs, knowing full well his own wife, Amanda, was upstairs in Patterson's room, eagerly awaiting the cattleman's return. Sikes hated the hypocrite Patterson for what he planned to do with Amanda now that he was safely beyond the reach of his own wife. Wallace Sikes would save Amanda from Patterson, even if he had to use the revolver. Once Wallace settled with Patterson, he would ride with Amanda to Waco on the two horses he had tied outside the hotel.

The clock mounted on the wall behind the registration desk said it was nine forty-five in the morning and the hotel clerk beneath the clock said nothing, just stared suspiciously at Sikes, who twirled the end of his black mustache, then refolded the newspaper, a story catching his attention. The decked headlines read:

75

**Wealthy subject of
English Crown
makes big plans
to start buffalo ranch;
Young investor
carries money satchel;
Fort Griffin likely location**

Snapping the paper as he moved it into the glare of the window light, Sikes avidly read the *Democrat*'s story:

Fools come in many forms, but never in such a glorious specimen as Jerome Manchester Paget, who calls himself a baron and a cousin of Queen Victoria herself. Whether you believe that or not, Paget is one of the oddest birds that has flown into these parts recently. Everywhere he goes, he takes a satchel full of money with him, intent, he says, on buying West Texas land and turning it into a ranch or refuge where buffalo can be raised for their hides like chickens are raised for their eggs. But the self-styled baron may well lay an egg himself when he tells his plans to someone less sympathetic to his story than this *Democrat* reporter. Fact is, money is still hard to come by in these parts and a man traveling around here with a satchel full of it shows he has more cents than sense.

The baron may have all the culture and refinement that a sheltered upbringing in distant England can afford a young man his age, but that doesn't prepare him to deal with the swindlers, the cheats, and the disreputables who inhabit the frontier beyond the established law. And right now, no place is farther beyond the law than Fort Griffin where he intends to implement his scheme. He reasons that the buffalo will one day be gone, though he admits to never having seen a single living buffalo, much less the herds of thousands that plague this state's western reaches and inhibit, as much as the savage Comanche did in years past, settlement of these lands. And on that day when the wild buffalo is about to disappear, he will be ready to start raising them like cattle and to fulfill the demands of tanneries for their hides. His idea is a dangerous one, not because of its utter ludicrousness, but because of the $25,000 he's carrying in his carpetbag.

With that kind of money to buy a ranch, the Baron is likely to get a plot of land, say the size of a grave. Just recently, another highly educated, but frontier ignorant Englishman bought the ranch in

New Mexico Territory while pursuing his fortune among men who were his royal inferiors. While their thinking wasn't as straight as his, their shooting certainly was. Now when an American fool is shot for his foolishness, he's buried and forgotten. But when an English fool is put out of his misery, it's an international incident as was the case in New Mexico Territory. An investigator all the way from Washington was sent to figure out the reason behind the killing and to satisfy the queen's demand that something be done. Nothing was ever done, short of the expenditure of good tax monies for a useless cause. We would prefer that the queen keep her royal fools on the island with her. After all, isn't that why God put water around England? If her royal highness should insist on allowing her royal relatives to visit our country with satchels of money, she should instruct them on safe investments in businesses like the *Democrat.*

Wallace Sikes nodded as he tore the article from the paper, then slipped the clipping inside his coat pocket. All of a sudden, Fort Griffin sounded more appealing than Waco. As Sikes straightened the paper, the bell on the door jangled, and he caught the profile of Patterson entering. Sikes lifted the paper up to shield his face and found himself staring at the rancher through the hole he had just torn. Patterson, smelling of tonic water strong enough to gag a spinster, held a bouquet of flowers. A bouquet for Sikes' wife, Amanda! And, even worse, Gregory Patterson wore a devious grin. Rage built in Wallace Sikes like steam in a defective boiler. He wadded the paper and threw it on the sofa. Patterson would suffer!

"Good morning, Mr. Patterson," said the clerk.

"Yes, it is," the cattleman replied, bounding up the stairs. A moment later, Wallace Sikes heard a door open on dry hinges, then close softly. He knew the kind of woman Amanda was and he knew that she would enjoy greeting Gregory Patterson.

Amanda Sikes stood before the mirror, brushing her long red hair, admiring its curl and bounce. She had to admit she was indeed a striking woman, her green eyes sparkling, her lips full and inviting, her cheeks round, slightly rouged, and her nose delicate. Her skin was as pale as a virgin's and her figure was seductive, funneling from her full bosom down to her tiny waist and then to her firm hips. She enjoyed the lust her figure brought to the eyes of a man like Gregory Patterson.

She licked her lips anticipating Patterson's return. He would be disappointed, of course, her greeting him fully dressed, but she preferred to tease. She had coyly refused his advances last night as she had each of the two preceding evenings, returning instead to her bed with Wallace. Amanda had insisted that Patterson take care of his bank business today before she gave in to his desires.

At the soft rap on the door, Amanda placed the brush on the dresser and smoothed the pleats of the brown riding suit with the high neck that would dash his ardor. Instead of buttons, the blouse was fastened with a dozen leather straps that fit into tiny buckles difficult for a man's stubby fingers to unfasten, particularly when he was in a hurry. With the buckles, she would control the pace. At the next rap on the door, she stepped across the room and past the bed. Unlatching the door, she opened it a hair to make sure Wallace hadn't followed. She smiled at Patterson. Slowly, teasingly, she pulled open the door which squealed on dry hinges. He stood with an arm behind his back, disappointment filling his eyes.

"I thought you would never come," she cooed.

He revealed his arm and a fine bouquet of spring flowers.

"For me?" she asked coyly, taking them from him and lifting them to her nose. "They smell as sweet as you."

He slid inside the door, looking both ways down the hall.

"I thought we might go riding together," she said, watching the disappointment deepen in the lines of his face as he surveyed her outfit and closed the door. "Over there," she said, tossing the bouquet on the bed.

His passion exploded. He lunged for her, wrapping an arm around her back and grasping her head with his free hand. With his powerful arms, he pulled her to him and their lips met in a crushing embrace. His mouth tasted of tobacco and his hair smelled of cheap hair tonic. As his hand moved toward her neck, she broke free of his lips and grabbed his encroaching fingers.

"Darling," she said softly, "we've all morning." She broke his grip and backed away. Planting both hands on her hips, she smiled. "Did you finish all your business? I don't want you to be thinking about anything else."

He nodded. "The deal's done," he said,

patting his coat pocket, then pulling out a stack of bills. "Ten thousand dollars," he said, all swagger and lust. He pulled a ten dollar bill off the top and tossed it on the bed after the bouquet. "You can buy you a pretty when we are done."

"Darling, please, put the money away. I want you."

His trembling fingers slid the money back in his coat pocket.

"Now, darling!" She closed her eyes and felt his big hands at her neck, fumbling with the top buckle. She took his hands in hers. "Darling, you are so excited. Let me help." She brushed his hand aside and let her nimble fingers unfasten, one, two, then three buckles while Patterson craned his neck for a glimpse of her pale skin. He licked his lips as perspiration beaded on his cheeks and forehead. "Darling, you are getting warm. Let me help you with your coat." She leaned forward and pecked him on his lips, then pranced behind him, taking his coat by the collar and letting it slide down his arms. Carefully, she folded the coat over the back of the room's one chair. As her arm slid from the coat, her hand hid the envelop of bills which she adroitly slipped from his coat pocket and into her skirt pocket.

"We'll not need that," she said, pointing to the revolver holstered at his hip. Her hand brushed against his buttoned fly as she unbuckled his holster. She took the revolver and placed it on the seat of the chair. The rest would be easy. She pushed him toward the bed, and Patterson seated himself at its edge. "Take off your boots, darling, and I'll handle the rest."

As he wrestled his boots free, she unfastened two more of the buckles, brushing her blouse open just wide enough for him to see a pale sliver of the flesh he desired to explore. Then she reached for his neck and slowly undid his tie, tossing it across the iron bedstead. He laughed at her frivolity. Next she unbuttoned his shirt and he wriggled his arms free. She took it and hung it on the bedpost. Her fingers then dallied on his trousers. Gregory Patterson fell back on the bed and arched his hips so she could pull his pants free. She tossed the pants across the room near the window. Laughing at her unpredictability, Gregory Patterson reclined before her in his white cotton union suit.

"Darling," she cooed, "it's getting warm, isn't it? Let me open the window, but we must remember not to be too loud or people on the street might hear us." She giggled suggestively as she scampered around the bed and squatted by the window. She lifted the window six inches. With her riding skirt screening her movement, she picked up his trousers and shoved them outside. Standing, she straightened her skirt and smiled. "You are a handsome man, Gregory Patterson." She tossed her head and began to unbuckle more of her blouse.

If Amanda knew her business, it was about time. She smiled as she opened the blouse. Patterson's eyes and his mouth widened. Amanda heard footsteps in the hallway, then a familiar cough. Her husband, right on time.

"Kiss me," she pleaded as she jerked her blouse open.

Gregory Patterson flew from the bed, a button on the back flap of his union suit popping. He flung himself at Amanda, taking her in his arms and kissing her madly just as the door crashed open, showering splinters across the room.

"What the hell?" Patterson yelled.

Wallace Sikes burst inside, revolver in his hand, rage in his voice. "You loose woman," he shouted.

Patterson tried to shake Amanda off and lunge for his pistol on the chair, but Amanda stuck to him like a leech.

"Don't kill him, Wally," she pleaded.

"Move, Amanda," Patterson commanded as he tried to shake loose.

"No," she cried. "He might shoot you, please listen to me, Gregory. I didn't think he would find us." She looked over her shoulder at Wallace. His eyes burned with anger. He couldn't stand her to be alone with another man, not even for a swindle. Hers was all an act, Amanda knew, but his was not. That was the danger of running a heist with him. He might go over the line and actually murder someone someday. That would ruin it all.

"I'll kill the both of you, now," Wallace cried, "rutting like animals, like vermin." He cocked his revolver.

Amanda felt Patterson's knees turn mushy and he slumped into her arms, then regained his composure. He tried to dance Amanda toward the chair, but she threw her weight against him as she pleaded with her husband. "Don't harm him, Wally. If you pull that trigger, you just as well kill me."

Hearing a noise behind him, Wallace spun about to see the hotel clerk's head peeking around the door. "This is my wife's and my business, not yours," Wallace cried. The clerk swallowed hard as he stood eye to eye with Wallace's revolver, then slipped meekly back down the hall.

Seeing his chance, Patterson suddenly plowed his arms through Amanda's grip, broke free and dashed for his revolver on the chair. Amanda grabbed at his arm, but missed. She stumbled ahead, her outstretched hands digging into flesh, then a triangle of cloth. She snagged the back flap of his union suit. Patterson tripped, then stumbled and fell headlong toward the chair. A gun exploded.

Amanda screamed at the retort. She felt Patterson's body go limp as she landed atop him. Her worst fears had finally come true. Wallace Sikes had killed one of her dupes. Real tears welled in her eyes now and the acrid smell of gunpowder stung her nose.

She pushed herself up from the body, then looked at Wally. The rage in his eyes had been replaced by fear. She must take charge before he panicked and ruined their chance of an alibi. She must put Patterson's revolver in his own hand, make it look like self-defense. Grabbing at the holster, she jerked Patterson's revolver free, but it slipped from her hand and landed on his head.

The rancher groaned. He was alive!

Amanda grabbed his pistol and looked for a place to hide it. She saw the chamber pot beneath the bed and scrambled to it, lifting the lid and dropping the pistol inside. She hurriedly fastened the buckles on her blouse.

Patterson was stirring, shaking his head and pushing himself up to his hands and knees. Beneath him, the shiny wooden floor was spotless, not a drop of blood. Then Amanda saw the black pucker of a bullet hole in the wall. Thank goodness Wally was a poor shot! With Patterson coming around, Amanda knew she must put on a charade. She must improvise, but would Wally follow her act?

She bent over Patterson, placing her hands upon his cheeks. "You're okay, thank goodness. I didn't know this would lead to trouble." Now came the tricky part, where Wally might snap. "I love you, Gregory Patterson, and wanted you so much, but I should have told you I was a married woman."

Amanda twisted her head around for a moment. Wally was still staring wide-eyed at his gun. Thank goodness!

Patterson mumbled something, then tried to push himself up off his knees, but his whole body trembled. He stared blankly ahead.

Amanda scrambled across the room and

grabbed the water pitcher from the wash-stand. Returning to Patterson, she poured half of it on the cattleman's head, saving the remainder for Wally and his daze.

Patterson sputtered and spit and rubbed the nasty knot he had sustained on the left side of his forehead.

"I'm sorry," she said, covering his face with gentle kisses. "I fear we best send for the marshal to protect us from my beastly husband."

"Huh?" Patterson said, pushing Amanda away.

"Maybe none of the papers will find out about this," Amanda said.

It hit Patterson like lightning. The marshal! The papers! "No," he managed. "My wife would kill me."

Amanda jumped up, planting her fists on her hips. "You're married? What kind of woman do you think I am?" she scowled.

"Just get out and take him with you."

Amanda let out a yip of joy. Then tossed the rest of the water into Wally's face.

He snapped back to the present. "What'd you do that for?"

She grabbed Wally's hand and pulled him through the door and down the stairs, dashing past the bewildered clerk. They bolted out the front door, Wallace finally coming

88

to his senses and jerking Amanda toward their two tethered horses.

Amanda went for one, jumping in the stirrup with one foot and swinging the other over the saddle as Wally untied the reins and tossed them to her. He climbed atop his horse. Together the horses carrying husband and wife galloped down the street past Gregory Patterson's pants. As she rode, Amanda patted her skirt pocket. Reassured that the packet of money was still there, she let out a whoop.

She followed Wally, but he turned west instead of south for Waco. "This isn't the way to Waco," she yelled, exhilarated.

"We're heading to Fort Griffin instead."

They pushed their horses hard all the way to Weatherford, sold their mounts there, and went to the stage station to buy passage to Fort Griffin.

Amanda excused herself to the privy out back and latched the door. She yanked the packet of money from her skirt pocket, knowing for the first time in her life what it was like to hold $10,000.

She started counting it, her pleasure diminishing the deeper she got into the money roll. It was small bills, all of it. And when she had counted it, the stack totaled but $2,000.

"The son of a bitch," she spat. "He cheated us."

CHAPTER 4

Baron Jerome Manchester Paget and his
damn rooster! Marshal Gil Hanson rubbed
his watery, bloodshot eyes and groggily
poured himself a cup of coffee. Each time
someone came within a cannon shot of the
baron's hotel window, the caged rooster
would cackle or crow, and the Englishman
would fire his revolver into the street. No
one had been hit for certain, though the
Tonkawa Cat Tails carried a suspicious
graze wound on his arm. Nonetheless, the
marshal felt obliged to check out each incident.

The gunshots had slacked off since the
first night, but not enough for the marshal
to get a good night's sleep. Hanson wondered why the baron never looked the worse
for wear. Maybe the Englishman was made
of stronger stuff than the marshal had
figured or maybe he didn't need much
sleep. The town still buzzed about the

baron, people gossiping about his comings and goings and whether or not he carried the money satchel. He always did. Folks kept up with the Englishman's activities like industrialists followed the markets, speculating on what he might do next, wondering who would ultimately deprive him of his money.

Hanson shook his head, trying to loosen the clabber that had collected after three nights of poor sleep. Outside the dark sky was softening around the fringes, a veil of pink slipping across the eastern horizon. Hanson gulped down the rest of his coffee, grabbed his hat and stumbled for the door. As he stepped out onto the plank sidewalk, Hanson heard Paget's rooster crow. He slammed his office door and plunged into the dwindling darkness. The stars overhead were fading and dawn's breath was cool and pleasant. Hanson cursed the darkness, cursed the rooster and, most of all, cursed the baron.

Stepping into the middle of Griffin Avenue, Hanson saw the usual lit buildings, the Bee Hive and a couple of the less popular saloons and a few cribs — different each night depending on whether men's tastes had been for plump or skinny, brown-haired or black — as the soiled doves finished cooing for the night.

At the end of Griffin Avenue, Hanson started to turn toward Planter's House, but he heard the crowing of Paget's rooster and spun the opposite direction toward the well-apportioned two-room adobe "Lop-Eared" Annie Lea used. Hanson angled for Annie Lea because her place usually wasn't active this time of night. Hanson knew he would have no trouble seeing who was visiting her because she always opened the window curtains. That was good for business. However, she never faced the window when she had a customer. That was bad for business since it exposed her mismatched assets, which men would pay to see.

Hanson slipped up beside the window and shook his head. There stood "Lop-Eared" Annie Lea in her black-stockinged legs, holding her loose blouse so wide open that she appeared as a butterfly ready to take to the wing. Beyond her, his mouth agape, his head leaning to the left stood Zach Fenster. Hanson shook his head. He'd be ready for female companionship himself if he were married to that prune Spinster Fenster. Poor Zach Fenster! Here he was the richest man in Fort Griffin and he couldn't get his wife to make him a meal, much less a pleasant bed.

Hanson moved on, figuring Fenster deserved a little privacy for the modest pleasure he spent his money on. Hanson retreated toward Griffin Avenue, winding up at the Bee Hive where Burley Sims laid out a food table that Hanson could sample as often as he liked. The marshal pushed his way through the swinging doors and glanced about the room, hazy with cigar and kerosene smoke and smelling of rancid men and perfumed women. One customer was slumped over a back table, unconscious or dead. Hanson nodded at Burley Sims, who was carrying a tray of dirty glasses to the bar.

"Rooster still keeping you up, Marshal?" Sims called.

Hanson grumbled as he ambled to the back table. Standing over the patron slumped there, Hanson toed at his chair, then kicked it. The man groaned.

"He's a live one, Marshal. I checked earlier," Sims announced.

Hanson circled toward the food, stopping at a table near the bar where Joe Loper played poker with two Bee Hive regulars, both with smiles on their faces. Hanson paused, staring over Loper's shoulder toward the mirrored backbar.

Loper pulled his hand to his chest, then

94

turned to stare at Hanson. "I don't like anyone looking over my shoulder when I play."

Hanson moved on. He hadn't paid attention to Loper's hand, especially after he saw how the slant of the backbar mirror offered Loper a glimpse of his opponents' cards. Hanson motioned for Burley Sims to join him at the food table. Sims left his tray of dirty dishes on the bar and approached the marshal. Hanson whispered, "Loper's eyeing your customer's cards in the backbar mirror."

Sims shrugged. "None are complaining about losses."

"Could be bad business, Burley."

"He just wants the Englishman's money. He makes enough to pay me my table fee and doesn't get greedy with my regulars."

The marshal took one of the tin plates stacked on the food table and helped himself to the dregs of last night's meal, the butt end of a burnt roast, a piece of hard bread flaked with cigar ashes, a couple cold potatoes and a spoon of canned oysters. He took a seat and ate slowly. About the time he finished eating, the game at Loper's table broke up, the two customers laughing and slapping Joe Loper on the back. Loper shook their hands, then yawned.

Hanson pushed himself up from his table and angled for the bar, taking one of Sims' cheap cigars. He bit off the end, spat it at a spittoon, missed his target, then stepped outside. Hanson wasn't much for smoking, but he enjoyed chewing on a cigar, especially those soaked in cheap rum. He leaned back against the saloon's cool adobe wall and stared at the pale blue of the morning sky and the long shadows of the emerging sun. Loper's two gambling opponents exited onto the street, departing in opposite directions.

Before Hanson realized it, Joe Loper stood beside him. It was eerie how stealthily Loper had approached.

"Marshal," he nodded, taking a pipe from his pocket and lighting up. His head was obscured by a blue haze of smoke.

Hanson studied the wooden pipe, especially its shiny patches of ornamental metal. The damn pipe was a reflector, one a gambler could leave on the table as he dealt and see what cards he issued his opponents. A man who carried a reflector pipe damn sure wasn't above using a backbar mirror to his advantage.

"What's your angle, Loper?" Hanson pulled the cigar from his lips, spitting a piece of tobacco on the walk.

Loper drew heavily on his pipe, then snickered at the sound of the baron's rooster. "Glad I'm staying at the Southern Hotel. They don't allow chickens."

"Just lice," Hanson replied, knowing the gambler was trying to change the subject. "What's your angle, Loper? You could have taken those two and you wouldn't have needed the backbar mirror to do it."

"I'll tell you the same thing I told Sims," Loper said, jerking his pipe from his mouth and stepping to the edge of the plank walk. He watched a lone rider approaching from the end of the street.

"Your angle, Loper?"

The gambler's voice rose in anger, but he never took his eyes off the approaching rider. "I want that fool Englishman's money."

"A lot of people want his money, Loper. Don't hurt him and don't cheat him or I'll come after you." Hanson poked the cigar between his lips.

Loper stood silent and transfixed, inspecting the horse and rider as they neared. The rider slanted forward in his saddle, his gun hand resting easily on his thigh, then pulled back on the reins until the yellow dun inched along. The rider looked slowly from side to side, taking in the details of buildings and the handful of people emerging with the dawn.

As the rider neared the Bee Hive, Marshal Hanson stepped beside Joe Loper and took in Hide Town's newest arrival. He wore a sneer across his lips and a patch over his left eye. His gaze bore into Hanson like an augur, then his right hand slipped from his thigh to the revolver at his side. Hanson realized the stranger had seen his badge. The marshal straightened, yanking the cigar from his lips and tossing it into the street.

"The son of a bitch," Loper said between gritted teeth.

"Who is he?" Hanson asked as his right hand fell to his pistol.

"One-Eyed Charlie Gatliff, as mean a son of a bitch as walks on two legs, Marshal."

"You know him, Loper?"

"We've had our disagreements."

Loper's veiled brevity increased Hanson's discomfort. "I ain't heard of him."

"He's been in South Texas mostly. I knew him in San Antonio. He must be in deep trouble to ever leave that part of the country. Some say he's killed as many as two dozen men in robberies. He's been known to strip their bodies bare and sell their boots, clothes, unmentionables and all, leaving them dead and naked. Other than that, he's a fine human being."

Hanson felt a cold chill shoot up his spine. Why were there always more bad men than lawmen?

Gatliff seemed to recognize Loper, and he spat toward the Bee Hive, then wiped his lips with the back of his torn sleeve. His tanned face was stubbled with several days' growth of beard. The well-oiled stock of a Winchester carbine poked out of its scabbard over the dun's rump like a serpent about to strike. Gatliff drew even with the Bee Hive, then turned the yellow dun in the middle of the street to face Hanson and Loper.

"Loper, I thought it was you," snarled Gatliff. "Long time no see. Last I heard you were a cripple."

Loper grunted. "The shoulder healed. Least you didn't leave me half blind."

A shrill laugh forced itself out of Gatliff's clenched jaw. "I ain't forgotten who gouged it out, Loper. I'll settle with you another day. I've business here."

Hanson took a step toward the rider. "What's your business?"

Gatliff growled. "The name's Charlie Gatliff. I'm looking for a friend of mine. Once I attend business with him, I'll be leaving town."

99

"What's his name?" Hanson demanded.

"Jerome Manchester Paget, calls himself 'baron.' "

Hanson felt his jaw drop.

Monk Partain groaned. "Dammit, why am I always the one that gets his head bashed?"

"You knew the plan before we left San Angelo," Surry Nettles shot back. "You should've backed out then." Nettles glanced both directions down the Fort Griffin Road, fearing riders might see them together, especially before he turned the two stolen geldings loose.

"Why can't I be the cripple for a change?"

Surry rolled his eyes. Why couldn't Monk Partain accept his fate in life? "Hard as it is for me to tell you this, Monk, you are too damn ugly to be the cripple. Besides, you've got a face that was made for bashing."

"Always thinking you're the handsomest damned son of a bitch that ever walked these parts," Partain scowled.

As if on cue, both men slid from their stolen horses, and stood facing each other. Rage pooled in Nettles like rain in a barrel. He jerked the reins from Partain's hands and tied both horses to a low branch of a live oak tree. From the rifle scabbard beneath his saddle, Nettles pulled a worn crutch, the wood slick from use and the cloth of the makeshift armrest black with dirt and sweat.

Partain, his eyes widening at the sight of the crutch, taunted Nettles. "Last time you did it, a schoolgirl could've hit me harder." Partain stroked his scraggly black beard and gritted his teeth.

Nettles tossed the crutch in the air, catching it by its foot. Gripping it with both hands, he took a half swing for Partain's head. "The stage'll be along in an hour or so." Nettles pointed to the west. "Five miles that way is Griffin."

"Get on with it," Partain commanded, then turned around and stepped toward the road. "Make sure I don't fall in the wagon ruts."

"Say your prayers," Nettles responded.

Monk stiffened.

Drawing back the crutch like a logger cocking an ax, Nettles swung with all his strength at Partain's head. The crutch hit with a sickening thud that turned Nettles' stomach.

For a moment, Partain stood like a sapling quivering in the breeze. Then he toppled over without moving a muscle. He landed with a nauseating thump, his head turning limply to the side, his nose spurting blood.

Nettles sighed. If Partain wouldn't pester him so, Nettles might feel sorry for him, unconscious and bleeding. Nonetheless, the lump that was rising on his head and the blood that was puddling beneath his cheek were convincing evidence that Partain had been waylaid and robbed by some bad man. And, when Partain regained his consciousness, he would have a terrible stuttering problem, a problem that only the healing touch of the Reverend G.W. "God Willing" Tuck could cure.

A final time, Nettles glanced both ways down the road to make sure he hadn't been observed. With no one in sight, Nettles rested the crutch on his shoulder like a soldier on parade and marched to the horses. He slid the crutch back in the scabbard and untied the reins of both horses. Nettles mounted, twisting in the saddle a final time to check on Partain. Once he had left Monk near an ant bed and Partain suffered the consequences for several days. The Reverend Tuck could cure stuttering, but not ant stings. "So long, Monk," Nettles said, "see you at the revival."

Nudging his mount away from Partain, Nettles turned the horses toward Fort Griffin. He would ride a couple miles, then scare the horses away. From there, he would limp into town on his cane and beg for handouts, maybe even try to find a job, that always built sympathy, and brought in a few more handouts. For Monk's sake, Nettles hoped this tale of a rich Englishman was true.

The stage rumbled along the Fort Griffin road, throwing up plumes of dust, spitting bits of grit and dirt and pebbles into the coach. Occasionally the driver spat tobacco juice which blew back into the coach as well. As a mode of transportation, it beat crawling, Flora Belmont figured, but not by much. She had ridden all the way from Weatherford with a red-haired woman in a plain riding suit and her doting husband. They had wanted to talk, but Flora did not have the heart for it, not after burying her fifth husband.

Not yet thirty-five and a widow five times over. It was terrible how tragedy had walked arm-in-arm with her through each marriage, how each husband had died suddenly, each leaving her considerable money. She had left Chicago when a couple of the papers had taken to calling her the "black widow." She had only lost three husbands in Chicago, another in St. Louis and her latest, God rest his soul, in Galveston. That's where she had picked up the trail of

Baron Jerome Manchester Paget. She had married and buried an industrialist, a publisher and a slaughter house owner in Chicago, a shipping mogul in St. Louis and a cotton broker in Galveston. But she had never had a chance to marry royalty. Until now!

By coincidence, his lordship the baron had arrived by boat in Galveston on Monday, the paper had carried the story on Tuesday, her husband had died on Wednesday and been buried on Thursday. Thursday afternoon, Flora Belmont had taken her grief to the bank and withdrawn $7,000 to assuage it. Her grief was so great that she couldn't stay in Galveston, not for the time being, of course. She would return and live in her late husband's mansion and dispose of the rest of his assets, but not before marrying his lordship, the Baron Jerome Manchester Paget, and bringing his fortune and title, with or without him, back to Galveston. She had hurried to start on the trail of Baron Paget, having time to pack only two trunks of clothes and the bottle of cyanide that she had had occasion to use five times previously.

The stage swerved at a slight curve in the road and she looked outside. Through her black veil and the shroud of dust tossed up by the stage, she saw something beside a live oak tree that caused her to gasp. It was a crumpled body with a full black beard like her latest husband, Bernard Belmont of Galveston. On the opposite seat, the red-headed woman, too, had been looking out the window, but she gave no sign of seeing a body. Was Flora's mind playing tricks on her? Had she killed one too many husbands? Surely the driver had seen it. But why hadn't he stopped? Was it an apparition of her late husband, come back to haunt her? Maybe she was getting old, maybe she was imagining things, maybe she had lost the stomach for the killing. But if that were so, she wanted the courage to marry once more and to bury one more husband, then she could bestow a royal title upon herself and live in riches forever. Lady Flora Paget! She liked the sound of that.

Across from her, she noticed the red-haired woman shift in her seat, wriggling her nose. Her doting husband, who had held her hand almost the entire way from Weatherford, shook his head. Then the odor hit Flora. She pulled a lace handkerchief from her beaded purse, then lifted her veil atop her hat and dabbed at her nose and the corner of her eyes. Vaguely, the stench reminded her of the aroma of her third husband, the slaughter house owner.

The stage tipped forward and started down into a broad river plain. Across the valley and beyond the river, Flora Belmont could see the scattered buildings that made up Fort Griffin. What she wouldn't do to find the right husband, she thought as she looked over this ragged town. Still she could not shake the memory of that specter she had seen beside the road a couple miles back. She hoped Paget didn't have a black beard like her latest late husband.

Shortly, the stage was splashing through the water and passing the edge of town, still at a gallop. Damn that driver, Flora Belmont thought. He jerked on the reins and pushed on the brake, the stage slowing, then sliding from the momentum. Flora Belmont was suddenly thrown forward in her seat and she grabbed for the window post to steady herself, but she missed it and fell forward against Wallace Sikes. He shoved her back against her seat. Before Flora Belmont could protest the rough treatment, the stage came to a stop. The instant the door swung open, Wallace Sikes burst out and landed on his feet.

"Hurry, Amanda, let's get to a hotel."

"Sure, darling, as soon as we can."

Quickly, she evacuated the stage.

Flora Belmont lowered the veil over her face and stepped outside where a crowd stood watching her. She saw an Indian, a handsome Army officer, a lawman and two boys scuffling before her.

"Hotel, ma'am, the Southern is the best around," said the taller boy. "I'm Alonzo Giddings, you can trust me."

Another, younger boy stepped forward. "Ma'am, the Planter's House is the only hotel in Fort Griffin with feather mattresses. And, the Planter's House is where royalty stays."

"Your name, young man?" asked Flora Belmont.

"Sammy Collins."

"Then Samuel, please lead the way and return for my two trunks," Flora said, her nose in the air.

"Just a moment, Sammy," interjected Amanda Sikes. "You say royalty lodges at the Planter's House?"

"Yes, ma'am," replied Sammy.

"We, too, want to stay there."

Sammy laughed at Alonzo Giddings. "Planter's House gets all the passengers off this one."

Giddings grumbled, then spun around and marched away.

Flora Belmont snapped her fingers to the

driver. "My trunks."

The driver, who stood opposite the law-man, waved her off.

Incensed, Flora Belmont marched to the driver's side. "Sir, I believe I told you I had two trunks to unload."

"I'll get them, dammit," Shorty DeLong replied, "but not before I tell the marshal about the body back down the road."

Flora Belmont smiled. She hadn't been seeing things after all. What a joy it would be to be married again, she thought. "Okay, young man," she said to Sammy, "could you introduce me to royalty?"

"I can arrange that," Sammy answered, "I'm his valet."

"And us, too?" asked Amanda Sikes.

"Sure," he replied.

CHAPTER 5

Marshal Gil Hanson made out the body propped against the lone live oak tree beside the barren road. As he reined up his fidgety roan gelding at the foot of the body, Hanson almost gagged. Death was never pretty, but this was as ugly a carcass as Hanson had ever seen, with warped head, crooked nose, closed eyes, scraggly beard, and bloodied face. The roan sniffed the air, then dipped its head and nibbled on the dry grass, its fear of death giving way to its appetite. Hanson noticed a stain of blood-soaked dirt and a trail of red droplets leading to the tree. The poor fellow had crawled into the shade before leaving this Earth to discuss with his maker the ugly face he had been given.

Hanson slid out of his saddle onto the ground and pulled a pair of hobbles from his saddlebag to cuff the roan's forelegs. He turned his gaze to the body. At least putrefaction hadn't set in. Circling the tree, Hanson examined the trampled grass and figured two horses had stopped. Finding nothing else, he approached the body and squatted, studying the man's boots, then allowing his gaze to crawl from the man's feet, past his knees, over his thighs, and up his chest to his bloodied face. What else Hanson saw did not register for a moment. Two open eyes!

Suddenly, Hanson leaped from his squat, a scream hanging in his throat, his hand grabbing at his Colt Revolver. His pistol was halfway out before he realized this was not a ghost, but a man. A man still alive!

"W-wa-wat-te-ter," the man mumbled.

Catching his breath, Hanson shoved the pistol in his holster and darted to his roan. He untied the canteen strap from his saddle, then fumbled with the cork, pulling it free and splashing water on himself. Bending over the man, Hanson held the canteen to his nose, hoping the aroma would revive him. The man's eyes were fixed somewhere beyond the horizon and his arms drooped at his side until Hanson pressed the canteen against his bloodied lips. As the water gushed into his mouth, his hands flopped up and grabbed the canteen. He suckled the water in gulps.

"Whoa, pardner, not so fast," Hanson said, jerking the canteen away from this roadside Lazarus. "What happened?"

The man lifted his hand and flinched as his fingers touched a great knot on the side of his head. "R-ro-rob-b-be-bed."

"How much?" Hanson asked

The Lazarus wiped at the dried blood caked in his beard, then gingerly lifted his head toward Hanson. "F-fi-fif-t-ty, m-may-b-be, s-se-sev-v-ve-ven-ty-f-fi-fiv-five. . . ."

Hanson doubted this fool had ever had seen fifty dollars in his life, much less seventy-five.

"C-ce-cen-cents," he sputtered.

Then no wonder the robber had tried to knock his head all the way to the Llano Estacado, Hanson thought. "What's your name, pardner?" Hanson corked the canteen.

"M-mo-mon-monk P-pa-par-t-ta-tain," he managed.

"This guy that robbed you, did he wear an eye patch?"

Partain shrugged. "D-do-don-don't k-kn-kno-know."

Maybe One-Eyed Charlie Gatliff had robbed Partain or maybe he hadn't. Damn shame Partain couldn't talk any better. If this robbery ever came to trial, Partain's

111

testimony would likely outlive the accused. "You stuttered all your life?"

"N-no-not b-be-bef-f-fo-fore I-I w-wa-was r-ro-rob-robbed," Partain replied.

"You do now." Hanson grabbed Partain's arms and helped him to his wobbly feet. "We'll ride double to Fort Griffin."

Partain grunted and, for once, didn't stutter.

Hanson helped the stutterer into the saddle. Bad as riding double was, it was better than having to bury someone.

When she bent over the open oven door, Aunt Moses looked like a skirted buffalo. She glanced over her shoulder at Sammy Collins. "It's about time you showed up," she said, standing up and clanging the oven door shut. The hot kitchen smelled of fresh bread, baked ham, canned corn, and boiled potatoes. "I should be grateful, all the business the baron's bringing, but it's making me a slave to the kitchen. Run down to Fenster's store and get one of those big tins of tomatoes. I figure I'll need that to feed this crowd."

"Okay," Sammy answered. Knowing it was almost closing time, he darted out the kitchen door, past the lean-to that was his room and around the side of the hotel. At the corner of the building, he ran past a man with a black patch over his eye, then raced as fast as he could to Fenster's store, reaching it just as Zach Fenster was hanging the "closed" sign. Sammy waved his arms. "Wait."

The store owner opened the door and motioned Sammy inside.

"Thanks," Sammy managed, heaving for air. "Aunt Moses needs a big tin of tomatoes. The baron's attracted us a lot of business."

"That baron," Fenster huffed. "Before he came, Beulah never talked to me, which is how I preferred it. Now, she talks to me all the time about the baron. It's baron this, baron that. She's shook the hand that's shook the hand of the Queen of England. So what?"

Sammy grimaced. "He's good to me!"

Fenster placed his hand on Sammy's shoulder. "Not that I don't care for the baron, Sammy. He's got a bit of charm, I admit, but not as much as Beulah harps on. Let me get your tomatoes."

The slick wooden floor creaked as Fenster strode to the back counter. He moved a ladder to the shelves which ran from floor to ceiling and climbed eye-level with the large canned goods. Fenster grabbed a tin, backed down the ladder and offered it to Sammy.

Sammy tucked the can under his arm like a stack of school books.

Fenster said, "I'll add it to the hotel's account."

Sammy nodded. "See you at supper." He dashed out the door, almost tripping over a straw-haired cripple hobbling by on a worn crutch. "Sorry," Sammy called over his shoulder toward the man he had never seen before.

"Don't be sorry," the man called. "Be thankful you can run."

Sammy sprinted down the street until a pig darted out from behind a water trough, squealing and nipping at his heels. The pig's snout bumped Sammy's heel and Sammy stumbled, tossing the tin of tomatoes forward as he tumbled onto the dusty street. The can rolled ahead, the stray pig giving chase. Sammy said a word Aunt Moses had banned, then shot up and dusted himself off.

"You all right, Sammy?" came a familiar voice.

Sammy looked up to see Marshal Gil Hanson riding on his horse behind a bearded and bloodied man. Sammy nodded, his face red with embarrassment, his eyes inspecting the man the marshal was

114

bringing in. Sammy couldn't remember seeing a homelier human being. Sammy gaped for a moment, then burst ahead for the tomatoes, kicking the pig solidly in the belly. The pig squealed, snorted, then scurried away. Sammy picked up the tin and raced on home.

Rounding the back of the hotel, he slowed down, caught his breath and slapped at the front of his shirt and britches a couple more times. Aunt Moses would jump him for sure now, complaining that he couldn't make his clothes go more than three or four days before she had to wash them. Taking a deep breath, he entered the kitchen.

Aunt Moses looked up from a pan of bread she was slicing and pointed to her work table. "Put the tomatoes over there." She shook her head. "You're a complete mess, Sammy, what happened?"

"A pig tripped me."

Aunt Moses scowled. "Why can't you make your clothes last longer so it'd be less washing for me?"

Sammy shrugged. He did most of the work on wash day, anyway.

"Go change so you'll be presentable for the baron at supper." Aunt Moses dropped her knife and headed for the canned tomatoes.

Sammy escaped the kitchen for his lean-to with its solid door, unbroken window and plank floor. It was about as weather tight as anything in Hide Town. At one end was his bed and a crate with a lamp on it. At the other end was a small table and two wobbly chairs. Between them was a petite laundry stove he used to heat water on wash days and the room on cold nights.

Slipping into the dusky room, he closed the door and began to unbutton his shirt. An odd feeling crept over him like the breath of a demon. It was as if he were not alone. As his eyes adjusted to the dimness, he turned around and caught his breath.

At the table not three paces away sat someone, an evil-looking man with a black patch over his left eye and a stubbly beard. He brandished a Bowie knife and was calmly carving on the table.

Sammy Collins eased toward the door.

"I wouldn't leave just yet, if I was you, boy," he sneered. "You go about your business while we visit. You understand?"

Sammy felt his knees tremble. "What do you want?"

"I want you to work for me, boy. That's all. I'll pay you a dollar a day." One-Eyed Charlie Gatliff swiped at the air a couple times, motioning with his knife for Sammy

116

to keep undressing.

Pulling his shirt off and throwing it behind him on the bed, Sammy faced this evil man and began to unbutton his pants.

"Boy, I want you to let me know what that baron is up to, what his plans are, that type of thing."

"Why should I?"

The man leaned back in his chair, his single eye affixed on Sammy Collins. "If a dollar a day won't convince you, maybe this will." Instantly, he flipped the knife in the air, caught the blade between his fingers, then flung it across the room.

Before he could move, Sammy heard the swoosh of the knife past his ear and the thud as it stuck in the wall beyond him. For a moment, the knife hummed from the impact's vibration. Sammy gulped.

"Tell me what the baron's doing, where he's going, who he's seeing, things like that. If you don't," Gatliff grinned, "I'll slit your belly and skin you from the inside out."

By the look in Gatliff's one malevolent eye, Sammy figured he meant every word of his threat.

Shooting up from his chair, Gatliff strode past Sammy for the knife. Sammy's breath froze in fear. Holding his unbuttoned pants at his waist, Sammy slipped to the opposite side of the room.

"You gonna help me?" Gatliff asked over his shoulder as he jerked the knife free and studied its sharp blade. Turning around, Gatliff slid the blade into its scabbard. "My Arkansas toothpick don't make noise when it cuts, but you will. First, you scream, then you gurgle and gasp and shortly you die, simple as that."

Sammy released his breath and gritted his teeth, trying not to look scared.

Gatliff stepped toward Sammy, who retreated until his back bumped against the wall. Gatliff reached for Sammy, putting his cold hands upon the boy's shoulders.

"What's your answer?"

Unable to respond through clenched teeth, Sammy nodded.

"And don't be telling nobody about this. You understand, boy?" Gatliff turned toward the door. "I left a twenty-dollar gold piece on the table for you. Payment in advance."

Even in the dimness, Sammy could see the table well enough to know Gatliff was lying.

"There's no money," Sammy challenged, proud of his daring until Gatliff spun around, his hand reaching for his waist. Sammy held his breath.

Gatliff's mean face parted into a narrow smile. "You ain't so dumb after all." His hand slid into his pocket and reappeared with a gold piece between his thumb and forefinger. He flipped it at Sammy.

As Sammy released his unbuttoned britches to snatch the coin, his pants slid past his knees.

Gatliff said, "I'll see you every day. You find me when I need to know things." With that, he jerked open the door and was gone.

His pants at his ankles, Sammy lifted the gold coin and studied it. He had never held twenty dollars in gold before, but neither had he ever betrayed someone like this. He lost himself in confusion, forgetting the time until he heard a shrill voice calling his name. Aunt Moses needed him in the kitchen.

Beulah Fenster stood with her arms folded over her meager bosom, glaring at her place at the table. Some woman dressed in black had had the audacity to take her seat. Each time Aunt Moses brought a platter of food into the room, Beulah would lift her abundant nose in the air, sniffing indignation instead of the aroma of fresh bread, baked ham, canned corn, boiled potatoes, and stewed tomatoes.

Except for Beulah Fenster, the regulars

were already seated. Zach Fenster in his accustomed place staring at the grieving Flora Belmont. Jake Ellis was intrigued by the red-haired woman in the dusty riding suit opposite him, but every time he glanced that way, the woman's husband growled.

Amanda Sikes enjoyed those furtive glances, knowing they would stoke the fires of ardor in her husband, who — much to his dismay — still had had no chance to satisfy his urgings since leaving Fort Worth. To her husband's left sat Colonel John Paul Jenkins, who conversed freely with Wallace Sikes while trying to get a better look at Amanda. While Wallace fought off the stare of Jake Ellis, the colonel was successfully reconnoitering Amanda.

Between Amanda Sikes and Flora Belmont was an empty chair for the Baron Jerome Manchester Paget. Beulah Fenster was plainly disturbed by the dilemma she faced. She could either ask the woman in black to move or she could rip her head off.

Beulah Fenster cleared her throat and tapped the woman in black on the shoulder. "Ma'am, you're in my accustomed chair."

Flora Belmont looked over her shoulder. "Beg your pardon, sister," she said with a twist of sarcasm. Slowly, regally, she arose from her chair, pushed it back, then stepped out of the way long enough to pull the empty chair beside her into the space just vacated by her own. With that, she sat back down in the same place, different chair. "There you are, sister!"

Beulah Fenster shook her head. "That's not what I meant."

"Sister, how can I know what you meant if you don't say what you mean?"

"I mean that's my place you're in."

Flora Belmont picked up her napkin and shook it of its folds. "It's not your place to tell me my place, sister."

Beulah Fenster realized she had made a mistake. She should have ripped the woman's head off to begin with. She might have attempted that delicate operation had not the baron entered the dining room. She moved the chair behind Flora into the empty space for the Englishman and walked around the table to the chair beside her husband. She snorted and seated herself, Zach Fenster sliding his chair away from hers.

Hotel proprietor Moses Miller sat at the head of the table, smiling because he had just counted the day's receipts. Thanks to the baron, business had never been better at the Planter's House. The baron attracted business like dung drew flies.

121

Entering the dining room, the baron paused, money satchel in hand, nodding to each of his acquaintances. "Good evening, ladies and gentlemen," he said, studying the seating arrangements. He lifted his hand and pointed to Beulah Fenster across the table from where she normally sat. "Madam," he said, "this is even better. Now I can more fully see your beautiful features."

Beulah answered with a so-there smirk, especially when she saw her husband rocking his chair still farther from hers.

The baron marched around the table, introducing himself to both Flora Belmont and Amanda Sikes, lifting the hand of each to his lips for a gentle kiss. Wallace Sikes' chair legs screeched against the hardwood floor as he moved to stand up and challenge the baron for undue familiarity with his wife, but Amanda kicked him under the table, and grabbed his thigh with her free hand.

"Please forgive my mourning, your lordship," said Flora Belmont, "but I just buried my fifth husband, who left me my fifth fortune."

The baron's head turned sharply. "Such bad luck, madam, for a woman so beautiful. And, so rich."

Beulah Fenster hid her snarl behind an

uplifted napkin.

The baron acknowledged the colonel and introduced himself to Wallace Sikes, then nodded to Sammy Collins and took his seat, sliding his satchel under his chair.

"I am famished," he announced, then looked across the table at Beulah Fenster. "How is the lovely Mrs. Fenster tonight?" he asked and again Beulah Fenster blossomed like a spring flower.

Her smile answered his compliment just as Aunt Moses sat down and nodded for Uncle Moses to give thanks. He did a fine job, mentioning several times the many blessings of prosperity.

When Uncle Moses finished, Aunt Moses started the food around and Jake Ellis initiated the conversation. "Found yourself any land to buy for your buffalo ranch, Baron?" asked the buffalo merchant.

"Indeed not," answered the baron, spooning a stewed tomato onto his plate. "I'm prepared to begin my search. I figure to inspect the wilderness for suitable land, well watered."

The colonel leaned forward as he forked a couple potatoes. "Too dangerous, Baron, you riding out there alone."

"I must warn you, governor," replied the baron, "that I am adept in the manly arts of defense, though having a guide would be suitable, provided he's honest and would not kill me in my sleep for my money."

The colonel laughed. "It'll take you a long while to find an honest man in Fort Griffin."

"How about Ike Mann?" suggested Zach Fenster. "He's a grizzled old bird, but as honest as they come. He's a buffalo hunter that knows the land and always settles his accounts at the store once he sells his hides."

Uncle Moses mumbled agreement. "Ike's an honest man, but he just don't bathe enough and always wants to spend the night here when he should stay in the camp with all the other hunters."

"I shall seek out this man called Mann," the baron said, smiling when others giggled at his funny. As the food circled the table from hand to hand, the baron took small portions of each dish before passing it on. He sat stiffly erect in his chair, his head straight, his shoulders square, his movements precise. He looked to Zach Fenster. "Governor Fenster, might you bring me a carton of .22-caliber cartridges tomorrow? I have discharged my pistol considerably the past few nights to discourage thieves."

"He'd be delighted to," Beulah Fenster responded before her husband could answer. "On the house."

The baron scratched his close cropped beard. "On the house?"

"It means free," Beulah Fenster answered with a smile.

"I would take them free only if you would do me the honor of delivering them, Mrs. Fenster, if your husband doesn't object."

"He doesn't!" she answered.

The baron nodded at Fenster and offered a smile to Beulah.

"Your lordship," interrupted Flora Belmont, "just what exactly does a baron do for a living?"

The baron twisted his head toward the impertinent Flora Belmont. "He does what all gentlemen want to do, madam."

From the end of the table, Aunt Moses gasped as if what all men wanted could not be discussed in mixed company.

The baron turned to Aunt Moses, offering her his most calming smile. "Like all gentlemen, a baron hunts, practices the manly arts, attends the races, yachts, frequents balls." Turning back to Flora Belmont, he finished. "That's how a baron lives."

"Not how he lives, your lordship, but how does he make his money?" Flora Belmont pressed.

"By inheritance, madam, much as I gather you have made your fortune."

She touched her napkin to her lips. "To the contrary, your lordship, I had to work to find five men with solid fortunes and weak hearts." Flora Belmont laughed.

At the end of the table, Aunt Moses dropped her spoon against her plate. "You would marry for money, nothing else?" she gasped.

"Five times, I have, sister, and I'm looking for a sixth." Flora Belmont was as adamant about her goal as Aunt Moses was aghast.

"In London," intoned the baron, "we are much more civilized than you here in the wilds. You have this strange notion that a marriage is made only of love. Marriage can be an arrangement of convenience. Indeed, I have come to America to expand my family's dwindling fortune through investments or through marriage to a woman of means, even a widow, provided she is of substantial means."

Amanda Sikes didn't like the direction the conversation was going. She hadn't had time to say a word much less snare the baron in her clutches and here this witch seated on the other side of him was already talking marriage and shared fortunes. It was time for drastic action.

126

She placed her fork on the table and dropped her hand to her lap, as if she were going for her napkin. Instead, she discreetly slid her hand under the table cloth toward the baron. If her husband realized what was happening, he might explode in a rage right here. But if Amanda didn't stake out her claim on the baron's affections, she might never have a shot at his money, even if it were dwindling.

Her hand touched his leg and he never flinched, nor changed his expression. Slowly, his head turned toward hers and she let the tip of her tongue trace the pink of her lips. He smiled. Amanda knew she, not Flora Belmont, had the baron's attention now. Suggestively, she patted his thigh, then felt a soft hand patting hers. As she turned to smile at the baron, her triumph turned to horror.

Both of his hands were on the table!

Amanda flinched, jerked her hand away and bent forward looking beyond the baron at Flora Belmont, who leaned forward as well, giving Amanda the haughty look of one who had filed first papers on a claim. Damn her, thought Amanda Sikes, disgusted that Flora Belmont would stoop to marriage just to steal a man's money. Amanda stared at Flora until both her hands reappeared above the table.

"So," concluded Baron Jerome Manchester Paget for Aunt Moses, "in England, especially among royalty, social standing and wealth are more important than sentimentality in making marriages."

Aunt Moses still did not understand. "But what if the man does not love his wife?"

The baron gave Aunt Moses a studied look. "That, madam, is what mistresses are for."

Aunt Moses sputtered, her face blushing. "A dreadful way of life," she replied.

"To the contrary," replied the baron, "it is a well-developed system. A gentleman in public with his mistress, keeps her on his left arm." The baron paused, looking to Amanda Sikes on his left. "A gentleman's wife is accorded the honor of his right arm." As he spoke, he turned this time to his right and Flora Belmont. "This custom of differentiating the left from the right prevents nasty misunderstandings among the slightly acquainted. And as most men have mistresses, so do most ladies have male companions. In England, among royalty, it is understood you never comment in public how little a lady's offspring resembles her husband."

Jake Ellis, the buffalo hide buyer,

scratched his head and spoke. "Baron, why did you leave a country with such grand customs, not to mention fine morals, and come to Texas?"

The baron pointed his fork at Jake Ellis. "Excellent question, governor. The fact is, all the inbreeding makes for some ugly women. And let me add, ladies, that were not both Beulah Fenster and Aunt Moses spoken for already, my search for a new baroness would have ended this very day."

Sammy Collins rolled his eyes, but Aunt Moses now wore a smile as broad as her hips. Sammy shuddered to think what English women must look like.

The conversation drifted to other things and then to dessert when Aunt Moses brought out a pan of apple cobbler fresh from the oven. She offered everyone a glass of sweet milk with it and the baron chose to pour his milk over his cobbler, then eat it with relish. "Another excellent meal," he said after finishing the last bite of cobbler. "I fear I must retire now for a good night's sleep."

Jake Ellis cleared his throat. "We all might get a good night's sleep if you'd quit shooting every time your damn rooster crowed."

"Indeed, governor, you are right. But I've considerable money that many men in this town desire. Once all men know I will not be intimidated by their rough ways, the sooner we can all get a good night's sleep." The baron pushed back his chair and arose. "Ladies, please excuse me and, gentlemen, good night." He nodded to each person around the table and picked up his satchel. "And, lad, might I borrow you to turn back my bed shortly?" the baron asked, looking all the time at Aunt Moses.

"Of course, it would be fine," Aunt Moses said, "because Sammy can finish up his chores afterwards."

"Good evening," the baron said, departing the room.

"Damned foreigner," scowled Wallace Sikes under his breath.

Sammy didn't like Wallace and Amanda Sikes. They had gotten off the stage with nothing but the clothes on their backs. He wondered if they had left somewhere in a hurry. When Sammy's cobbler bowl was clean as a sun-bleached skeleton, he asked to be excused and walked to the Englishman's room. His pocket held the twenty-dollar gold piece that One-Eyed Charlie Gatliff had given him to spy on the baron. He had never felt richer or poorer. Reaching the baron's room, he knocked. In a moment, Sammy heard the baron kicking the wedge loose from beneath the door.

The door cracked, then swung open. Sammy sighed and entered, the rooster in the corner cackling at his entry.

"Why the long face, lad?"

Sammy felt too embarrassed to tell the truth, to admit how he had betrayed the Englishman to that evil man. "Did you mean all you said about the English women being ugly and Beulah and Aunt Moses being so pretty?"

The baron laughed. "Goodness no, lad. That is the art of flattery. They most definitely are not prettier than the average English woman, nor are Amanda Sikes and Flora Belmont."

"I don't trust that Sikes woman and her husband." Sammy moved across the room to turn down the baron's bed covers.

"It's hard to know who to trust, lad. That's why I value you as someone I can trust and talk to."

Sammy's head drooped. Not an hour ago he had betrayed the baron for a gold piece that now seemed to burn through his pocket into the flesh of his leg. He couldn't stand it. "You can't trust me."

"What lad?"

"Some one-eyed fellow threatened me before supper, saying he would kill me if I

131

didn't post him on your comings and goings. He promised me a dollar a day if I did."

"Goodness, lad, I hope you took him up on his offer."

Sammy hesitated before admitting the truth. "I did."

"Good for you, lad, good for you!"

"You mean you're not mad?"

"No, lad, no. I'm not hiding anything. Tell him whatever I'm doing, where I'm going. I've no secrets."

Sammy shook his head. "He's an evil man who could kill you."

The baron smiled. "I can protect myself, lad."

"He scares me."

The baron nodded. "Indeed, you must be careful as will I."

"Do because you're the only real friend I've got. I don't know what I'll do when you leave."

The baron cocked his head. "Maybe I'll take you with me to London, make you my permanent valet."

Sammy let out a whoop. A baron, a member of royalty, offering him an escape from Fort Griffin. "But you must be careful."

"Indeed I will, lad, but we must both be careful. Should the occasion arise that someone says a message is from me, do not believe him unless he knows the sign we will agree upon now. And if he knows it, do whatever he says."

"A sign?" Sammy scratched his chin.

"Remember 'London Bridge is falling down.' That shall be the sign that the message is authentic. If the messenger tells you 'London Bridge is falling down,' do whatever he says, no matter who he is."

"Yes, sir," Sammy replied, wondering if one day soon he might actually see London Bridge.

CHAPTER 6

Tugging his hat in place, Marshal Gil Hanson glanced at the unlocked cell where Monk Partain was sleeping off the knot on his head. Though the baron's rooster had been quiet during the night, Partain hadn't, talking deliriously in his sleep, something about always being the one to get busted on the head. Oddly, Partain didn't stutter in his sleep.

Hanson ambled outside in the early morning cool and turned toward the Bee Hive for breakfast. Walking past two buildings, he heard a high-pitched scream and a clatter amid the empty barrels and clutter. His hand flew to his revolver as a terrified tomcat with a stub for a tail shot past him down the street.

Hanson relaxed. Damn fool Tonkawa! In a moment, Cat Tails emerged from the darkness, holding his trophy overhead like a warrior with a new scalp.

134

The marshal shook his head and moved on, looking warily around the street. Half the town was waking after a night's rest, the other half passing out after a night's debauchery. Hanson barged into the Bee Hive. A dozen men with stony faces, lethargic eyes and dwindling drinks barely realized his presence. In the back, Joe Loper sat alone at a table, practicing his card manipulations. Burley Sims invited Hanson to a free meal. Hanson obliged himself, grabbing the last boiled egg, a good chunk of roast beef and a slab of hard bread before pouring himself a cup of coffee. He moved to Loper's table.

"Mind if I join you, Loper?" he asked and sat down.

Loper shrugged and kept practicing false cuts and shuffles.

Hanson toyed with his food. "You and Gatliff go back a ways?"

Loper's fingers froze and his eyes stared beyond the marshal toward the past.

Chewing a bite of greasy roast, Hanson awaited details, but got none. Loper was hiding something. The marshal sopped up some grease with his hard bread and pointed his fork at Loper. "You figure Gatliff'd kill the baron?"

Slowly, Loper nodded. "First chance he gets."

Hanson shook his head. "I can't watch the baron all the time."

Loper studied the marshal. "I can help."

Hanson wondered about Loper's angle. What was the gambler pulling on him? "How's that, Loper?"

"Put out the word I'll kill any man that harms a hair on the Englishman's head."

"What good would that do, Loper?"

The gambler pushed himself back from the table, wriggling the fingers of his gun hand. "Would you want to take a chance against me, Marshal?"

Hanson saw a dead calm in the gambler's steely eyes. The marshal shook his head.

The gambler relaxed. "As the law, you can't bully folks like that. I can and it might save you trouble and the baron his life."

Hanson studied the gambler. "Give me your word you won't hurt the Englishman."

Loper grinned. "A gambler's word ain't worth the paper it's not written on."

The marshal nodded.

"I won't harm him, Marshal, as long as you don't interfere when I involve him in a card game."

Hanson considered Loper's offer. If the gambler kept his word, Hanson had made a good deal. If the gambler didn't, Hanson was no worse off than he was now. "It's a deal, Loper." With nothing else to discuss, Hanson finished his breakfast. Loper resumed card practice.

Hanson was about to pick up and leave when he saw the saloon door swing open. In hobbled a lame man, a gnarled crutch under his right arm and a tin cup in his left hand, dragging his crooked right foot behind him. He was a handsome man, with hair the color of fresh straw and a slight smile that showed both the determination and the pain of trying to overcome his deformity. Hanson stared at yet another stranger in Fort Griffin.

Surry Nettles cursed under his breath. The marshal had taken Monk Partain to jail yesterday and Nettles had seen nothing of him since. Was the marshal wise to Monk and himself? Nettles thumped his crutch into the floor and dragged his crooked right foot behind him. He thumped, dragged, thumped, dragged all the way to the bar.

The bartender stood with arms folded across his chest. "This ain't a charity house, fellow."

Nettles grimaced and shook his head. He'd see that the Reverend Tuck took care of this smug son of a bitch for insulting an emissary of a man of God. The Reverend

Tuck, for all his many shortcomings, looked out for his shills, attacking in his sermons those who had offended Monk or Surry. And a saloon made such an easy target with all its drunkenness, gambling, and dissipation.

"What's food cost?"

"Food's free with drinks, two bits without."

Nettles dropped his head. "That's more than I got." He waited, hoping the barkeep would show an ounce of human pity and share a plate of God's bounty with him.

"Payment in advance," the barkeep said with a smile.

"I'll work for a meal, sweep up, wash glasses," Nettles pleaded.

"No cripples are gonna work for me," Sims answered emphatically. "Bad for business."

The Reverend Tuck had always warned Nettles to control his anger at moments like these. Revenge upon the unmerciful and the unholy was to be reserved for the reverend himself. Nettles gritted his teeth, fighting the impulse to clobber the barkeep. His anger dulling his senses, Nettles realized someone had approached the bar. When Nettles turned, the first thing he saw was a badge. He gulped.

"Morning," the marshal said, "when did you get to town?"

"Yesterday," Nettles replied, his blood racing.

"We don't get many cripples. How'd you get here?"

"Walked some, rode a freight wagon most of the way," Nettles lied, wondering what the marshal knew.

Nodding, Hanson stuck his hand in his britches pocket. "Maybe I can help you." With that he tossed a quarter in Nettles' tin cup. "Now, Burley, he can have a meal, on me."

The barkeep nodded. "Have at it."

"Thank you, Marshal, thank you very much."

The marshal waved his thanks aside. "How'd it happen, your foot?"

"Wagon accident," Nettles replied. "My ma took the wagon to church one Sunday while my pa worked in the field. The horse spooked and the wagon overturned on me, ruining my leg."

Hanson shook his head.

"Ma always blamed Pa for working in the fields on Sunday, said God was punishing him for not keeping the Sabbath holy."

"A real shame, though seems like your pa should've come out the cripple." Hanson slapped Nettles hard on the back.

Nettles stumbled a bit, shifting feet and crutch. He hoped the marshal hadn't noticed the movement of his lame leg.

The marshal nodded amiably at Nettles. "Enjoy your breakfast and stay out of the street when Shorty DeLong drives the stage through town. He's run over women, children and animals, so he wouldn't think twice about trampling a cripple."

Nettles accentuated his nod with a smile.

Cat Tails had an incredible thirst, a craving that mere water would not quench, not after a full night stalking his latest feline victim. Cat Tails wanted whiskey, but he had no money and no barter goods. Fondly, he remembered Dung Foot, just off the stage a few days back pulling from his odd parfleche a funny piece of paper. Cat Tails had exchanged that odd paper for a full bottle of whiskey at the back door of the Bee Hive. That odd bag held enough paper to quench Cat Tails' thirst for life. If only Dung Foot hadn't placed that rooster in the hotel window!

Now, Cat Tails desired to chop off that rooster's head as much as he one day dreamed of catching a live buzzard with his bare hands or snipping the tail off a live fox or, even more dangerous, clipping the tail off a skunk before it could spray him. Dung Foot's first night in town, Cat Tails had actually gotten his hands on the cage and was prepared to remove it when the bird cackled. Cat Tails had ducked as a bullet came whistling from the room, grazing his arm. A light sleeper, Dung Foot was also a good shot.

Cat Tails slipped between buildings, moving stealthily toward the Planter's House, hoping to slip up on Dung Foot and take his odd parfleche. He snapped his teeth when he saw the man he called "Evil Eye" standing near the hotel, apparently stalking the same prey. Cat Tails slipped to the huge pecan between the hotel and Government Hill. With an agile grace, he grabbed a low branch, swung himself up and into the tree to watch and wait. He had nothing else to do.

Around mid-morning, Cat Tails saw Evil Eye saunter up to the hotel. A few moments later, the youth stepped outside, nervously looking both ways down the street, then peeking around the hotel corner before motioning for Evil Eye to meet him in back. Once Evil Eye disappeared around the side of the building, Sammy Collins slipped after him.

No sooner had the youth left, than Dung Foot scurried out the hotel door, moving quickly down the street and, to Cat Tails' pleasure, toward him. Dung Foot carried the parfleche in his left hand and a walking stick in his right. Cat Tails could feel his thirst abating because shortly Dung Foot and his satchel would pass beneath him.

Cat Tails patted the sheathed knife at his belt and worked his way through the tree to a sturdy branch that drooped over the road. He could jump Dung Foot and take his parfleche. Cat Tails could almost taste the whiskey.

Dung Foot advanced toward the tree. Cat Tails glanced at the hotel. No sign of Evil Eye. Cat Tails licked his lips as he positioned himself to jump Dung Foot, grab his bag and run. Cat Tails' head bobbed to the cadence of Dung Foot's stride. Cat Tails picked out a twig on the road. When Dung Foot reached that point, Cat Tails would jump. Dung Foot neared, then stepped on the twig. Cat Tails pushed himself away from the limb and fell earthward, landing nimbly on his feet, not three paces from Dung Foot.

Jerking his knife free of his sheath, Cat Tails motioned to the parfleche and grunted

142

in his guttural tongue. Dung Foot only smiled.

Baron Jerome Manchester Paget stopped dead in his tracks, highly amused by this display of aboriginal arts. The Indian mumbled, then waved his knife at the baron's satchel. Paget shook the bag in his left hand and the gold-headed cane in his right. "No!"

"*Si*," replied Cat Tails in his limited Spanish.

"See what?" Paget answered.

Cat Tails' face clouded with confusion.

The baron punctuated his refusal with a wave of his cane.

"*Si*," Cat Tails repeated.

"See what?" Paget replied.

Exasperated, the Indian lunged for the bag, swinging his knife.

Nimble afoot, Paget jumped back a step.

The Tonkawa growled like an animal.

The baron held up the bag. "You want?"

"*Si*," Cat Tails repeated.

The baron dropped the bag at his royal feet. "There!"

A smile as broad as a crescent moon pushed through the clouds of doubt on Cat Tails' face. Waving the knife at the baron, Cat Tails lunged for the bag, grabbing it by its maroon leather handle.

The baron jumped back a single step and deftly raised his cane, swinging it for Cat Tails' head. The cane popped against his skull.

"Oooowww," screamed the Indian, dropping the bag and grabbing his ear. Cat Tails lunged for the baron with his knife.

Nimbly stepping aside, the baron tripped Cat Tails as he flew by. In one graceful move, Paget brought his cane to his chest, grabbed the bottom end with his left hand and pulled. Suddenly, he unsheathed a sword with a razor sharp stiletto blade.

Surprised by Dung Foot's agility, Cat Tails crashed to the ground and instantly rolled over on his back, lifting his knife.

Paget kicked the Indian's hand with the point of his shoe and the knife went flying. Then before the prostrate Indian could react, Paget straddled him, holding the tip of his sword at Cat Tails' throat. The Indian's eyes were as big as wagon wheels. What had been a triumphant smile melted into a terrified grimace.

"Amigo, amigo," the Tonkawa repeated.

"You go away," the baron ordered, lifting the blade tip from the Tonkawa's throat and backing away.

The Indian clambered up, grabbed his knife, and sprinted off.

144

Calmly, the baron re-sheathed his blade, then strolled to his satchel, retrieved it and continued his promenade, as if nothing had happened.

The baron ambled beyond the ramshackle huts and adobe hovels that circled Hide Town's ragged perimeter, then moved among the tented camps of the buffalo hunters. Hides were stretched, bundled or stacked like furry warts upon the ground. The stench of rot was overpowering and the baron shook his head at the flies that swarmed around the ricks of hides. Rats scurried ahead of the baron, a few plump, belligerent ones pausing to stare as he passed.

The baron came upon a swarthy man, hunkered over a skillet, frying a few thick slices of saltpork. By his greasy beard, buckskin shirt and leggings slick from filth, Paget figured him a hunter. The hunter's squinty eyes watched the baron as if he were a thief. As the baron neared, the hunter arose, slowly straightening his six-foot-six frame until he towered over Paget.

"You looking for work or you just lost, green pea? Either way, you don't look our type," growled the hunter.

"Actually, governor, I'm seeking the camp of Ike Mann."

"Governor, am I? Don't tell me you're president."

Paget laughed. "Indeed not, governor. I am Baron Jerome Manchester Paget, late of London now of Fort Griffin, Texas."

"That a fact?"

"Indeed, governor. Now, Ike Mann's camp?"

The hunter started to toy with stringing the baron along, but he caught a whiff of burning saltpork. The hunter squatted down over the popping skillet and cut loose a string of epithets. "You're bad luck, green pea, so get along. Ike camps toward the creek. You can't miss his camp. He paints the spokes of his wagon wheels red."

"Thank you, governor," Paget said as he moved on, wrinkling his nose. He preferred the odor of the rotting buffalo flesh to the smell of the hunter's charred saltpork.

After wandering among various camps, wagons and tents, Paget spotted a camp laid out around three freight wagons with red spokes. A grizzled hunter was busy greasing the rear axle of the nearest wagon. Paget remembered having seen this man being refused a room at the Planter's House the day he had arrived in town on the stage.

As the baron approached, Ike Mann slapped a thick, goopy brush against the

146

worn spindle. "What's your business, English?"

"Didn't know you knew me, governor."

"You're that fool that makes no secret of toting money around."

"You speak your mind, governor. Everyone said you were an honest man. I like that," the baron responded.

Mann poked the stiff bristled brush in a can of grease. "You didn't come to visit so state your mind."

"Land, governor. I want to buy land to start a buffalo ranch."

Mann pointed to a coffee pot on the fire. "Want a cup of mud?"

"Mud?"

"Coffee!"

The baron waved away Mann's offer.

Mann took a tin cup off a nail in the wagon and swung his arm in a wide arc, flinging dregs everywhere. He lumbered to the fire and grabbed the coffee pot handle with his bare hand. Paget grimaced, but Mann showed no discomfort as he poured the steaming liquid.

"English, did I hear you say you're starting a buffalo ranch?"

"That's right, governor."

Mann took a swallow of the hot coffee. "Damn foolish idea. Buffalo migrate. They don't work like cattle."

The baron shook his head. "Land for ten thousand will suffice. I need help to find that land. You're the man. I'll pay."

Mann drew deeply on his coffee. "Your money could buy me a reputation as an idiot."

Paget opened his satchel for Mann to see inside. "You could spend your reputation."

Mann hawked and spat in the coals, which popped, sputtered, and spat back. Mann scratched his beard. "I ain't going nowhere until I can get a fair price for my buffalo hides and pay off my men."

Closing his satchel, Paget nodded. "Perhaps, governor, I can help. At Planter's House, I board with a buyer named Jake Ellis."

"He's the problem," Mann replied, spitting into the coals again. "I've got close to 6,000 hides to sell. With them selling for three dollars in Kansas, they should bring a dollar fifty here. He's offering half that, waiting us out until we have to sell at his price. Then he'll turn around and sell hides for three dollars or whatever the going price is in Kansas by then. We did the killing, we did the skinning, we did the drying, we did the baling and we did the hauling. All he does is stay on a feather mattress in the

Planter's House and wait us out so he can profit from our sweat and risk."

"Governor, if I can persuade Jake Ellis to give you a dollar fifty a hide, will you show me land?"

Mann pondered a moment. "If you can convince Ellis to give me a fair price, then you can talk Uncle Moses into giving me a night on a featherbed."

The baron nodded. "I'll work that out once we get back."

"Payment in advance on the featherbed," Mann replied.

"It'll be arranged, governor," Paget replied. "Allow me a few days to converse with Jake Ellis."

"English, you're a strange varmint," Mann said, "but let me give you one warning. Put in writing any deal you make with Jake Ellis."

The baron grinned. "Indeed I will, governor, indeed I will."

Beulah Fenster waited patiently in the rocker on the front porch of the Planter's House, her hand wrapped around a carton of .22-caliber cartridges. Her husband had forgotten the baron's request, but not her. She had marched to the store and reminded him. Zach Fenster had scowled, and she had

149

seen disgust in his eyes. He should be so smug, visiting Lop-Eared Annie Lea weekly. Beulah considered knifing him for infidelity, but she doubted that would regain his affection and knew it would threaten her monied existence.

She wore her prettiest dress, a pink cotton cloth with a full ruffled front that gave substance to her otherwise modest bosom. She wore a broad-brimmed hat that she tied under her chin with pink ribbons. To fend off the warmth, she swished a silk fan in front of her face. She smiled when she finally saw the Englishman approaching the hotel, carrying satchel and cane. He walked with an arrogance that said he was the superior of every man in town. She knew the feeling, certain she was better than any woman around.

Seeing the baron made her heart flutter and her knees tremble. Her breath accelerated. Her hand fanned faster in a futile effort to cool her passion and the heat of her flushed face. She hoped he would notice her dress, her hat and, most of all, herself. She recalled the language of the fan from her etiquette training and placed the fan on the left side of her bosom, a sign that the baron had won her heart. Surely, he would recognize the signal as sophisticated as he was. However, as excited as she was, Beulah Fenster felt something amiss, something dreadfully wrong.

A man wearing an eye patch trailed the Englishman, stalking him like a predator follows its prey. She nervously patted her bosom with her fan. As Paget neared, she called out to him. "Baron, please join me."

Acknowledging her with a smile, he dashed up the porch steps and strode immediately to her. Stopping in front of her rocker, then clicking his heels, he took her hand in his and kissed it. "How is the lovely Mrs. Fenster today?"

"Flattered," she blushed, "but worried."

"And why, madam?" the baron asked, releasing her hand.

Beulah Fenster lowered her voice. "Don't turn around just yet, but there's a man following you."

Paget dropped his English club bag and took a seat on the porch railing so he could see the street. "Indeed, you may be right. Several times, I have seen him the last few days."

The one-eyed man approached.

"Governor," the baron said, "my name is Baron Jerome Manchester Paget. Yours would be?"

"Charlie Gatliff," he answered dourly.

"Governor, have you been following me about this morning?"

"Nope," sneered Charlie Gatliff, pointing at the baron's satchel. "I've been following your carpetbag about."

"And why?" Paget asked, crossing his hands over his chest.

"I wanted to be around in case you left it somewhere."

"You best not follow me, governor."

Gatliff sneered. "I can understand you not wanting me around, especially you being with a woman as ugly as that cow there."

Beulah Fenster caught her breath, her face heating with rage.

The baron barged down the steps. "Kindly take that back or I shall whip an apology from you!"

Gatliff widened his stance and let his gun hand fall to his side, his fingers wriggling dangerously near his revolver. "I don't need much of an excuse to kill you," Gatliff snarled.

The baron tossed his cane on the porch, then took off his hat and flung it for an empty chair. Paget turned to Beulah Fenster. "I cannot let him talk to you like that."

"Come to your senses, Baron. You'll live longer as a coward."

Paget ignored Gatliff, unbuttoned and removed his cutaway coat, folding it crisply and hanging it over the rail. Next he slid his arms out of the shoulder holster, giving the gun to Beulah Fenster. "Should he threaten you and I be unable to defend you, shoot him."

Beulah Fenster's face turned pale as she took the gun. "You don't have to do this for me, Baron," she gasped.

"Indeed, madam, I will not have one as lovely as you insulted by a common ruffian." He turned to Gatliff. "I propose we settle this through the manly arts, governor."

"Manly arts?" Gatliff asked.

"By fists."

"A gunfight'd be a less painful death for you."

Paget unbuttoned his ruffled sleeves and rolled them up, staring as Gatliff unbuckled his gunbelt and knife scabbard. He draped the belted weapons over the porch rail.

Just then Sammy Collins walked around the hotel and froze in his tracks. "What's going on?"

"Stand back, lad," Paget commanded. "I'm about to teach this ruffian some manners for insulting the lovely Mrs. Fenster."

Faster and faster Beulah Fenster fanned herself. Never before had men fought over her. She felt like a princess in a fairy tale.

His sleeves rolled up, the baron undid his tie and unbuttoned his collar. That done, he lifted his fists and stepped toward Gatliff.

Staring a moment, Gatliff then laughed sinisterly. With the toe of his boot, he scratched a line in the dusty street. "Cross that line and I'll kill you."

"Take back your insult."

"She's a cow," Gatliff repeated.

Instantly, Paget jumped across the line, his fists cocked, his jaw squared for battle.

Surprised at Paget's sudden move, Gatliff swung his right fist for the baron, who deftly dodged his punch and then launched one of his own. His blow glanced off Gatliff's cheekbone. The one-eyed man cut loose a yelp, not so much from the pain as from the surprise that the baron had landed a blow so easily.

Gatliff straightened and held his fists in front of his jaw as the two men circled each other, oblivious to the shouts of men along the street announcing a fight. A couple of times Paget feinted and Gatliff flinched backward, then Gatliff feinted, but the baron stood his ground. Gatliff lunged toward him, but Paget danced out of harm's way. "I'll get you," Gatliff shouted, charging again at Paget, who merely backpedaled out of reach. Next Gatliff moved in slowly, steadily, his fists flailing for the baron, striking only glancing blows on Paget's shoulders and arms.

Paget, more controlled in boxing style, punched selectively, half of his punches hitting their targets until Gatliff's face began to pucker with red welts and his nose began to drip blood.

A clump of men circled around the pugilists as Gatliff leaned toward Paget, swinging his fists without effect at the Englishman's head. Gatliff had taken several punches to the face and began to shield his head from the baron, leaving his midriff open. Paget moved in, focusing on Gatliff's belly. One, two, three punches plowed into Gatliff's stomach and his breath exploded like air out of torn bellows.

Gatliff gasped for air, his shoulders drooping, then caught a breath and lumbered toward the nimble Paget. The Englishman launched a right at Gatliff's nose, glancing off his jaw instead, and then threw a right into Gatliff's soft belly. Enraged by so much abuse, Gatliff lunged forward into Paget, knocking him to the dusty street. Both men rolled around in the dust, Gatliff swinging wildly, his punches hitting the ground more often than the baron.

Paget jumped to his feet as Gatliff climbed onto his hands and knees. Paget shook his fist over Gatliff's bloodied and bruised form. "Apologize," he shouted, "apologize."

Screaming his rage, Gatliff clambered up to his feet and began to circle Paget again.

The baron lowered his fists from face to shoulder level and stuck his jaw forward, daring Gatliff to hit him, baiting the gunman's anger. "Apologize to the lady, governor, and we'll be done with this foolishness."

Gatliff swung at Paget, his fist missing by three feet.

The baron laughed. "You Americans brawl. We English box."

Gatliff rubbed his bloodied face, then charged the baron. But before he could strike the Englishman, Marshal Gil Hanson jumped between the two men and clamped Gatliff in a bear hug.

"The fight's over," Hanson yelled. "Who started this?"

Beulah Fenster pointed at Gatliff. "He did."

"It's okay," the baron interrupted. "He'll not insult the lady again."

Gatliff grunted, but his muscles relaxed and Hanson released his grip.

The baron approached the marshal. "Had

he apologized to the lady, constable, I would not have beaten him so soundly."

Shaking his bloodied head and rubbing his bruised cheek, Gatliff stepped toward the marshal and the baron. Coming within reach of the baron, Gatliff suddenly knotted his hand, drew back his arm, and plunged his fist into the baron's nose. Surprised and hurt, the baron staggered with his own nose bloodied, then collapsed in the street, groaning.

Hanson grabbed Gatliff's arm and twisted it behind his back. "You're going to jail. Somebody bring his gunbelt." Hanson turned to the baron. "You okay?"

The baron grimaced as he touched his bleeding nose. "I'll survive once my eyes stop watering."

Holding the baron's satchel and gun, Beulah Fenster wormed her way through the crowd. "I'll care for him," she called. "I'll tend his wounds."

CHAPTER 7

As the marshal marched One-Eyed Charlie Gatliff down the street, Joe Loper grabbed the bad man's gunbelt and trailed the marshal. A worried Sammy Collins pushed his way through the crowd surrounding Paget. The baron had not only survived his encounter with Gatliff, but had also gained a measure of respect among the men of Fort Griffin, not to mention the women. Both Flora Belmont and Amanda Sikes had appeared from nowhere, trying to elbow Beulah Fenster out of the way so they could doctor the baron themselves. The baron was being helped to a sitting position by Flora Belmont on one side and Amanda Sikes on the other while Beulah Fenster stood angrily by, holding the baron's satchel and shoulder holster.

The Englishman shook his head and rubbed his red, bloodied nose. "Mr. Gatliff does not play by the Marquis of Queensberry rules," he said.

Sammy watched Beulah Fenster, Flora Belmont, and Amanda Sikes shoving for position like hogs around a trough of slop. The baron shook his arms free of Amanda Sikes and Flora Belmont, then stood up on his own. For a moment, he wobbled and the three women closed in around him, each grabbing him. He flinched at their touch and once again shook his arms free of their grip. He took his shoulder holster and satchel from Beulah Fenster, then nodded at Sammy Collins.

"Come along, lad," the baron said, stepping past the three women and through the curious circle of spectators toward the hotel.

Beulah Fenster raced ahead of him to the porch and gathered his hat, his coat, and his gold-headed cane, handing them to him as he passed. Silently, the baron took his belongings. Beulah Fenster's faced drooped in disappointment that he did not linger with her. The disappointment turned to anger at the sound of Amanda Sikes' voice.

"Oh, Baron," called Amanda with a toss of her red hair, "I'd be glad to attend your nose and your other needs." She licked her lips.

"You brazen hussy," blurted Flora Belmont, then turned to the baron. "Your lordship, I should be glad to dine with you and discuss certain investment possibilities and financial opportunities, including marriage, if it might be mutually beneficial."

"Me a hussy?" challenged Amanda Sikes. "Listen to yourself."

"Ladies, please," the baron interrupted. "There's been enough fighting for one day. If you can't act like ladies, I'll not be interested in either of you. Beulah Fenster is certainly a lady in her thoughts and deeds."

Amanda Sikes and Flora Belmont frowned, then glared at Beulah Fenster and her newfound smile.

The baron nodded as he entered the hotel, Sammy moving quickly down the hall with him. As soon as they entered his room, the nervous rooster began to crow in its cage. From habit, Sammy picked up the cage and wedged it in the window while the Englishman tossed his carpetbag on the bed, then dropped his other belongings nearby.

Sammy sighed. "It's all my fault. I told Gatliff where you were going, and he followed you back from the hunter's camp."

"Lad, it's not your fault. Furthermore, I insist you keep telling him my every move. The more people that know what I'm doing, the safer I am. The fisticuffs began when the one-eyed chap insulted Beulah Fenster and said she was ugly."

Sammy grimaced. "But she is ugly, no?"

Without hesitation, the baron nodded. "Ugly indeed."

Shrugging, Sammy stepped toward the washstand and poured a pitcher of water into the basin. "I don't understand."

"Beulah Fenster is taken with me more than my money. Amanda Sikes and Flora Belmont only want my money, lad."

Sammy soaked a cloth in the cold water, then squeezed out the excess and offered it to the baron, who seated himself beside his money satchel on the bed.

"You do it," Paget instructed Sammy.

Gently, Sammy dabbed the wet rag around the baron's nose, then more vigorously he rubbed blood from his close-cropped beard. "I don't want to tell the one-eyed man your plans."

"Now, lad," the baron replied, "he's paid you, has he not?"

Sammy nodded.

"Then do it. None of my plans are secret, lad. I want everyone to know where I am, who I'm with, what I'm doing. It's safer for me that way."

"He's a mean man."

"He's a ruffian, lad, but I showed everyone

I can stand up to brigands. Everyone thinks me a dunce for bringing a bag of money here to start a buffalo ranch. Everyone's been laughing behind my back about what a fool I am since I stepped off the stage that day into a pile of droppings."

"But I'm still scared you'll get hurt or killed."

The baron shrugged. "No need to be. You still remember the coded message I'll send you if I'm ever in trouble or need you to follow someone else's instructions?"

"London Bridge is falling down."

"That's right, lad. Whoever brings you that message, you do whatever he says, no matter who it is."

Sammy lowered his head. "Something else scares me. You said you might take me when you left, didn't you? I want to go so bad, I've worried you were just funning me."

The baron reached out and roughed Sammy's hair. "When I leave, I'll take you with me, lad. That's a promise as solid as the British empire."

Sammy just smiled.

"One thing more, lad. Find Jake Ellis and tell him I've some business I'd like to discuss with him. Too, I'll need a writing table and a good chair as there's other matters to attend as well."

162

"Yes, sir," Sammy replied, tossing the stained washcloth back in the wash basin and escaping out the door.

One-Eyed Charlie Gatliff sat in one corner of the marshal's office and Joe Loper leaned against the opposite wall. Between them at his desk stood Marshal Gil Hanson, his hand nervously tapping the butt of his revolver. Hanson wasn't sure it had been wise to allow Joe Loper in his office with Gatliff. At least it had given Hanson an opportunity to send the stuttering Monk Partain away. Now, though, Hanson felt like a man standing between two locomotives headed full throttle at one another. With a collision inevitable, Hanson just hoped no innocent bystanders were hurt, himself included.

Hanson pointed at Gatliff. "Stay away from the Englishman."

Gatliff crossed his arms over his chest and leaned back in his chair against the adobe wall. "And what if I don't, Marshal?"

Before Hanson could respond, Loper answered with a voice low and menacing. "I'll kill you, Gatliff."

"Since when are you deputy marshal, Loper?" Gatliff laughed. "And as town marshal, Hanson, your jurisdiction doesn't extend beyond the town limits, now does it?"

Hanson grunted that Gatliff was correct.

"His doesn't," Loper interjected, "but mine does. If you harm the Englishman, I'll kill you."

Gatliff laughed again. "Is the marshal gonna get a cut of your take when you cheat the Englishman out of his money?"

"Difference is, Gatliff, you'd take his money and kill him to boot."

Gatliff sneered. "Call yourself the law and hide behind the badge, both of you, but you're no better than me trying to steal his money."

Hanson's hands closed into fists. Forgetting his fear of Gatliff, Hanson stepped toward him, silently shaking his fists. Sometimes you compromise the law to protect it. Hanson knew that, but how could he explain it to an insidious lawbreaker like Gatliff?

"It's true, isn't it, Marshal?" Gatliff laughed.

Hanson scowled. "For helping keep the Englishman alive from your type, Gatliff, I'm allowing Loper the opportunity to get a chance at him in a card game. He's promised the Englishman won't get hurt. That's more than you've promised."

Gatliff laughed. "A gambler's word isn't

any better than a murderer's word, now is it? Or any better than a lawman's?"

Hanson advanced on Gatliff, drawing his fist back until he felt a pair of hands grab his forearm.

"Easy, Marshal," Loper said. "He's just riling you because he likes his chances against you, whether he's armed or not."

Hanson took a deep breath, the muscles in his arm relaxing, though his jaw was tight with anger. The marshal was tired of both men, neither of whom he trusted. He was tired of the Englishman and the problems the fool had created for Hide Town. Hanson could handle his own against the typical Fort Griffin riff-raff, but these two were more sinister, more devious. He wanted nothing to do with either of them. Hanson threw up his arms. "Get out of here, Loper, and go about your business."

Loper nodded. "Sure, Marshal, just watch out for that snake."

Gatliff stepped toward Loper, lifting his fists. Marshal Hanson pulled his revolver. For a fleeting moment, fear glinted in Gatliff's solitary eye, but it disappeared so quickly that Hanson wondered if it had ever been there to begin with.

"Sending witnesses away, Marshal, before you shoot me?" Gatliff taunted as Loper closed the door.

Hanson waved his gun at Gatliff's face. "You've got a big mouth and a way of riding folks hard. No harm better come to the Englishman."

"Then you better keep me in jail."

Hanson lowered his gun and shoved it back in his stiff holster. "I don't want to look at you all the time, Gatliff." Hanson retreated to his desk and picked up Gatliff's revolver. Unlatching the cylinder, Hanson dumped the bullets into his palm. Then he snapped the revolver's cylinder shut and offered the bullets to Gatliff. "Put 'em in your pocket."

Gatliff obliged.

Next, Hanson shoved Gatliff's gun back in his holster and placed it in a chair. "Get out of here, Gatliff. Carry your gunbelt out by the buckle. No sudden moves." Hanson pulled his own pistol and cocked the hammer. "Move."

"Mighty friendly of you, Marshal," Gatliff answered, picking up his holster.

"Just get out, Gatliff, and stay away from the Englishman."

As the gunman left, his laugh sent shivers up the marshal's spine.

"Afternoon, Baron," Jake Ellis said as he

stepped up onto the shaded porch of the Planter's House. "Sammy Collins said you needed to see me." Ellis smiled at the Englishman's red swollen nose. No man in Fort Griffin deserved a beating more than the arrogant Englishman who held court every night at supper, the women fawning over him. Until the Englishman came along, Ellis carried sway as the most important man in Fort Griffin. He was the major purchaser of buffalo hides. Ellis figured he was still the wealthiest and most important man in Hide Town, though everyone talked about Baron Jerome Manchester Paget as if the Englishman was.

The baron, his money satchel at his feet, eased up from the rocking chair and extended his hand, a warm smile upon his face. "I've a proposition for you."

Ellis pumped the baron's hand, thinking it soft and effeminate, the hand of a man who had never worked at anything but leisure. Ellis squeezed hard against the soft flesh, yet the baron seemed not to notice.

After greetings, the baron settled back into the rocking chair and brushed the side of his tender nose. "As you know, I am here looking for land to start a buffalo ranch."

Ellis clucked his tongue and settled into a chair opposite the baron's. "I wish I had your smarts, Baron. Here I am buying and selling hides by the millions and not worrying about the future of the hide trade and here you come, completely foreign to the business, and anticipating the future." The fool, Ellis thought, taking in the baron's proud smile. How foolish the aristocracy must be to bask in such meaningless praise. How vain of the baron to believe that his English intellect was somehow superior to men who had not only survived this hard land but also had made a prosperous living at it. Aristocrats were little more than leeches that sucked the lifeblood and vigor out of a country.

The baron held his tender nose in the air. "Few around Fort Griffin are as perceptive as you, governor, about my plans."

And none are as stupid as you, thought Ellis, offering the baron a pleasant nod instead of his actual thoughts. "How can I help?"

"Governor, I must hire Ike Mann to escort me about the wilds."

Ellis leaned back in his chair, not quite sure where this was leading. "Sounds like you need to be talking to Ike."

The baron propped his elbows on the arms of the rocker and held his hands fingertip to fingertip in front of his face.

"Indeed I have, but Mr. Mann can't leave until he pays off his men, and he can't pay off his men until he sells his hides."

Ellis grinned. "Why, I offered to buy all of Ike's hides just yesterday, yet he refused."

"Governor, Ike Mann said with hides selling for three dollars in Kansas a fair price was a dollar fifty, but you were only offering half that."

Ellis nodded. "That's right and the price keeps dropping. That may be the best bid I'm able to make Ike this year. Things are so unpredictable and freight costs are going up. Ike may be able to get a better price in Kansas if he freights them up there and sells to another buyer. I can't offer more than seventy-five cents locally."

The baron accordioned his fingers as he pondered the situation. "Surely, you can make Mr. Mann a better offer. I need him and, unlike you, I cannot afford to wait. I need him to show me land available for purchase. Then I must hire workers, buy fencing, and capture a herd of buffalo."

Now Ellis licked his lips. Wouldn't it be satisfying to swindle an arrogant aristocrat? "Wish there was something I could do, Baron, but I can't go against the market." Ellis fought to contain a smile because he controlled the market in Fort Griffin. He would get three dollars a hide when he sold, but that didn't mean he had to pay the hunters anywhere near that. After all, every penny he whittled the price below a dollar fifty was a penny that ultimately wound up in his pocket.

"I need Ike Mann," the baron persisted. "He needs a dollar fifty a hide and he has maybe 6,000 hides."

Ellis shook his head. "Price is down to seventy-five cents a hide now." Ellis leaned farther back in his chair and waited.

The baron stroked his chin, then stopped when it seemed to affect his tender nose. "Perhaps I could pay the difference, governor, between your offer and his demand."

The Englishman had more money than sense. There had to be a trick! But even so, what could it be? At seventy-five cents a hide, the baron would pay $4,500. That was a steep price just to have someone nursemaid him out in the wild. "This is an unusual proposal."

"Indeed. You would pay Ike Mann the full dollar fifty, then I would pay you in English pounds before I left or in Yankee dollars once I returned from my inspection of the wilds."

Ellis shook his head. "American money only!" There was the rub. Of course, Ellis

170

preferred the money in advance, but what did he stand to lose. If the Englishman didn't come through, he could still make a tidy profit in Kansas buying hides at a dollar fifty. If things worked out, the Englishman's money would be a big windfall. Still, Ellis hesitated.

"I shall provide written papers on our agreement, governor."

Ellis stared at the baron, still not believing how big a fool the Englishman was. No wonder the British had lost the Revolutionary War. "Your word is certainly good, Baron, though paper does eliminate the possibility of misunderstandings."

"Absolutely," responded the baron. "Would you care to accompany me to my room so I can write up the documents?"

"Certainly." Ellis pushed himself up from his chair, as anxious as a pickpocket to conduct business.

The Englishman grabbed his satchel and arose. With a sweep of his hand, he motioned for Ellis to proceed. Ellis accompanied the Englishman past the registration desk and down the hall, neither man speaking. As they reached the door, the baron twisted the handle and entered just as the door across the hall opened up. Ellis looked behind him in time to see a flash of Amanda

Sikes in a chemise.

"Baron," she called softly, then instantly realized her mistake. "Oh, how embarrassing," she said, her blushing face confirming she spoke the truth. She slammed the door at Ellis.

The hide buyer entered the baron's room, nodding to the caged rooster. "So that's the fellow that's kept me awake so many nights."

"Indeed he is," the baron said proudly as he shut the door and tossed his satchel on the feather mattress. "Everyone thought me the dunce when I acquired him."

Everyone was right, Ellis figured as he looked at a room that was the mirror image of his own, excepting the caged rooster with its peculiar aroma and a writing table with chair near the window.

The baron took the chair and arranged his writing materials, ink well to his right, pen at his palm, paper before him and envelopes to the left beside a tin of matches and a stick of sealing wax. He picked up the pen, dipped it in ink and began to write on the top sheet of paper. Ellis moved over his shoulder and read each sentence as it appeared in Paget's ornate, effeminate handwriting. Every word in his fancy script carried numerous appendages, like a soldier decorated with various medals. The baron finished the front of the paper, then held it up and shook it to help it dry. Then quickly, he laid it down and began to write on the back. When he was done, he signed it with an elaborate signature, dominated by the bold "B" in his title of "Baron."

Picking the paper up, the baron read it quickly to Ellis, who agreed to buy all of Mann's hides at a dollar fifty apiece. Paget agreed to pay in American dollars half as much per hide to Ellis once the baron returned from his land inspection. Ellis nodded greedily as the baron completed reading the document. When the baron offered Ellis the pen, the hide buyer snapped it from him, dipped it in the ink well, and signed the document instantly.

The baron picked up the paper and blew on Jake Ellis' signature until it seemed dry. Picking up two matching pieces of stationery, the baron sandwiched the written contract between them, then straightened the three pieces of paper together. "The extra sheets'll keep the front from smudging," the baron said as he folded them in thirds. Placing the contract aside, the baron plucked an envelope from the stack, but his careless elbow knocked the signed contract to the floor. "How clumsy," he said, bending over and grabbing the papers. Straightening back up in his chair, the baron grinned as he pressed the folds into the paper sheets.

Ellis answered with a smile, knowing this piece of paper would cost the baron $4,500. He watched as Paget slid the paper into the envelope, then picked up a sulfur match and struck it against the end of the writing table. The match took to flame, and the baron picked up the stick of sealing wax and held it over the back of the envelope. Quickly, the heat produced tears of wax which dripped on the flap, sealing the envelope in three places.

"Indeed," said the baron, "that should seal the deal, governor." He blew out the match.

"Yes, sir," replied Ellis, rocking confidently on the heels of his shoes.

The baron offered the envelope to Ellis. "Upon my return, present me with this promissory letter and I'll pay you. It's a pleasure doing business with you, governor. I assume you will make your offer and payment to Ike Mann before dinner, will you not?"

"I certainly will, sir." Ellis spun around and departed, barely containing his laughter until he got out into the hall.

"Get away from me." Amanda Sikes pushed

her husband aside.

Wallace Sikes moaned like a frustrated puppy.

Amanda shook her red hair like a mop and folded her arms across her chemise. "We've got to get his money before anybody else does."

"But it can wait, just a while longer," he said, approaching her with his arms outstretched, his eyes longing for what was beneath the chemise.

Amanda stamped her foot. "No, no, no, Wally. That's final." She turned her back to him.

Wallace sighed and slumped into the room's one chair. "We got $2,000 out of Fort Worth. Why can't we just enjoy our money now, have a good time without worrying about where our next money is coming from?"

Amanda spun around. "Wally, you need to think bigger. And, we don't have $2,000 any more. I had to buy new clothes and there aren't any fine dresses in Fort Griffin, not the type that would impress a baron."

"Baron, huh?" growled Wally. "I don't care about a baron, just you Amanda. Sometimes I want to give this up."

Amanda planted her hands on the pleasant curves of her hips. "And do what? Starve or get a job?"

Wallace winced at her words. "No, but you know how it drives me crazy knowing you're in another man's arms. The close call in Fort Worth tells me it's time to quit. And what if I didn't break in before . . . before . . . well you know, before one of them . . . ," he said with both fire and fear in his voice.

"I know, Wally, but I can hold my own against any man."

He shook his head. "But it's me just not knowing, not knowing what's going on that drives me crazy."

"But, darling," she cooed, "you can't go fishing unless you bait your hook, you know that. I guess we could give it up. I don't know what you'd do, but I guess I could take in laundry."

Amanda watched Wallace melt at the thought. "No, no, you're too beautiful for that," he said, his eyes moistening with tears.

He was just too sentimental at times, Amanda thought as she walked to him. She placed her arms on his shoulder and pulled him to her. Wallace leaned forward in his seat, resting his cheek against her flat stomach. She knew the urge was building in him again, yet she relished manipulating him. It made him much better, much later.

He tried to stand and brush against her bosom, but she pushed him back down in the chair.

"The answer's still no, Wally."

Her husband slumped into his chair. He sighed and shook his head. "Why do you treat me this way, Amanda?"

"Because I love you," she replied flippantly. "Anyway, we don't have time."

"It's three hours to supper," Wallace pleaded.

"I know, but I've got to decide which of my new dresses to wear." She moved to the bed, picking up each new dress and holding each close against her like she would a dance partner.

Wallace grunted at each one, not caring, especially not when Amanda was choosing it to attract another man.

Amanda settled on a dark green one and she undressed before him, taunting him with her body as she slowly, seductively put on her underthings and then her dress. As she buttoned up the front, she smiled at Wallace. Though he watched, his eyes were glazed over.

"Wally, darling," she said, stepping to him and patting his shoulder. He pulled back from her. He was in a childish mood now. "Wally, darling, we've got to come up with

177

some way of outsmarting Flora Belmont or she'll get the money before we do."

Her husband sighed. "She's so pushy it would take more than us to stop her. Take the whole damn cavalry."

"That's it," Amanda shouted, then danced around the room. "Wally," she cried, running to hug her husband, "you are so smart. Why can't I think of things like that?"

"Huh?" Wallace answered, scratching his head. "What things?"

"The cavalry," Amanda danced around the room again. "The colonel, of course. We must convince him Flora Belmont adores him."

"Sure," Wallace Sikes replied, "we just sashay right up to him and say 'Colonel, Flora Belmont is more interested in you and your Army pay than she is in the baron and all his thousands.' I'm sure he'll believe that, coming from such a good friend of Flora's as you."

"Now, now, Wallace, you are missing the potential of things. You keep thinking of the broad plan and leave the details to me."

"What a brave man you were this morning, Baron," Beulah Fenster announced at the dinner table. "I have never seen anyone as gallant as you."

178

Zach Fenster stared at his wife, his lips pursed like he had bitten into a sour pickle.

The baron coughed and held up his hand. "A vile insult, unbecoming of your charm," he replied. "It doesn't merit repeating."

"And the baron would never have been touched by that evil man," continued Beulah Fenster, "had he not let down his guard when the marshal broke it up."

"Fascinating, isn't it," said Zach Fenster. "Fact is, that's all I've heard all day. Is there anything else we might discuss?"

"Indeed there is," replied the baron. "Thanks to Jake Ellis," Paget nodded across the table, "I've a guide to take me into the wilds to look for ranch land. Governor Ellis made a fair offer to relieve my guide of his hides so he could escort me."

Amanda Sikes caught her breath and, by feminine instinct, she knew Flora Belmont was just as surprised as her with that announcement. When she leaned forward in her chair beside the baron, she saw Flora Belmont looking at her as well. Glares of mutual hatred passed between them.

Colonel John Paul Jenkins spoke up. "When are you planning this expedition, sir?"

"We'll leave day after tomorrow," the baron replied. "It should take but a week to find a suitable site."

"I see," replied the colonel.

"Can I go?" Sammy Collins asked.

"No, Sammy," replied the baron. "I need you to stay here and watch after my rooster."

"You need anybody to watch after your carpetbag?" Zach Fenster asked sarcastically, drawing a scowl from his sour puss wife.

"And who's your guide to be, sir?" asked the colonel.

"Ike Mann," replied the baron.

"If he wants a room here," Uncle Moses interjected from his end of the table, "tell him we're full up. He's the stinkingest buffaloer I've ever smelt, and I've smelt a lot of them in this town."

CHAPTER 8

He barged into the Bee Hive, the swinging doors clattering behind him. Conversations stopped mid-sentence and one by one, every head, every pair of eyes turned toward the front. The laughter caught in every throat, the merriment evaporated in every smile, and the lust shriveled in every heart. Burley Sims caught his breath. Nothing could be worse for business than this. A flood, a tornado, a fire, anything but this man.

The intruder stood with his feet spread apart, his left hand on his hip, his right hand gripping his weapon and moving in an arc from man to man, each fearing his unforgiving gaze. Standing in the door, he was silhouetted against the bright noon light of another day, a day that until that moment had been as good as any other in Fort Griffin, but no more.

Burley Sims could stand it no longer. "Aw damn," he cried, "a preacher!"

"Not just a preacher, barkeep, but a Baptist preacher," he barked.

The customers hissed.

"The Reverend G.W. 'Gawd Willing' Tuck," he announced, "here to serve the will of Gawd and minister to the needs of man."

Burley Sims collapsed on the bar, propping his elbows between two empty beer mugs and burying his face in his palms. "Why this, why now?"

Around the room, the Bee Hive's patrons looked ashen and frail, the thick smoke giving them ghostly features.

The reverend cleared his throat. "Who might the proprietor of this den of iniquity be?"

Several patrons pointed at Sims, still bemoaning his fate.

"Why this, why me?" he mumbled, shaking his head in his palms.

As Tuck strode to Sims, several men scraped their chairs against the wooden floor as they stood up and aimed for the door. "Hold it," Tuck shouted and every man turned to stone, especially when each saw the weapon in the reverend's right hand. The Bible once there was tucked under his left arm and a revolver had taken its place. "Nobody's leaving alive."

Meekly, the patrons retreated to their seats.

Nodding his satisfaction, Tuck reholstered his revolver and took his Bible in hand. He marched to the bar, spotting Surry Nettles in a corner leaning on his crutch and Monk Partain, a wicked knot still visible on his head, standing by the food table.

As Tuck approached the bar, Sims shook his head free of his palms. "Why the Bee Hive? Why me?"

"Yours, sir, is the biggest den of sin in Fort Griffin," Tuck replied, folding his right arm across his chest so that his Bible covered his heart. "To save Fort Griffin, I must fight sin in its darkest pit."

Sims groaned.

"Fort Griffin is evil, but decent people want to purge its wicked ways of liquor and gambling and loose women."

Sims spun around to the backbar and picked up a bottle of whiskey. Uncorking it, he planted it against his lips and irrigated his sinful thirst. Reluctantly, he lowered the bottle.

"I am but a humble man of Gawd, a poor man of Gawd," Tuck continued. "Yes, indeed, a poor man of Gawd. For all my good deeds in Gawd's service, I have but a dollar to my name."

A knowing grin creased Sims' face. "You want a bribe, is it?"

Tuck slammed the Bible against the bar, leaving Sims bewildered. "I can preach against sin or I can preach against hell."

Sims scratched his head. "Huh?"

"If I preach against sin, all the saloons will lose money. And by my count, there are eight saloons, four dance halls, three gambling dens, and Gawd only knows the number of cribs with wicked women. With so much sin and not a single church, I could start a church and plague you for an eternity."

Sims drew deeply on the liquor bottle.

"Or, barkeep, I can use your saloon as my cathedral for one night, tonight, to preach against hell."

Shrugging, Sims wiped the liquor from his lips. "It'll just drive my business to other saloons for the night."

"Not," Tuck shot back, "if you convince them to close."

"They'd laugh me out of town," Sims gasped.

"And, they'd laugh themselves out of business," Tuck replied. "Unless they close tonight, I'll start preaching tomorrow against sin and that means against every saloon, every dance hall, every gambling den, every house of carnal pleasure. I'll start my holy war tomorrow unless every man and woman who works or uses those places attends my sermon and contributes freely when my hat is passed."

"Sounds like a bribe to me!"

Tuck slapped the bar again with his well-thumbed Bible. "I have not asked for a penny from you, just the use of your saloon for one night. I can lead you to the collection plate, but only Gawd can convince you to give."

"I want to think about it, Reverend."

Tuck smiled as he lifted his Bible to his heart. "I'll be back at seven o'clock to begin my sermon. You've plenty of time and men here to get the word out."

"But, Reverend . . ."

"Good day," Tuck said, spinning around on his heels.

He was halfway to the saloon door when he suddenly stopped and stared at Monk Partain. "You look troubled, fellow."

"H-hu-hun-g-gr-gry," Partain sputtered.

The reverend reached into his coat pocket, pulling out a single greenback. "My last dollar," he announced, handing it to Monk and looking around the room. "There's money for food and for someone else in need." His gaze stopped on Surry Nettles leaning on his crutch. The reverend pointed to him. "Share my generosity with the crippled lamb over there."

The Reverend Tuck strode out the door before Monk Partain could say, "T-th-tha-than-thank y-yo-you."

"I don't get it," said Wallace Sikes, his exasperation building like storm clouds and needing release, release that was unlikely for awhile, not when Amanda was in one of her scheming moods, and she was always in a scheming mood when it came to money.

"Hush," Amanda said from the room's single chair. She sat with a cigar box in her lap, writing a note atop it on stationery she had bought that afternoon at Zach Fenster's store. In as delicate a hand and as inviting a tone as she could manage, she composed a message to Colonel John Paul Jenkins. Finishing the note with a smile, she held up the missive to the window light, then winked at her husband.

Wallace shrugged. "Read it."

Amanda smiled, rattling the note to prolong Wallace's curiosity. "My Dearest Sir," she began, "I have relished dinner with you these past evenings and feel myself attracted to you more than any man I have ever known. And yet, it is so frustrating that we have not had an opportunity to be alone. Though we must still be discreet to avoid the gossip of others, I should like to meet you thirty minutes after dark beneath the great pecan tree just up the road from the hotel. Perhaps we can discuss our futures. Remember to keep this our secret and ours alone for now. Flora Belmont."

Wallace coughed. "Flora Belmont didn't write that."

Amanda rolled her eyes. "The colonel won't know that."

Wallace crossed his arms. "And, if Flora didn't write it, then she won't be there to meet him."

Impatiently, Amanda grabbed the cigar box and arose from her chair. "Now, you've a letter to write."

"Amanda, nobody's gonna believe a letter from me."

Exasperated, Amanda pushed her husband into the chair. She slapped the cigar box in his lap and put pencil and a clean sheet of paper atop it.

Wallace grabbed the pencil, hating how Amanda always took charge.

"Write what I say."

Wallace angered at her command. After all, he was the man, the husband, the boss of this marriage. Though she made it up to him in other ways, he still chafed at her bossiness.

"Madam," Amanda dictated, "I would like to discuss matrimony with you. Please meet me thirty minutes after dark beneath the pecan tree by the hotel. I shall be devastated if you fail to come. Tell no one of our plan and do not mention it at dinner. Your admirer." Amanda paused to re-read the note over her husband's shoulder.

"Are you done?" Wallace asked, impatiently tapping the pencil against the cigar box.

A suggestive smile upon her face, Amanda grabbed the note and folded it in half.

"I don't get it," Wallace said.

Amanda giggled and danced around the room. "Don't you see? We have one delivered to Colonel Jenkins and we'll slide the other under Flora Belmont's door. She's been watching us and the baron's room and would create a ruckus if she knew I was visiting the baron in his room. Tonight, she'll think it's the baron inviting her for a rendezvous. While she's out, I'll get in his room and get him in a compromising situation. Then you break in and catch me in his arms. Fire a couple shots and we'll scare the money out of him."

"You are so devious," Wallace said.

Wallace tossed the cigar box on the bed. He lunged from the chair and captured Amanda's narrow waist. "Now?"

Amanda pushed him away. "Not now, Wally," she answered. "I must finish the envelopes and see that they are delivered."

Wallace's head and spirits sagged.

Amanda giggled. "After we take the baron's money, then we can celebrate, you and I, together." She licked her lips.

Ike Mann was loading buffalo hides into the wagons Jake Ellis had sent around while a dozen other grizzled hunters stood nearby, scratching their chins at the dollar-fifty price Ike Mann had commanded for his hides. No one else had received such a price in the six weeks since the first outfits had brought in their winter kills. Mann just let the men talk, enjoying their odd theories about his bargaining prowess. He seldom glanced their way, though his ears listened intently as he helped his crew load the wagons. Only when several of the hunters took to making catcalls and lewd remarks did Mann glance away from a bundle of hides he was wrestling into a freight wagon.

There at the head of those men, oblivious to their insults, stood the baron, his satchel in one hand, his cane in the other, his bowler hat atilt on his head.

Mann shoved the hides in the wagon and turned to rescue the baron. "Get along now, fellows," Mann commanded. "The baron's a friend of mine."

The hunters just hurrahed the baron more until Mann issued a threat. "You fellows clear out, and I might put in a good word for you with Jake Ellis. Anybody that wants a dollar-fifty for his hides better skedaddle, pronto."

After a little nodding among themselves, the buffalo hunters slipped back toward their camps. Only after they were out of hearing range did Mann grab the baron's hand. "I'll be damned, English," said Mann, furiously pumping Paget's hand, "you must've had some talk with Jake Ellis. He paid me a dollar-fifty a hide and everybody's wondering how I got double what he's offering them."

"Excellent, governor, excellent," said the baron, tapping the hard-packed ground with his cane. "Will your affairs be concluded so we can leave tomorrow? And you'll provide me a mount?"

Mann nodded. "Only problem is, English, seems like there's one thing you're leaving out of our deal."

"The feather bed, of course," answered the baron.

"You work it out with Moses Miller?"

The baron shook his head. "I had less luck with him."

Mann grimaced. It was a small thing for sure compared to getting the full price for his buffalo hides, but it was a matter of pride as well.

"Governor, we must improvise." The baron outlined his plan.

Mann grinned. The baron was keeping his promise after all.

Sammy had just completed emptying the hotel's one spittoon and was about to escape his other chores and find the baron when Uncle Moses grabbed him at the kitchen door.

"There's a letter on the front desk that needs to be delivered to the fort and Colonel Jenkins," Uncle Moses said, jerking his thumb toward the parlor.

There had been a time when Sammy Collins would have loved an excuse to visit the fort proper, but that was before Baron Jerome Manchester Paget came to town. "Yes, sir," he said half-heartedly, retreating from the back door, tromping through the kitchen, trudging past the dining room table and marching into the entryway. He found the sealed envelope on the desk, tucked the letter in his britches pocket and headed out the front door for Government Hill

At the top of the hill, he saw the black troops scurrying about while lethargic white officers, their arms crossed, just stared. Something must be up, Sammy thought. Most times the enlisted men were left to attend their chores on their own while the officers hid in the shade discussing whatever officers talked about.

Sammy crossed the parade ground and entered the small anteroom of the headquarters building. "Halt," cried a clerk seated at the desk. Through the open door of an adjacent office, Sammy saw Colonel John Paul Jenkins hunkered over his desk studying a map. "State your business," the clerk demanded.

Sammy jerked the envelop from his pocket. "For the colonel," he announced.

Colonel Jenkins glanced up from his map, nodding at Sammy.

"I brought you a letter," Sammy said as the clerk grabbed it and carried it to the commander's desk. "See you at supper, Colonel."

Jenkins shook his head. "Not tonight. I'm taking troops out into the field tomorrow morning."

Sammy shrugged. "Injun problems?"

"An affair of international significance. Protecting a citizen of a foreign power," the colonel said.

It didn't make sense to Sammy, but he figured he had asked enough questions.

The colonel took the envelop from his clerk and ripped it open. As he read it, a puzzled look gave way to a smile. "On second thought," the colonel said, "maybe I'll make dinner after all."

Sammy retreated out the door, ran across the parade ground, then jogged down Government Hill road and angled for the hotel.

At the Planter's House, Uncle Moses stood on the porch, hands on his hips. "What took you so long? Amanda Sikes wants a bath before supper. I've dragged the tub in. The water's boiled and ready for you to tote. Your work's slackened since the baron came. You need to pick it up."

Shrugging, Sammy strode past Uncle Moses and headed for the kitchen, where Aunt Moses was waiting, her arms crossed.

"You're gonna kill Uncle Moses, him having to drag that tub to the Sikes' room. Go see if they are ready for the water."

"Yes, ma'am," Sammy said, slipping out the kitchen door and down the hall to the their room. He lifted his arm to knock, then froze at the sound of Wallace's voice.

"You want me to shoot the baron or not?"

"Wally," Amanda replied, "I'll tell you a final time. After I get in his room, give me twenty minutes. Then break the door down and make a lot of noise. Fire your gun a time or two so people'll come and catch the baron with his pants down. Just don't shoot me."

There was a pause.

"I don't like this, Amanda, not a bit," Wallace said.

"You're getting squeamish, Wally."

"You're getting too brazen, Amanda."

"No," Amanda answered, "I'm getting rich."

Sammy tiptoed back down the hall. What was he going to do? The baron would likely not take the threat seriously, nor would the marshal. Sammy could think of only one man who might be able to stop this scheme.

One-Eyed Charlie Gatliff!

Colonel John Paul Jenkins couldn't keep his mind on business, not since he had received the letter from Flora Belmont. Though Flora was not as lovely as the red-haired Amanda Sikes, she was likely wealthier, maybe wealthy enough to hire a cook for

194

Fort Griffin.

The poor grub the past three weeks had put the post on edge. The men grumbled at everything. The food was so bad that the post hospital, where many malingerers went for a few days of bed and plentiful food, was now empty. At night, the troops would slip out of their barracks and hunt for rabbits or, some said, go into town and kill the cats or one of the stray hogs if they could get it.

By going out on patrol tomorrow, the colonel would at least get the troops out in the field where everyone shared hardship and grub. Jenkins and his troops would tail the baron wherever he went, making sure nothing untoward happened to him. Many were the details that the colonel needed to attend before leaving on patrol. Jenkins lifted the letter to his nose hoping to detect the fragrance of Flora Belmont. The paper smelled like paper. He had heard of women sending letters sprinkled with perfume. Maybe that would come later. He relished the possibility. No woman had ever been so straightforward and it excited him. Though there was work to be done, a good officer delegated his tasks.

Hiding the letter, Jenkins called his clerk. "I must attend to matters in Hide Town tonight. Assign all my duties to others."

"Yes, sir," the clerk said, saluting smartly.

"And," Colonel Jenkins added, "have one of the troopers heat water and draw my bath."

Supper was nearing and Aunt Moses kept Sammy Collins busy, setting the table, then sharpening the carving knife, and now peeling apples for a cinnamon desert. He took the knife and circled apple after apple, leaving corkscrews of peel on the table. Looking out the back door and hoping to glimpse Charlie Gatliff, he nicked his thumb, drawing a bead of blood.

Aunt Moses waddled by and shook her finger at Sammy. "Cut a thinner peel or there won't be any apple left."

"Yes, ma'am," he replied just as he saw Gatliff pass by the back door. He dropped the knife on the table and knocked his stool over as he hit the floor. "Woodbox empty. I'll get more firewood," he said, then bolted outside before Aunt Moses could stop him.

He dashed to his lean-to door, motioning for Gatliff to join him. Shortly, Gatliff was inside the dingy room with him. Sammy took a deep breath and started rattling off the problem, his words bouncing off the wall like hailstones.

"Whoa, kid," Gatliff interrupted. "Start again."

Sammy caught his breath. "Tonight in the baron's room. Amanda Sikes plans to distract him."

"Distract him?"

"Then Wallace Sikes'll break into the room, shoot him for being friendly with his wife. They'll take his money."

Gatliff grabbed Sammy by the shoulders. "You sure?"

He nodded. "I overheard them when I went to fetch bath water."

"Does the baron know?"

Sammy shook his head. "He might not believe it."

"He's a sap, ain't he?" Gatliff shook the boy's shoulders. "I've got to get inside so I can keep an eye on the baron's room."

"I don't know, how," Sammy shrugged. "All the rooms are full and there's no place to hide in the hall."

Gatliff released the boy's shoulders. "They won't try anything until after dark. Come dusk, I'll circle the hotel. If anyone leaves, go to their room, whistle when I pass and I'll crawl in through the window."

"I hope this works." Sammy nodded, then slipped back outside and around to the kitchen.

Aunt Moses welcomed him back with a scowl. "I thought you were going for fire-wood."

"No," Sammy grinned, "I had to drop some logs in the outhouse."

Aunt Moses' face reddened and her cheeks bloated.

Sammy turned away to keep from laughing at her reaction.

The tension around the dinner table seemed as thick as her late husband's beard and Flora Belmont couldn't figure out why. Of course, Beulah Fenster was her same effusive, boring self, fawning over the baron who could do no wrong in her ugly eyes. And every time Beulah Fenster spoke, her husband would roll his eyes like he was embarrassed to be in the same room with her, much less married to her. Neither were Wallace and Amanda Sikes a picture of marital harmony. They sat sullenly side by side, Amanda offering the baron a haughty smile while her husband just stared.

Sammy Collins frowned like he didn't feel good while Aunt Moses glanced resentfully around the table as if she were getting tired of fixing meals for so many. Jake Ellis had bored everyone with his complaining about the drop of buffalo hide prices, and Uncle

Moses seemed almost asleep in his chair.

The Englishman dined quietly, nodding periodically to some inane comment by Beulah Fenster or rubbing his close-cropped beard. The baron had been courteous to Flora when he sat down but aloof since then. Of the people at the table, Colonel John Paul Jenkins perplexed Flora the most. The colonel, attired in his dress uniform, kept staring past Wallace Sikes, past Amanda Sikes and past the baron at her. Flora had offered him a courteous smile and that only seemed to encourage him. The colonel was freshly shaved and reeked of poor judgment from the tonic water, thick with the aroma of sour lilacs, he must have liberally doused upon his cheeks. She thought him rather handsome and restrained. Flora liked men who held their emotions. The colonel was one, the baron another. Restrained men were easy to kill.

But one thing bothered Flora Belmont. Had the baron really fallen for her enough to write a note for a rendezvous? He seemed too reserved to commit such thoughts to paper. Doubt still plagued her, even after the baron finished his bowl of apple cobbler and excused himself. Picking up his money satchel, he strolled out the door and toward the hallway leading to his room. Flora watched him depart, wondering what type of husband he would make.

Shortly, Flora Belmont arose from the table and marched to the door, her nose held intentionally high in the air. She said not a word to anyone for they were all so plebian, nowhere near the equal of a lady who was destined to become a baroness. She stopped a moment at the sound of Beulah Fenster's voice.

"Good riddance," Beulah said.

Her embarrassed husband coughed as if the noise would overtake and disguise his wife's words before they reached Flora Belmont's ears.

The room grew quieter yet with an eerie hush. Then Flora walked on. She would not lower herself nor her station by responding to an insult from such a crude — not to mention ugly — woman.

As she passed the baron's door, she was tempted to knock, tempted to question him about the note. While her curiosity drew her to the door, her instincts pushed her toward her own room. She slipped into her room, which buzzed from the flies that had flown in through the partially open window. Flora thought of changing dresses, but that might raise suspicions when she left. She thought about a touch of perfume, but discarded the notion for the same reason. It might draw attention to her like the tonic water on the colonel had caught her notice.

She was anxious, restless, ready for dark. Anticipation throbbed in her veins. Too impatient to stay in her room, Flora Belmont patted her hair, straightened her dress, then slipped into the hall. Someone had already lit the kerosene hall lamp, earlier than usual. She eased past the baron's door and the Sikeses' door across from it, thinking she detected a slight quiver at the couple's door, as if someone behind it had been spying through the crack.

In the parlor, she was startled by Sammy Collins reclining on a wooden bench, holding his stomach like it ached. He was illuminated by a low burning lamp that cast a sickly pallor over him. He seemed to perk up as she passed. Outside on the porch sat Moses Miller and Jake Ellis, rocking and smoking in the twilight. She could feel their eyes upon her as she marched down the steps and crossed the street, not stopping until she stationed herself in the darkness of the brooding warehouse opposite the hotel. From this vantage point, she could see the front of the hotel as well as the baron's side window with the protruding chicken cage.

The street was quiet, the saloons and

dance halls strangely silent. It was bizarre and so quiet that she was all the more scared when she realized a man had stopped not a dozen feet from her in front of the warehouse. Flora Belmont held her breath and hugged the wall so that this ghostly shadow might not see her. This apparition glanced her way and her heart seemed to jump into her throat, but the ghostly figure did not appear to spot her. Flora Belmont realized why when she noticed his left eye was unnaturally dark, like a deep pit. This man was the one called One-Eyed Charlie Gatliff. Flora Belmont shivered.

As he passed, she watched him cross the street, walking suspiciously close to the baron's room, then disappearing in the darkness to the nervous cackling of the baron's rooster. No sooner had Flora Belmont calmed her pounding heart, than Gatliff appeared again from the other side of the hotel. He circled wide of the porch to avoid the stares of the two men enjoying their cigars there, then approached the warehouse again, pausing a moment not ten feet from Flora before moving on. The dangerous Gatliff was circling the hotel for some reason.

Five, ten, fifteen, twenty minutes she waited and one, two, three, four times Gatliff circled the hotel. In all this time, Flora Belmont had seen nothing of the baron and too much of Gatliff. Then as Gatliff disappeared around the hotel again, Flora heard the rooster's call, more nervous than before.

Squinting in the darkness, she just made out the cage being pulled inside and a big hulking figure dash for the window, then crawl in. Immediately, she made out a second smaller figure with a satchel emerging from the hotel. It had to be the baron. The rooster took up the cackle again as the chicken cage reappeared in the window.

Flora Belmont smiled. Though she didn't understand who had entered the room, Flora decided the baron was shrewd to leave by the window where few, if any, would know he had departed. The baron played on the common notion that he always left the rooster in the window when he was in his room. For a moment, Flora Belmont could not decide whether she had rather steal his heart or his money. Old sins, though, were hard to break.

And then, as if to perplex her further, she thought she heard the robust singing of "Amazing Grace." And, the hymn seemed to be coming from one of the saloons. The night, the mood, everything was so inexplicable and yet so exciting. Catching her breath, she ambled toward the pecan tree, fighting the urge to run.

Warily, Sammy Collins eased himself up from the hard bench by the door. He glanced into the dining room to make sure that Aunt Moses wasn't watching, then at the porch and the undulating glow of Uncle Moses' cigar. Sammy slid away from the bench and tiptoed toward the hall, cursing Wallace Sikes for lighting the hall lamp so early but blessing Flora Belmont for leaving her room. He just hoped she stayed away a good while. Otherwise, there would be hell to pay if she returned and found Gatliff inside.

At Flora Belmont's room, Sammy looked behind him to make sure no one was watching, then opened the door and slipped in like a thief. Quickly, he started across the room for the window, running into the end of the iron bedstead. He grumbled to himself and made a wider arc around the bed. Reaching the window, he opened it fully, the dry wood screeching and screaming as if alarming all of Fort Griffin. Sammy stood guard by the window, waiting, sweating, hoping to catch Gatliff. Then he heard the cackle of the rooster. Had Gatliff passed the baron's room as he circled the hotel? Sammy shoved his head outside. Hearing a twig snap, he pulled back, then emerged again like a dazed turtle from its shell.

And there he was! Or was he? Sammy whistled softly.

The man came closer.

Sammy caught his breath, then let the air out in a great sigh. It was Gatliff.

Gatliff was beside the window instantly and still that wasn't fast enough for Sammy.

"Anyone else in there, kid?" Gatliff asked.

"Nope," Sammy replied.

"Then get out of the way."

Sammy obeyed and Gatliff pulled himself through the window. No sooner was he inside than Sammy stuck his leg out the window.

"Not so fast, kid," Gatliff said.

Sammy's mouth went dry. "I gotta go," he whispered.

"Show me the baron's room."

Sammy gulped and scurried around the iron bedstead. At the door, Sammy cracked it slowly as Gatliff looked over his shoulder. "Second one down the opposite side of the hall.

"Good enough," Gatliff said. "Now get your tail out of here."

"Yes, sir," Sammy whispered, spinning

away from the door and moving quickly for the window, forgetting the bedstead again and stubbing his shoe.

"Quiet, dammit," Gatliff scolded.

Sammy didn't answer. He was at the window, then out onto the hard-packed ground. All of a sudden, he could breathe freely. He had this urge to shout and celebrate his escape, but instead he slipped quietly to his lean-to. He opened the door, slid inside, then closed the door. He stood catching his breath and letting his pounding heart slow down. And when he had calmed down, he realized something was amiss.

Someone else was in the room! Sammy's chest tightened.

"Hello, lad," came a familiar voice.

Sammy couldn't believe it. He jumped to the upended apple crate by his bed and grabbed a candle and tin of matches. Striking a match against the rough wooden wall, he touched the flame to the candle making a ball of light appear in his hand. Sammy turned to face his visitor. "What are you doing here?"

The baron smiled. "I came to stay the night, lad, on your floor, get accustomed to sleeping on the hard ground before I start my expedition."

"But why give up a featherbed when you

don't have to?"

"I had to."

Sammy scratched his head. "But why?"

"Lad, the man that'll be leading me on my inspection tomorrow wanted a night in a featherbed as payment."

Sammy felt his jaw drop open. "You mean Ike Mann's spending the night in your room?"

"Indeed, lad, indeed."

don't have to?"

CHAPTER 9

Her heart pounding, Flora Belmont rushed toward the giant pecan tree. Above her, the night was moonless and cloudless, the stars sparkling like jewels against the black sky. Ahead of her she could just make out the mushroom silhouette of the tree. For once in her life, she felt vulnerable to a man. Nearing the tree, she patted her bosom as if that might slow her heaving breath and her pounding heart. Stopping beside the massive tree trunk, she wriggled her nose at the sickly fragrance of sour lilacs, an aroma she had smelled before but could not place. A dark hulking shadow seemed to step out of the tree trunk.

Flora jumped and caught her throat. "Oh, you startled me!"

The black shadow stood motionless, then ghostly arms reached for her and pulled her closer. Flora gasped with anticipation as a strong hand found its way behind her neck, pulling her lips to his. Up close, the baron seemed taller than she remembered. She melted as he crushed his lips against hers. Breathless from excitement and his prolonged kiss, she arched her back to break away for air. She tried to escape those iron arms, but they controlled her like a doll.

Something was terribly wrong. The baron was bearded, yet this man, except for his mustache, was clean shaven. The aroma? The sour lilac odor? She recalled the dinner table. She gasped through the kiss. This was not the baron at all, but rather Colonel John Paul Jenkins. Where, then, was the baron? Had she not seen him climb out his window?

Flora was appalled. And yet, she was strangely attracted to this powerful man, a man accustomed to the rigors of the Army rather than the ease of bookkeeping like her five deceased husbands.

Gradually, his muscled arms relaxed and allowed her to pull away from his lips. When he spoke, his voice had the low peal of embarrassment, like the sound of distant funeral bells. "I couldn't control myself, not after your note."

"My note?" Flora gritted her teeth, realizing she had been taken. Her mind awhirl, she played coy, stalling for time to consider the note's real author. It had to be the Sikes couple. Amanda and Wallace Sikes had duped both her and the colonel, dammit. Had the baron left the hotel to meet Amanda somewhere else? Flora, for the moment, didn't care. Even if Amanda and Wallace Sikes stripped the baron of his money, they couldn't steal his title!

"No decent woman," the colonel apologized, "has ever shown a liking for me."

None still has, Flora thought as her own checkered past flitted through her thoughts. The colonel pulled her tightly against him and she turned her cheek and pressed it against the coarse wool of his uniform. Here was a man unlike her five late husbands, a man who was at once strong and vulnerable. He awakened some maternal instinct in her, some instinct that had been lost since the day her father had beaten her and tried to use her as he would a disreputable woman for hire. Yes, the colonel had fairly attacked her with his kisses, but he had not groped at her like other men.

"So much to talk about and so little time," he said softly.

Flora Belmont was torn, not knowing whether or not she wanted to string this foolish man along.

"When the baron pulls out of Hide Town

tomorrow, I'll follow him with a patrol to make sure nothing happens. Trouble'll find a man who carries $25,000 in a carpetbag. What I couldn't do with money like that. Marry a fine woman like yourself and settle down, quit the Army life."

"You've no family?"

The colonel growled. "Not since father died. He was a hard man and not much of a family man."

Flora Belmont sighed. "My papa, too." She lifted her head from his chest and kissed him, impulsively. Perhaps this was a man worth keeping.

"Unlike you," the officer continued, "I've never married. That's not to say I've led a celibate life, but I never found someone like you to settle down with."

Flora was both flattered and intimidated by the colonel. He had fallen so easily for her without her as much as lifting a ring finger to him. He seemed so sincere, unlike her courtship with her five late husbands.

"I must get back to the fort," the colonel said softly, "but I wanted to see you before I left and would like to see you again, Flora Belmont. May I? It can get lonely out here."

"Yes," Flora Belmont whispered. For the first time in her life, she felt vulnerable to a man, and she rather liked it.

211

Reluctantly, the colonel released her. "Good night and goodbye." He slipped away into the night.

Flora Belmont stood watching, even though she couldn't see him in the darkness. She still wanted the baron for his title, but now she thought she might want the colonel for herself. She felt as foolish as a schoolgirl. Time was lost in her thoughts. When she finally turned back to the hotel, she had no idea how long she had stood alone under the tree.

Yellow rectangles of light seeping out of curtained windows lit the hotel. Puddles of the jaundiced glow collected on the front porch now vacant, Uncle Moses and Jake Ellis having finished their cigars and conversation. Flora Belmont bounded up the steps and inside. Uncle Moses sat behind the hotel desk, glancing up as Flora passed. She felt her face blush as if Uncle Moses could read her infatuation with the colonel. She hurried down the hall, past the baron's closed door. Was the baron inside or not?

Glancing across the hall, she was surprised to see an open door and to glimpse Wallace Sikes sitting on the edge of his bed, his head in his hands. She thought she heard him sob.

Everything was too perplexing to decipher

so she simply marched to her room and closed the door on a strange day.

Amanda dosed herself liberally with perfume, enhancing her seductive charms. The baron would not, could not resist her. No man ever had and no man ever would when she set her mind to seducing him. Wallace Sikes paced the room angrily, the jealousy building in him like a volcano about to erupt. The thought of another man kissing his wife, scorched his mind like molten lava. He paced sullen, anxious, crazy, belligerent, and mean. Amanda controlled him by suggestive looks of the reward she would bestow upon him after the deed was done. Until then, she couldn't resist teasing him a bit as she tightened the lid on the perfume bottle.

"How do I look? And smell?" She pranced before him.

He grumbled and stared, his eyes afire like twin embers.

She shook her head so her auburn hair shimmered seductively. "Do you like it?"

"No, dammit, no," he scowled, his voice a low rumble.

"You don't like my hair?" she cooed.

"I don't like this, this tempting fate." He ran his fingers through his hair. "If any man ever, you know, got . . ."

"Got through," Amanda teased.

Wallace took a deep breath and exhaled so fast the air whistled as it crossed his lips. "I don't know what I'd do."

Amanda crossed her arms over her ample bosom. "We can stop, Wally, if you find work for this kind of money."

Wallace lowered his head. "Little chance of that."

"I'll not take in laundry or cleaning work, Wally. You know that. I want the finer things in life. You're the one that suggested the Englishman, not me."

Wallace shrugged. "I do it to keep you, Amanda."

Amanda licked her lips. "You enjoy the rewards, don't you?"

Wallace looked up at the ceiling, then sighed. "Sometimes I wonder if it's worth it." He gave his wife a tepid smile.

Amanda crossed the room to him and placed her hand beneath his jaw. Lifting his chin, she kissed him gently. "Don't worry. Give me twenty minutes, then barge in and rescue me, my gallant husband."

He nodded, though a corpse would have shown more enthusiasm.

Amanda ran her fingers down her dress. "I'll be thinking about you." She marched to the door, cracking it open and looking both directions down the hallway. It was vacant as she stepped out, the wooden floor creaking an alarm that a crime was about to be committed. Amanda took a deep breath and rapped on the baron's door. "It's Amanda," she whispered. "I need to see you." She twisted the door knob and pushed, the door budging only a fraction. The baron had wedged a door stop under the door. "Please," she repeated, "I need to see you."

No answer.

She placed her ear against the door. "I've come for you," she said a little louder, fearing someone else might hear. She knocked again, harder. The rooster cackled. Then she heard the rattle of the iron bedstead and the creak of the floor as the baron approached the door. She heard the door wedge being kicked loose, then watched the door swing partially open, the baron hidden behind it.

Amanda jumped inside before someone spotted her. Instantly, the door shut and Amanda heard the wedge being toed back in place. Amanda had not expected the smell. That rooster had evidently made quite a mess. Amanda hoped she could tolerate it for twenty minutes. She moved toward the window, setting the rooster to cackling. "I couldn't wait any longer," she said. "I need you unlike any man I've ever met."

The baron grunted.

Even though she could not make him out in the darkness, she knew the sound of a man needing a woman. It would be a challenge to hold him off twenty minutes. "If you'll light a lamp, I'll undress for you," she cooed.

"Nope," he answered gruffly.

Amanda stood by the window and began to unbutton her dress in the soft breeze that took the edge off the room's foul odor.

"Would you care to help?" she asked seductively.

"Nope."

He didn't sound right, Amanda thought. Maybe it was the anticipation. Maybe he realized he was being set up. Maybe he held a revolver in his hand. She did not know because she could not see him. Amanda swallowed fear, not for herself as much as for Wallace. Surely the Englishman hadn't figured all of this out? Surely this would work as planned. She heard the creaking of the floor as the baron moved for the bed. The bed rattled under his weight as he fell

on the mattress. The rooster took to cackling.

Amanda danced away from the window
until the odor made her dizzy, then she
retreated back to the window and a whiff of
fresh air. "I've wanted you, ever since I saw
you," she said as she let her dress slide to
the floor. For once, she felt awkward and
nervous, uncertain what to do next. Usually
by this time, her victims were pawing all
over her, but not the baron. He was stoic
and that made him unpredictable, maybe
even dangerous.

"Would you like to rub my back? I'd like
that," she offered.

"Nope," he answered.

Damn him, thought Amanda, for dispens-
ing with the preliminaries. Now, Amanda
was really worried. She'd spent no more
than five minutes in the baron's room and
still had fifteen minutes before Wallace
would rescue her. Amanda's mind raced for
ways to stall him.

"Now," he growled and slapped the bed
where he wanted her.

Amanda gulped. She must stall him. But
how? She must stay away from the bed. She
wished for a lamp or a candle or even a
match, any light that might allow her to read
his eyes and gauge the depth of his passion.

217

She heard the bed creak. He was arising. She heard his footsteps on the plank floor. He was coming for her. Amanda moved to get away, but she could not see him and ran into an outstretched arm, covered with thick hair. The arm and its mate collapsed around her. "Slowly," she pleaded.

His powerful arms lifted her off the floor and his hands began to tear at her garments. He smelled of decaying flesh as he brought his acrid mouth to hers. Amanda lifted her knee, aiming for his groin, but he anticipated the move and trapped her knee in a vise between his legs. Amanda grabbed for his head to push him away and gasped. This man had shoulder-length hair.

This was not the baron! She fought against him, but he was too strong. He leaned backward toward the bed and started to fall like timber before an ax. He took Amanda down with him, the bed rattling and bouncing and creaking. For an instant, she pulled herself from his lips.

"Wally," she cried before he pressed his rough lips and unkempt beard against her face. Amanda panicked. This had never happened before.

Wallace sat in his room, holding his pocket watch in his left hand, his revolver in his right. The minute hand was frozen on the watch's face. It seemed to move as slow as a calendar. The time terrified Wallace because every minute increased the chance Amanda would be violated. He wished now he had never read of the baron in that Fort Worth paper.

The uncertainty of what Amanda was doing to this man or, even worse, what he might be doing to her tortured Wallace. His gaze bore into the watch face. The minute hand, if it advanced at all, moved unseen like the onset of disease. Finally, five minutes passed and another eon before the minute hand had moved ten minutes. Then, Wallace heard something that sent his heart to pumping ice water through his veins. It came like a scream with his name on it, a scream that gasped for air and then was drowned in the unknown.

"Wally," came the sound from across the hall.

It was Amanda. Something had gone awry. Wallace shot up from his chair, throwing his watch on the bed, flinging the door open, and jumping madly across the hall. Raising his gun to his chest, he pressed his ear against the door but could hear nothing over his pounding heart and the rooster. He held his breath and still heard the rooster and something else, something bouncing like a bed. Then he heard a muffled scream.

It was Amanda! She was in trouble!

Wallace grabbed the door handle and twisted. The door budged but a fraction. Something had been wedged beneath it. Wallace backed away from the door and lifted his foot to kick it in. That was when he felt the cold metal of a gun barrel against his temple.

"That ain't your room, now is it?"

Before Wallace could react, his revolver was wrenched from his hand. Wallace slowly looked from the door to this assailant. It was a grizzled man wearing a patch over his left eye.

Tucking Wallace's gun in his belt, One-Eyed Charlie Gatliff nodded toward Wallace's room. "Let's wait in there."

His lips trembling, his eyes watering, Wallace shook his head. "But my wife?"

Putting his ear to the door, Gatliff paused a moment, his eye and his gun still fixed on Wallace Sikes. "Sounds like she's having a good time to me."

"No, no, no," Wallace pleaded. "Why are you doing this?"

Gatliff shoved Wallace Sikes toward his room. Motioning to the bed with his gun. "Sit."

"Why, why?" Wallace was almost delirious.

Gatliff sneered. "I've been trailing the Englishman since Galveston, and I'll be the one to take the fool's money."

Wallace Sikes, like his spirits, sank into the feather mattress while Gatliff leaned against the side wall where he could not be seen from the hallway.

Wallace saw Flora Belmont pass and he thought he observed a smile on her face. He wondered what Amanda would think, him not rescuing her, him failing to get the baron's money so they could get out of Fort Griffin. They still had good money from their Fort Worth job.

Maybe a half hour passed, maybe more. Wallace couldn't be sure because everything had run together in a blur of emotions that seemed to last an eternity. However long it was, the door across the hall finally came open, just a crack at first, then the width of an eye and finally the width of a head, Amanda's head. Bewildered and ashamed, Amanda looked both ways down the hall, then flung the door open and raced to her husband, holding her dress in front of her. Her hair was as mussed as her expression was wild.

Amanda stood, crying and staring. She

tossed her dress aside. "Oh, Wally," she cried, "it wasn't the baron. Why didn't you come when I screamed?"

Her husband shook his head and with a twist of his clenched fist pointed toward the side wall with his thumb. "Him."

Gatliff touched the brim of his hat with his forefinger. "Howdy, ma'am. Nice outfit you're wearing. Your husband's right. He tried to save you, honest he did, but I had other plans."

"Why?" Amanda managed.

"I want the baron's money for myself. After I get it, you can do whatever you want to him." Gatliff laughed, then pushed himself away from the wall and marched past Wallace and a confused Amanda Sikes. "I hope you both enjoyed this as much as I did." His laugh was low and sinister as he marched out the open door.

Wallace stood up and inched toward his befuddled wife. He stroked her auburn hair, gently patting it back into place. "We've got money left from Fort Worth, Amanda. Let's just leave town now, and forget this," Wallace pleaded.

Amanda shook her head and stomped her foot on the floor. "When I leave Fort Griffin," she said, "it'll be because the Englishman's a broke and broken man."

Marshal Gil Hanson was stunned. Every saloon, every dance hall, every den of ill repute was closed. Except the Bee Hive! As Hanson walked toward Burley Sims' saloon, religious hymns pricked his ears. What had come over Fort Griffin? Whatever it was, Gil Hanson didn't trust it. Maybe it was a lawman's instinct or maybe it was the doubts of a man who had seen too much of the sordid side of life to have much hope for the spiritual side. Hanson patted the revolver at his side. It was about all a lawman could put his faith in, that and his wits. Of course, the marshal's wits had been tried since the arrival of the baron. It seemed as if every crook in West Texas had converged on Fort Griffin to relieve Paget of his money.

As Hanson approached the Bee Hive, the gospel singing reached an off-key crescendo, then ended. Hanson squeezed inside the saloon packed with every bartender, every gambler, every dance hall girl, every piece of human trash from the foot of Government Hill to the muddy banks of the Clear Fork. If Hanson could just up and send the whole lot to prison, he'd do the respectable folks of Fort Griffin and all of the state of

Texas a grand favor. Frontier civility what it was, the women sat in chairs while a couple of the more comely ones occupied the laps of men who looked as if they would be doing something more than praying once this meeting was over. Some men sat on the edges of tables while others, the gambler Joe Loper included, stood along the walls, their arms folded across their chests.

Hanson studied the room, looking for Charlie Gatliff. Just before dusk, the marshal thought he had seen Gatliff walking around the Planter's House. Hanson didn't spot Gatliff, but he saw just about every man who gave Fort Griffin its dark side and all the women who gave it their back side, including Lop-Eared Annie Lea, the most exclusive soiled dove of them all.

Though the room abounded with low-lifes, Hanson's gaze kept falling on two men, his eyes instinctively drawn to the cripple Surry Nettles and the stutterer Monk Partain. Even in the crowd, both men stood out. When a man in a black frock coat jumped atop the bar and held up a Bible, Hanson smiled and nodded to himself as his gaze moved from the preacher to the cripple and the stutterer. Surry Nettles and Monk Partain, Hanson decided, were the reverend's shills, in town to be healed by the preacher.

As the preacher stomped on the walnut bar, Burley Sims popped up from his seat on a nearby beer barrel. "Don't scar the bar."

The crowd laughed until the preacher scowled. "Sinners," he shouted with a voice that could have toppled the walls of Jericho. "All of you." He stomped his boots again on the bar.

Grimacing, Burley Sims climbed meekly back atop the beer barrel.

"G.W. 'Gawd Willing' Tuck's my name, the Reverend Tuck. We just sang because singing is good for the spirit. Now I'm gonna preach because preaching is good for the soul, and your souls need the salve of salvation, the balm against abominations." Tuck shook his well-thumbed Bible at the assembly.

Across the room, men and women shifted in their seats or shuffled their feet. It would be a long sermon!

Tuck looked about the room, waiting for the restlessness to stop. When he was satisfied that he had everyone's attention, he began. "I can preach against sin or I can preach against hell. You are the sinners and you can decide. This is a town that has no church and needs one as badly as Sodom and Gomorrah. Those towns were destroyed by the wrath of Gawd Almighty. So, too, will be Fort Griffin if it does not repent."

Slapping his Bible, the Reverend Tuck turned and walked to the end of the bar by Burley Sims, then turned around and stalked the other direction like a great cougar ready to pounce upon a grazing doe.

"I could build a church here or I could move on after two weeks of revival. You damnable sinners will decide that for me."

From the back of the room, a man who had had too much to drink wobbled to his feet and shook his fist at the pastor. "Why don't you just go on now?" he managed.

Faster than the multitude could say "amen," the reverend flung back his frock coat, jerked his revolver free, and fired into the wall over the drunk's head. Almost before anyone could react, the revolver was back in his holster. "Challenge me," the reverend shouted, "and you challenge the word of Gawd Almighty."

The drunk hushed.

"I'll speak the word of Gawd Almighty and you'll listen or be damned. That is His commandment to me and mine to you. I'll preach from the thirteenth chapter of Genesis, the thirteenth verse. Genesis Thirteen Thirteen, an unlucky number as ever was created and it is appropriate that this is for this iniquitous town. The verse proclaims, 'But the men of Sodom were wicked and sinners before the Lord exceedingly.' "

Tuck snapped the Bible shut. "You are all sinners, you gamble, you dance, you whore, you drink, you fight, you slop with all the hogs of iniquity." Tuck stomped on the bar, and Burley Sims buried his face in his hands, wondering about the salvation of his furniture.

"Not only are you dancing, gambling, drinking, whoring, fighting sinners, but you are that exceedingly, so sayeth the Lord Gawd Almighty and so sayeth me, Reverend Tuck. You know that. I know that. The Lord Gawd Almighty knows that. So, too, do the upright people of this iniquitous community know that, but they haven't spoken out against you and against sin. And, do you know why?"

By his iron gaze, the reverend challenged someone to answer. No one said a thing. "And, do you know why they haven't risen up against sin, the goodly and Gawdly people of this community? Because," he shouted, "they haven't had a leader, a man whose voice could be heard above the calamitous noise of your wickedness. Now, I can be that voice. Like the voice of Gawd, my voice'll not be stilled. I can preach against sin exceedingly or I can preach against hell. If Gawd leads me to preach against sin . . . ," Tuck paused, his eyes surveying the room, his head shaking disapprovingly at what he saw, ". . . then I shall preach against you agents of Satan and raise an insurrection of righteousness against you.

"Or," Tuck paused and smiled upon the crowd, "I can preach against hell. Now, there are bad people like yourself and good people like those who aren't here tonight. Both the good and bad need to be saved. So, I could preach against hell and try to reach all those in need of being plucked from Hades. Or, I can preach against sin and the wickedness of those in this room. There is sin aplenty in this town, sin that must be fought and conquered. Yet, there are so many souls who need the hell scared out of them. All I need now is a sign from Gawd Almighty to show me whether to preach against sin or to preach against hell. I don't know the sign but maybe you can think about it as I pass my hat among you."

Marshal Hanson shook his head. This was extortion, not a sermon. The only sign the Reverend G.W. "God Willing" Tuck could possibly understand was a dollar sign.

With his free hand, the preacher took off

his hat and pitched it to Burley Sims. "I want to pray," Tuck said, "and when I'm done Mr. Burley Sims will pass the hat around. Remember the text of my sermon, Genesis Thirteen Thirteen, an unlucky verse if ever there was one. But maybe if you give exceedingly you can show the Lord Gawd Almighty that this is not the Sodom He thinks it is. Maybe you can show Him that you have generous hearts and generous spirits beneath your sinful flesh. And that would make me happy, make me want to let this be my last sermon against sin while I'm in Fort Griffin. Let's bow our heads and pray."

Tuck stared around the room, then bowed his own head. "Lord Gawd Almighty, we come to you today, asking for deliverance from evil, asking for direction in our lives, asking for forgiveness of these despicable sinners and asking for a sign that should show me, your humble servant, Thy will in Fort Griffin. Is it to fight sin, which needs to be fought on the devil's own field of battle, or is it to fight hell and save the souls that will otherwise perish in eternal damnation?

"And if these sinners respond by offering freely of the riches they have gained through their sinful ways, I shall know to preach against hell in Fort Griffin before I move on. Lord Gawd Almighty, please help all of us here to do Thy will. Amen."

Burley Sims popped up and toted the reverend's hat from person to person. "What all that meant," Sims called out, "is that if we don't give big, the reverend is gonna make things tough on us."

Tuck held his hand up. "Give only what Gawd Almighty leads you to give because I am powerless to make you give."

Sims jumped up on his chair. "Just bribe him. We don't want a crusade against sin. Next thing you know we'll have the women of this town joining the Temperance Union, attacking drinking, attacking card playing, attacking dancing."

Around the room, men began to dig into their pockets.

Tuck lifted his Bible heavenward. "A thousand dollars would be a sign Gawd wants me to preach against hell instead of sin."

The men dug deeper into their pockets and the soiled women about the room, stuck their hands in their blouses, pulling out coins and rolls of bills.

From the back of the room, Joe Loper called out. "Hey, Reverend, how about performing some miracles while Burley's passing the hat? You do perform miracles, don't you?"

Tuck's lips curled into an unholy snarl. "I have cured people before," he said, shaking his Bible at Loper.

"How about curing the cripple for us?" Loper challenged.

"Yeah, yeah," came a chorus of support.

Tuck grimaced as he looked at Surry Nettles. "Gawd Almighty cures only when the lame have faith."

"What about Lop-Eared Annie Lea," someone shouted.

"Annie Lea! Annie Lea! Annie Lea!" Men and women took to chanting her name.

Lop-Eared Annie Lea stood up from a chair and waved a handkerchief. "Over here, Reverend," she called, then made her way to the bar, squeezing between tables, chairs and bodies. "I'm deformed," Annie Lea called out.

"And make a darned good living from it!" yelled someone.

Burley Sims followed in Annie Lea's wake to the bar and dumped a hat full of money at the preacher's feet and then waded back into the crowd to collect more filthy lucre.

Tuck stared at the money, licking his lips.

Annie Lea stood at the foot of the bar, unbuttoning her blouse, then lowering her chemise. "Can you even these up?" she challenged. The men in the saloon exploded in shrill whistles and loud clapping.

Tuck glanced from the money at his feet to Lop-Eared Annie Lea's most famous assets. His mouth dropped open and he bent down so his wide eyes could get a closer look.

Annie Lea jerked her blouse shut. "Come any closer and you'll have to pay just like everyone else." Annie Lea eyed the money on the bar. "Looks like you could afford a peek, if you want."

Tuck stood transfixed, staring at Annie Lea even as Burley Sims dumped another hat full of money on the bar. The reverend snapped back to reality when Annie Lea spoke. "You better count it, Reverend, to see where God is leading you," she said, then turned and retreated to her seat.

Tuck squatted and began stabbing at the bills and coins, gathering the paper in his hand and stacking the change on the counter. The crowd began to murmur, impatient for Tuck to finish so they could get on with their sinning. As the reverend worked, Marshal Hanson moved to the bar to discourage any of those gathering around Tuck from helping themselves to his tithe.

The marshal was at Tuck's elbow as the

preacher finished tabulating his take. A smile worked its way across Tuck's face as Burley Sims jumped up on the counter and lifted his arms for quiet.

"Preacher," Sims said, "what's your total?"

"Eleven hundred and thirty-seven dollars," he called out.

The room erupted in spontaneous cheers and applause.

"I'll preach against hell," Tuck shouted, though few could hear him over the celebration.

Hanson grabbed the reverend's arm. "Preacher, I'm Marshal Gil Hanson, and I figure I ought to escort you out of here with that much money."

Still appearing in a daze from Annie Lea, the reverend picked up his hat and plopped it on his head, then began to stuff the wads of money in his coat and pants pockets.

"Where you staying, preacher?" Hanson asked as the reverend snatched the final coins from the bar.

"I'll stay in the finest hotel in Fort Griffin," he said.

"That would be the Planter's House, only place in town with feather mattresses, but it's full up and has been ever since the baron showed up."

Tuck's daze seemed suddenly to disappear, like fog before the sun. "The Planter's House or nothing else. Show me the way!"

Hanson grunted and steered the preacher outside. Reaching the hotel, Marshal Hanson was surprised to see Uncle Moses behind his desk.

"I'd like a room, sir," Reverend Tuck announced.

Hanson shrugged. "Uncle Moses, I told him you were full up, but he had to see for himself."

"Not any longer," Uncle Moses said, pushing the guest register toward the preacher.

"Not the baron?" cried Hanson in surprise.

"Nope," Uncle Moses replied. "Wallace and Amanda Sikes. Oddest thing, too. An hour or so after dark, they came out and said they were packing up and moving to the Southern Hotel. No reason or anything like that, but I don't believe I ever saw a couple as dumbfounded as those two. It was like they had seen a ghost or something."

"So, you have a room for me?" The preacher smirked at Hanson. "You see, Marshal, our Gawd Almighty does indeed work in mysterious ways."

CHAPTER 10

Astride a barrel-chested bay gelding, Ike Mann rode to the Planter's House, a smile unfurling across his bearded face. Behind him trailed a gentle roan saddled for the baron and a pack mule loaded with supplies. Spotting the Englishman on the porch, the buffalo hunter let his grin balloon. "Morning, English," Mann proclaimed, "I'm obliged for the best night's sleep I ever had!"

"Feather mattress made a difference, did it, governor?"

"That and the companionship, English. I hadn't had that much fun since I first saw Lop-Eared Annie Lea."

Baron Jerome Manchester Paget shrugged, uncertain what Mann was referring to.

"English, you mean you ain't heard of Annie Lea? She shows fellows her bosom."

The baron rubbed his close-cropped beard. "Airs her dairy, does she?"

235

Mann scratched his head. "I ain't heard it said that way, but it's so." Mann studied the baron, taking in his plaid trousers, his swallow tail cutaway coat, his black ascot, and his bowler. "This ain't a dress party, English. You sure that's how you want to go?"

The baron nodded. "Anyone that sees me must know I'm a gentleman." The baron picked up the satchel of money at his feet.

"You bring any hardware, English? You might need it."

"Hardware?"

"Yep, a gun," answered Mann, bending and slapping the big buffalo rifle in a scabbard strapped to the side of his bay.

The baron grinned, patting his coat beneath his left armpit. "I'm prepared."

Mann shook his head. "If it'll fit under your arm, English, it ain't nothing but a peashooter. If they get close enough for you to use it, you just as well try to make friends."

Paget laughed as he stepped off the porch.

"English, where we're goin' you'll see a lot of land, but no owners. It's state land until you settle up with the land office. Are you bringing anything but money you won't need?"

"The lad has my belongings out back."

"Let's get your warbag and ride west,"

Mann replied.

The Englishman took the reins from Ike Mann and, in spite of the carpetbag, climbed easily into the saddle.

"You've ridden before."

The baron rattled the reins and the blue roan stepped lazily forward. "Many times on more spirited horses than this, governor."

Mann touched the heel of his boot against the flank of his bay and the gelding started for the corner of the hotel. "Your roan is a gentle animal, but a good one with strong lungs and good endurance. If we find trouble, the roan won't let you down."

The baron followed Mann around the hotel. At the lean-to, the Englishman called for Sammy Collins. The boy emerged, holding a canvas satchel. Sammy's face sagged with a frown. Ike Mann dismounted and took the satchel.

"Cheer up, lad. I'll be back in a week or so," the baron said.

Sammy shrugged and pointed to the big pecan tree. "You may have more trouble than you can manage." There beneath the tree's umbrella of mid-morning shade sat a dark brooding figure on horseback. "One-Eyed Charlie Gatliff'll be tailing you, just waiting to bushwhack you."

"Bushwhack?" the baron repeated, as he

tied the maroon handle of his satchel to the saddle horn.

"Ambush. It means ambush."

The baron glanced over his shoulder at Mann. "He'll protect me from Gatliff. And, with Gatliff following us, Ike Mann won't get any ideas about taking my money, either."

Sammy shrugged. "You've an odd way of looking at things."

"Not odd, lad, different," the baron said, extending his hand.

The youth shook it vigorously. "Keep your eyes open."

"Indeed, lad, I will, and remember that I've one more eye than Charlie Gatliff to keep watch."

Sammy laughed and reluctantly released the baron's hand.

The baron straightened in his saddle as Ike Mann gave a final tug to the hemp rope that secured the baron's warbag to the supplies. Then, Mann hoisted his big frame into the saddle and the bay seemed to sag a moment beneath the buffalo hunter's weight.

"*Adios,* boy," Mann said, touching the greasy brim of his wool hat, "I'll take care of English here."

Sammy Collins bit his lip and offered a slight nod as Mann and the baron turned their horses around. Sammy followed them to the street in front of the hotel and waved as they moved over to Griffin Avenue and turned, Charlie Gatliff trailing fifty yards behind them. Activity in Fort Griffin stopped as Mann and the baron passed. Men halted their chores and pointed at the baron or his satchel. A couple of men even noticed Gatliff following in the Englishman's wake, one taking off his hat and holding it over his heart like he might for a funeral procession. A couple of women of questionable repute threw the baron kisses.

At the end of the street, Mann veered off the road that led up Government Hill and maneuvered among the camps of the buffalo hunters still jealous over the price he had extracted from Jake Ellis. Most of the men howdied Mann and watched the baron, elbowing one another as they mocked his dress.

One of the hunters stood atop a rick of dried buffalo hides and pointed back toward Hide Town. "You're being followed, Ike. That damn patch-eyed feller."

Ike nodded. "Once we get clear of town I'll put on a shooting demonstration."

The fellow on the buffalo hides laughed. "That'll make him keep his distance, won't it, Ike?"

"At least out of range," Mann replied.

■ ■ ■ ■

From the bluff atop Government Hill, Colonel John Paul Jenkins watched through a pair of field glasses as Baron Jerome Manchester Paget emerged on horseback from the buffalo hunters' camp. Behind him some fifty yards rode a solitary man on a yellow dun. The colonel turned his mount around and rode toward the stables where the surly men of Troop F of the Tenth U.S. Cavalry, Colored, awaited orders.

"Sound the bugle," commanded Jenkins to his adjutant. Instantly the order was passed and the bugler pulled his brass horn to his lips, sounding the call. Hurriedly finishing their cigarettes but not their grumbling, the troopers climbed into saddles as empty as their stomachs. These were men who hadn't received a decent meal in weeks, men who would eat field grub for who knew how long. Their eyes simmered with anger, a rage that would only be doused by a full stomach, not some meaningless expedition toward the High Plains.

Gradually, the men organized their troop, four riders abreast, and upon command, they started down the road to Hide Town, the tromp of their horses' hooves throwing

240

up a veil of dust. With Colonel John Paul Jenkins in the lead, the cavalrymen descended Government Hill and cut through the buffalo hunters' camp. Several of the hunters hooted and hollered at the black soldiers.

Jenkins heard the insults, but ignored them. He had other things to think about like last night under the pecan tree. He could not believe his boldness with Flora Belmont. She was a woman unlike any he had ever met before. She played her emotions like a hand of poker. She was stoic and inviting, sensual and yet dangerous. Never had the colonel met such a woman and never had he wanted to be around a woman more. Maybe now was the time to resign from the Army and find some other work, maybe settle down with Flora Belmont.

Jenkins stood in his stirrups and looked back over his shoulder at his troops. All the black men glared at him, their eyes as full of hate as their stomachs were empty of food. The colonel weathered their stares, hoping for one last glimpse of Flora Belmont or, better yet, wishing she might see him leading soldiers. Disappointed, he settled into his saddle and rode for a few miles.

The sky overhead was a pale blue and the fresh grass of late spring was scattered green around wildflowers of red and orange and yellow and blue, colors that would make Flora Belmont a spectacular bouquet. The cottonwood and pecan trees bordering the Clear Fork of the Brazos shimmered in the gentle breeze that wafted down the long valley. Never before on patrol had Jenkins noticed the flowers and the trees and the grass, at least not like this. Sure, he had seen landmarks and forage and water holes, but never nature. Taking a deep breath, the colonel watched the land nearby, not the distance before him. That was when the adjutant at his side spoke.

"Colonel, they're stopping." The adjutant pointed at Gatliff, who was sitting easy in his saddle, and beyond him at the buffalo hunter and the baron. Ahead buzzards circled in the air.

"Whoa," said Ike Mann, holding his hand up. "Trouble!"

The baron reined his roan in. "It shouldn't be too much trouble, not with the Army behind us."

Mann pointed to dozens of circling buzzards.

"Vultures?" asked the baron.

"Buzzards," Mann answered, "mean something's dead or dying." The buffalo hunter stood in his stirrups, studying the terrain ahead. "Whatever's in trouble is over that rise."

Settling back into his saddle, Mann slowly pulled his Sharps Big Fifty buffalo gun from its scabbard. "Just in case," he said.

"Me, too, governor," the baron replied, slipping his hand under his coat and pulling out his .22-caliber revolver.

Mann grinned. "Flash that artillery around too much, English, and you may scare off the cavalry."

The baron nodded. "I'm ready."

Mann laughed and nudged his horse forward toward the rise, the pack mule following reluctantly. Near the crest of the hillock, Mann pulled back the gelding's reins and rose slowly in his stirrups, then sat back down, sliding his buffalo gun into its scabbard. "It's only Cat Tails," Mann sighed.

"Cat Tails?" the baron asked as he rode up beside Mann.

"That crazy Tonkawa that hangs around town and clips the tails off stray cats."

The baron stared at Cat Tails spread-eagled upon the ground more than a hundred yards away. In addition to the buzzards overhead, a half dozen on the ground cautiously approached the body.

"These vultures, governor, they eat carrion?" the baron asked.

"Whenever they can get it," Mann replied.

The baron lifted his revolver. "I cannot abide such an indignity, even for an aboriginal."

Mann pointed toward the baron's pistol. "Put the peashooter away, English, and just watch."

Reluctantly, the baron complied. "I protest that such an indignity can be allowed upon the body of even an aboriginal."

"Just watch Cat Tails."

The baron shrugged and studied the buzzards approaching Cat Tails, occasionally spreading their wings as if they might take to flight. They would stride in, then back out and put their heads in a clump as if they were deciding how do divide up lunch. One by one, they would advance toward Cat Tails, then back away. With their red pimpled faces and their black gangly wings, they were ugly, ungraceful birds. They kept inching closer to Cat Tails, making short advances but shorter retreats, winding up just a little closer to the body with each advance and retreat.

"What's the fun in this, governor?" the

baron asked.

"He ain't dead, English."

"What?" the baron shouted.

"Shhhhh," Mann answered. "If you scare the buzzards away, Cat Tails might kill you."

The baron gulped.

"I seen this once before. Cat Tails trying to catch a live buzzard."

"But why?"

"Who knows the mind of a Tonkawa?" Mann's voice turned to a whisper. "Those buzzards are getting close."

Two buzzards advanced within Cat Tails' reach. They paused, looked at one another and then stepped closer, one moving in toward the head and shoulder, the other approaching the armpit and chest.

Mann let out a low whistle. "I don't know how that damn Indian can hold his breath so long. That close, the buzzards have got to see him breathe."

The one advancing toward the armpit, got within pecking distance of Cat Tails chest. For one brief instant, Cat Tails and the two closest birds were frozen. In the next instant, Cat Tails exploded with his arms springing like a steel trap at the bird beneath his armpit. The bird spread its wings to fly, but Cat Tails grabbed its leg as the other startled birds took to wing, squawking and rejoining the buzzards circling above.

Cat Tails held the buzzard's twitching leg and fought the buzzard's thrashing wings. The wings flapped against his chest until Cat Tails fell to the ground, pinning the bewildered buzzard. The buzzard's flapping wings pummeled his face and chest before he jerked his knife from its scabbard and sliced at the bird's neck. The bird went limp. Cat Tails jumped up, lifting his knife and his trophy above his head. Cat Tails whooped and hollered and danced, finally bending over the bird carcass, plucking a handful of tail and wing feathers and shoving them beneath his headband.

"He finally got his buzzard," Mann said, "but I figure the bird was old, blind, or as crazy as Cat Tails himself."

"A strange ritual, this aboriginal display," the baron said.

"English, no one'll believe what we just saw." Mann shook the reins on his bay and the gelding started toward Cat Tails. The baron followed and soon Cat Tails ran to greet them, gesticulating wildly, chanting his guttural language. As he approached Mann and the baron, Cat Tails shoved his knife back in its leather scabbard and began to gesture. With his right hand, the Tonkawa shook his index finger at the baron. Then with his index and middle finger upright, he lifted his hand to his forehead with his palm facing the baron. He raised his fingers in a spiral curve above his head.

Mann interpreted the gesture. "Cat Tails says you're good medicine, which means good luck as best a white man can translate it." Responding in sign language, Mann lifted his right hand to his forehead, his fingers bunched. He rotated his wrist, making a horizontal circle with his fingers.

Cat Tails smiled, then cut loose a shrill yell and darted away, whooping and hollering.

"What did you tell him?" the baron asked.

"That you thought he was plenty loco."

"Loco?"

"Crazy. He thought it a compliment."

The baron watched as Cat Tails ran gleefully toward the top of the rise. Then suddenly, the Tonkawa dropped to his knees.

Mann laughed. "Maybe I should've told him the cavalry was following."

Then, Cat Tails scurried just below the crown of the rise, making a wide swath so Gatliff and the cavalry could pass. In a moment, Cat Tails had disappeared in the grass, hiding himself.

Mann and the baron rode ahead, past the buzzard carcass and toward the west, where only Indians and a few well-armed white men had previously trekked. Well after noon, they ate in the saddle the jerked buffalo tongue Mann carried.

Toward dusk, Mann angled north toward a clump of trees bordering some unnamed creek. Mann pointed to a herd of pronghorn a quarter mile to the south. The antelope stood frozen, watching Mann and the baron and then Gatliff and the cavalry. As Mann came within a hundred yards of the creek, he pulled up on the reins and halted his bay.

"It's time I sent Charlie Gatliff a message," the buffalo hunter said, climbing down out of his saddle and jerking his buffalo gun from its scabbard. Back down the trail, Gatliff halted. Behind him the cavalry stopped. Mann tied the reins of his bay around his wrist and made sure the pack mule was securely tied to his saddle. Then he lifted the buffalo gun and rested it on the saddle as he pointed the gun south. He inserted the longest cartridge the baron had ever seen into the breech of the Sharps Big Fifty.

"Steady, boy, steady," he said to the gelding as he took aim at the biggest antelope in the herd. "Watch the farthest one to the left, English," Mann instructed. No sooner had he spoken than the buffalo gun coughed loudly and spit fire. The bay jumped and the mule kicked at the air, but Mann held the reins tight and calmed the two animals by force. The reverberations of the shot sent a deadly whisper over the flat land. The antelope went down with a thud and the rest of the herd broke for the distance, disappearing in the grass and the dusk.

"Excellent shot, governor."

Wordlessly, Mann shoved the buffalo gun back in its scabbard and climbed into his saddle. He turned the bay around, then stood in his stirrups. "Gatliff," he yelled, "that antelope is for your supper."

Gatliff touched the brim of his hat, but gave no other response.

"Come any closer than two hundred yards anytime the rest of the trip and I'll put your other eye out."

Gatliff touched the tip of his hat again and rode to fetch the downed antelope.

"Would you really shoot him?" the baron asked wide-eyed.

"If he don't keep his distance."

The baron gulped. "Don't shoot him unless I give permission."

"Whatever you say, English," Mann replied, nudging his horse toward the clump of trees where they would bed down for the night.

They made a simple cold camp, eating more jerky. By dark, the baron saw Gatliff's campfire more than two hundred yards away and beyond it the several fires of the cavalry.

Colonel John Paul Jenkins cut loose with a string of epithets that singed the ears of his fellow officers. Why had that damned buffalo hunter shot that antelope? Jenkins had planned for his men to kill a half dozen of them so they would have fresh meat for supper. Even at the head of the column he had picked up the grumbling when the troops had been ordered to eat lunch in their saddles. Then he had heard their curses as they had bitten into petrified squares of hardtack which they swallowed with sips of warm water from their canteens. As night closed in, Jenkins felt every pair of eyes burning into his back. Maybe he was just as edgy from having nothing more than hardtack for lunch and supper.

But all those white eyes in all those black faces kept staring at him. And as darkness enveloped the prairie and the troops began to build fires of dried buffalo chips and grass, the soldiers' eyes began to simmer white hot and the flesh of their faces disappeared in the darkness. Jenkins took his bedroll and saddle and moved to the perimeter of the surly camp. Every clump of men he passed spoke in whispers or stared silently, their gazes like daggers in his back. There was no merriment, no joking, no laughing, no pranks, no levity, just simmering eyes and smoldering stomachs growling with hunger.

Jenkins fixed his bed away from most everyone else, save his adjutant, and used his saddle as a stool until the last glowing embers of the brief fires died away. Though the eyes had disappeared in the darkness, Jenkins knew they were still there, still staring, still simmering. His nerves taut, his mind reeling with suspicions, Jenkins was too tense to sleep, though his tired and aching body craved rest after the twenty-five miles the troop had covered. He walked the perimeter of the camp, checking the guards and the horses. He spoke to no one for fear someone might shoot at his voice.

Cautiously, the colonel made his way back around the camp toward his bed. In the darkness, the camp seemed indistinct with many forms and shapes moving about or hulking nearby. Were those real or merely monuments to his imagination? Then something odd struck the colonel, something that he had seen but not realized until now. He had not prohibited smoking and yet not a single glow from a pipe or even a cigarette was visible among his men. His men smoked like all troopers and he had never seen soldiers too tired to smoke. Never!

Were the men planning to murder him for executing the cook? Jenkins swallowed hard and looked around, but could barely see three feet in front of himself. Jenkins called softly to his adjutant.

"Over here," came the reply.

Colonel Jenkins stumbled that way, tripping over his saddle and falling onto his bedroll.

"You okay, Colonel?" called his adjutant, a little too loudly to Jenkins' way of thinking.

"Fine, fine," Jenkins replied sharply. "I'm turning in."

The evening air was cool, but Jenkins did not slide under his cover, nor did he take off his boots. He waited, he listened. His ears began to play tricks on him like his eyes before that. He felt a chill run down his spine, a chill that came not from the evening air, but from fear. He could not stay on his bed.

Jenkins threw back the cover on his bedroll, then reached for his saddle. As quietly as he could, he dragged it atop his bedding, then covered it with his blanket. Taking off his hat, he dropped it at the head of the bed. Then he crawled twenty feet farther away from the circle of his troops and stretched out in the grass. He lifted the flap of his holster and pulled out his revolver.

He waited and waited and waited and nothing happened. His eyelids grew heavier and heavier and then he dozed off for a time. For how long, he could not be sure. Then he was startled from his slumber. At first, he thought it was the rustle of the breeze among the trees down by the creek. Then, he thought it was the sound of barefooted men on the move through the grass. He blinked his eyes, but he could see nothing, only shapes and forms that were certainly more imagined than real. Then gunfire started, not twenty feet away.

One, two, three, four gunshots, then more, the flashes of the pistols lighting the air for brief instants and all Jenkins could see were white eyes. And the flashes of revolvers pointed at his bedroll. Five, six, seven, eight more times guns exploded with a thud into the colonel's saddle and hat and bedding.

Jenkins lifted his pistol and fired from the ground at the men attacking his bedroll.

"Run," shouted one of the troopers as they stampeded. Jenkins grimaced. He had missed, but the camp fell silent.

Finally, Jenkins' adjutant spoke. "You okay, Colonel?"

"Nary a scratch," Jenkins said loudly.

He was answered by the hisses of his men.

Jenkins stayed in the grass the rest of the night, his gun in his hand. Except for the changing of the watch, the camp was subdued. Come morning, he pushed his aching body up from the ground. He was stiff and sore but alive. He still carried his revolver and he waved it for any eyes that might be watching. He marched to his bedroll and toed at the blanket, filled with bullet holes.

"Lieutenant," he ordered his adjutant, "have the bugler sound."

The adjutant grumbled, pushed himself out of bed, jerked on his boots and went for one of the troopers.

As he walked back to his own bedroll, Jenkins picked up a trooper's hat and smiled. This was the hat of one of his would-be assassins. He poked his finger through a crease in the crown, then studied the hat as the bugle sounded. From the low angle Jenkins had fired, the bullet had sliced through the front brim and cut a vee out of the crown. Another two inches lower and the trooper would still have been attached to the hat, though perhaps not all of his brains.

The men of his troop climbed out of their covers, glancing curiously at the colonel, then stretching and yawning and massaging the stiffness of their muscles.

"Lieutenant," Jenkins shouted, twirling the trooper's hat around his finger. "See that the men line up with their hats. Whoever's missing a hat will be executed and left on the prairie to rot."

The soldiers gasped.

"Yes, Colonel," the lieutenant said dejectedly.

Jenkins smiled, then turned toward his bedroll to collect his own hat and roll up his bedding. Behind him, he heard one man laugh, then another and another. Jenkins turned around in time to see a covey of hats being thrown in his direction. When the final hat dropped from the air, every enlisted man was wearing a smile instead of a hat.

Jenkins cursed and shoved his pistol back in his holster, then hooked the flap. "Disregard that last order, Lieutenant," Jenkins said. "We'll have a cold breakfast and be in the saddle ready to pull out when the Englishman does." Jenkins folded his blanket and bedding and then examined his saddle. Pulling out his pocket knife, he extracted three slugs embedded in the leather and wood frame and slipped them back in his pocket with his knife. Finally, he picked up his hat and stared at it for a minute before pulling it down on his head. The troops would not get another chance at him, not on this patrol. He'd bed down the rest of the journey with the buffalo hunter and the baron.

"What was all the commotion about last night, Colonel?" Ike Mann looked up from a nice fire where he was roasting a couple rabbits he had shot earlier in the afternoon. "Me and English worried the Comanches had come back."

Jenkins dismounted. "Some of the men thought they saw Comanches and turned scared."

The baron stepped over to Jenkins and extended his hand. "Indeed a pleasure, Colonel. Care to join us for dinner? It's not Aunt Moses's cooking, but it's still food."

Jenkins nodded, then looked back down the trail. "Why's Gatliff following you fellows?"

"Ike thinks he's out to kill me and take my money," the baron laughed. "I think he's just trying to keep Ike from killing me and taking my money."

Mann laughed. "You don't owe me anything, not after the romp you arranged for me on the feather bed."

The baron chuckled. "Seems one of the women at the hotel slipped into my room, thinking I was there, but I'd promised Ike the use of my feather bed. Ike sure had a good time with her."

Jenkins felt his face redden. "It wasn't Flora Belmont, was it?"

"Absolutely not, Colonel," the baron answered emphatically. "It was Amanda Sikes."

Jenkins felt his breath return as he pulled a pair of hobbles from his saddlebag and hobbled his horse. Then he stepped toward the fire, feeling the buffalo hunter's and the baron's gaze upon him.

Mann cocked his head as the colonel squatted down by the fire. "Did them troopers think you was Comanche or can the Army only afford moth-eaten hats for its officers?"

"In the excitement, one of the men shot my hat a few times."

Mann eyed Jenkins skeptically, then motioned for Jenkins to take a seat on the ground. "Rabbit's about done."

Jenkins sat down. "You fellows sure eat better than the Army. You mind if I eat supper with you the rest of the way, even throw my bunk in with you."

"Not at all, Colonel," answered the baron.

Mann pulled a spit from the fire and jerked one of the two rabbits off the stick. The meat sizzled and popped and Ike dropped the rabbit into his lap, then tore the roasted carcass in half, tossing one slab to the baron and the other to Jenkins.

Jenkins hoped the aroma of rabbit wafted to the soldiers he had left behind. He had ordered another cold camp and had prohibited the men from firing their guns at animals for meat. He enjoyed the fresh meat, relishing every bite, picking the bones clean and tossing them back into the fire. "Seen any land you like, Baron?"

"Not yet, Colonel. Ike tells me the best water and grass is about two days ride more. I'll be ready to buy it and start my buffalo ranch," the baron said, patting the satchel at his side.

After they finished eating, they stared at the embers a while, then began to stretch and yawn, before turning in for the night.

When Colonel Jenkins joined Ike Mann and the baron for supper two days later, the Englishman was all smiles.

"This is the place, Colonel," announced

the baron.

Ike Mann seconded the baron's comment with a nod. "All the land beneath the Caprock and between the north and south forks of the Double Mountain branch of the Brazos River. It's good land."

"You can find more grass above the Caprock," Jenkins countered.

"True," Ike Mann answered, "but the water's better here, English."

"I'm satisfied," the baron said.

"Well, Baron, now that you've found your place," Mann asked, "what do you plan to do?"

"Go to the capital — Austin, isn't it? — and file for the land. And then, I'll find a woman to marry."

Jenkins smiled, thinking of Flora Belmont. "Any ideas who the lucky lady'll be, baron?"

The baron nodded, grinning shyly. "Flora Belmont."

Jenkins clenched his jaw and tried to hide his snarl.

CHAPTER 11

The Reverend G.W. "God Willing" Tuck had no other explanation for it except the will of God. Monk Partain and Surry Nettles, though, blamed it on Tuck's leisurely pace from San Angelo, the reverend arriving in Hide Town one day, sleeping late the next, and missing the wealthy Englishman as he took his money into the Caprock country. Though God was a font of endless miracles, a preacher had only so many and right now Tuck could count just two — Monk Partain and Surry Nettles. Tuck could have easily decided how to play those two miracles, if only he knew when the baron would return. If Tuck waited too long to heal them, he would lose folks' interest. But if he cured them now, he must produce another miracle to soak the baron.

Tonight, he would deliver his first sermon since he had preached in the Bee Hive. He had taken from the Bee Hive $1,137 and the burning memory of the soiled dove that had lowered her chemise. He had never seen more fertile ground for a miracle than her bosom, if only he had the faith in himself to heal her. People would come from miles around to see such a great miracle. Tuck decided he would heal Monk Partain and Surry Nettles that night, a mere prelude to curing Lop-Eared Annie Lea.

Suddenly, the religious fires were burning in him. Performing miracles and watching the wide-eyed, slack-jawed amazement in the faces of the naïve made preaching enjoyable. It didn't matter that it was the same miracle he had performed time and again at rural prayer meetings. Country folk always believed and felt obliged to help the work of God by giving of their meager belongings. The fools!

Tuck pulled on his coat, then fished his shirt cuff out of each sleeve. Tuck patted the revolver beneath his frock coat in case God needed any help in keeping the crowd in line. He ran a comb through his flowing gray hair and nodded his satisfaction into a mirror over the washstand. Taking his hat, he positioned it like a crown on his head. Lastly, he picked up his Bible and left the hotel.

On the street, Tuck opened his Bible and

pretended to be reading scriptures as he strolled the half mile to the Clear Fork where he planned to perform. Families by the wagon load had already gathered amid the trees and folks visited or fixed supper. Reaching the sermon site, Tuck mingled with people, introducing himself, helping himself to portions of their supper, then moving past the rows of makeshift wooden benches to his platform, an overturned wagon bed stripped of wheels, axles, and seat. With its tailgate to the Clear Fork, the wagon bed was a hyphen between the makeshift seats and the creek behind. Earlier, Tuck had tied a rope head high between two trees and clothes-pinned to it two woolen blankets borrowed from the Planter's House. The makeshift stage curtain bisected the front from the back of the wagon bed, providing a backdrop to keep hecklers from standing behind him or making faces at the crowd. Further, the blankets would screen Monk and Surry when the time came to heal them. Tuck liked what he saw, especially when men, goaded by their wives, began to hang lanterns from the trees. Darkness was the perfect time and lantern light the perfect illumination for miracles.

As eight o'clock neared, the crowd grew

and gathered on the makeshift benches while Tuck strode back and forth on his platform, working himself into a holy fervor, hoping people would think he was beseeching God for help in dealing with the sins of Fort Griffin. He saw Uncle and Aunt Moses with Sammy in tow. Tuck smiled. Then he saw the marshal. Tuck frowned. Lawmen were sometimes skeptical of preachers, though Tuck could not understand why a lawman of a lesser law should suspect a practitioner of a higher law. It seemed against the natural order of things.

Just before starting time, Tuck watched Surry Nettles hobble in, moving toward the packed front benches. Tuck knew Surry wasn't looking for a seat but for a place to fall. Surry found his opportunity when a little boy darted into the aisle, bumping his crutch. Surry staggered, then tumbled to the ground. Several men jumped to help him while an embarrassed mother grabbed her son and swatted his behind.

Tuck jumped from his platform, offering his help. "Are you okay, my crippled lamb?" Tuck asked, his voice smooth as oil.

Surry nodded. "Thank you, Reverend, and the rest of you as well."

One woman, taken by Surry's handsome looks, scooted her brood together and offered Surry a seat beside her.

"Thank you, ma'am," Surry replied.

When Tuck stepped back upon the platform, he saw Monk Partain standing behind the benches, looking for a place to sit. Tuck's throat tightened when he saw the marshal approach and quiz Monk. Tuck knew he must start the service before the marshal had time to ask Monk too many questions.

Tuck lifted his arms to the heavens and called out in a deep, mellifluous voice. "Good evening, ladies and gentlemen and young ones," Tuck smiled, especially when the marshal backed away from Monk. "Welcome to our prayer meeting for singing, shouting, praying, and raising Gawd Almighty tonight. Let's begin with the singing of 'Shall We Gather at the River,' a goodly Baptist song."

Tuck started the singing, the women joining in readily, the men grudgingly. Not even Tuck knew all the verses so they just sang the first verse six times then stopped. All the time the preacher studied the crowd, looking for troublemakers, men especially who might make the evening difficult. Except for the marshal, Tuck saw no one particularly worrisome.

Holding his Bible in his right hand, Tuck

lifted it toward heaven. "Let us pray," he shouted. Tuck prayed and prayed and prayed, fifteen minutes by his estimate. Nothing beat tiring a crowd out better than covering the multitude of sins that Satan had strewn in life's path. If Tuck could not convince folks to repent, at least he could exhaust them so they would be too tired to sin. When he finally said "Amen," several men echoed the word, more out of relief than affirmation.

Then Tuck opened his Bible and shook it in the faces of the people as he began his sermon. "The sixth chapter of John, the twentieth verse, reads, 'But he sayeth unto them, It is I; be not afraid.' And I say unto you it is I, the Reverend G.W. 'Gawd Willing' Tuck, be not afraid of me for I am here today to save you from everlasting damnation in the pit of hell. You think it's hot in West Texas? It's a thousand times hotter in hell and that's where you're going, unless you repent and seek the everlasting forgiveness that comes from being saved by the grace of the Lord Gawd Almighty and being baptized from head to foot by a Baptist instead of being sprinkled by some other well-meaning but misled preacher."

Tuck flipped through his Bible and stomped his feet against the platform. "Matthew, twenty-fourth chapter, thirty-third verse, says it well and speaks straight to you, each and everyone, unless you have repented. It reads . . . ," Tuck slapped the pages of the Bible for emphasis, ". . . 'Ye serpents, ye generation of vipers, how can ye escape the damnation of hell?' That is how it reads and it is written to you just as it was written to the sinners and pagans and disbelievers of the days when blessed Jesus strode upon this earth with his holy feet. As sinners, you are no better than rattlesnakes, crawling upon your belly across Gawd's world. Do rattlesnakes fly in the air to be closer to Gawd? They do not. Only birds do! Do rattlesnakes sing the praises of their Maker? They do not. Only birds do! The pagan rattlesnakes hiss and rattle the miseries of Satan. Like sin, the rattlesnake hides in the path of life, ready to strike your leg and bring you down. And where do rattlesnakes live? In a hole in the ground so they can be closer to Satan, closer to his evil ways, closer to hell's heat."

The reverend, by now glistening with sweat, jerked off his hat and wiped his forehead with the sleeve of his coat. He enjoyed the fearful countenances scattered throughout his audience, but was taken aback by the broad smile on the marshal's face. Tugging his hat back in place, Tuck plowed ahead. "Until you are saved, you are no better than rattlesnakes, no better than the dirt they crawl on. If you die without the redemption of the Lord Gawd Almighty's one and only Son, your buried soul shares the ground with the rattlesnakes, close to hell for all eternity.

"But if you are redeemed, your soul shall fly with the birds and be close to the Lord Gawd Almighty, today, tomorrow, and forever. Hallelujah, ain't it grand, people, that Gawd has given us a way to escape the snakes and the burning fires of hell? What you decide tonight can be the difference between hell, yes, or hell, no."

Tuck pranced around the platform, gesticulating to make points, slapping his Bible against his leg, pointing an accusing finger at the worshipers. It was time to give Monk and Surry their cues. Whenever he started talking about miracles, they would know it was their night to be healed.

"But to be saved from hell, you must be redeemed and to be redeemed, you must have faith. The man who has faith can work miracles. Why, I've seen preachers that show their faith by handling snakes, the devil incarnate. I kill snakes like Gawd smites sin. I believe in greater miracles, miracles that can be performed even today. I have the power to do it because I have the faith, but I can't perform miracles except on a person who truly believes."

Tuck paused and looked about the crowd, his gaze stopping on the marshal whose grin was wider than before. The preacher's eyes and the marshal's met for a moment, the marshal pointing with his finger toward Monk Partain. Damn, thought Tuck. The marshal must know Monk and Surry were shills, but there was no way to stop them now for he had already given them the cue. Tuck caught his breath.

"There are those among us with problems. There's not a problem too big for Gawd, not a sickness he can't cure, not a malady he can't mend. Even the worst sickness of all — sin — he can cure. If you believe in Gawd and want to be saved, you can be cured, too. Is there anyone among us?"

The question hung in the air for a moment, then Surry Nettles pushed himself up from the bench, leaning on his crutch.

The preacher shook his head. "My crippled lamb, do you believe? Do you really believe?"

Surry's face clouded with doubt and his eyes began to water. "I believe," he said, his voice breaking, "but I don't know if I believe enough."

Oh, God, could Surry Nettles perform? Tuck loved him for it. By the time Surry Nettles hobbled up front, there wouldn't be a dry eye among the women, and many a man would be fighting his composure. Tuck extended his arm to Surry. "Come, my crippled lamb, take my hand and let your faith soar."

Tears began to trickle down Surry's face. He bit his lip and sniffed. "I don't know."

Reverend Tuck waved his arm at Surry Nettles. "Come on, my crippled lamb, the Great Shepherd wants to heal you through me."

Surry hobbled a step, his crutch catching the corner of the bench ahead of him. He toppled forward onto the ground. Men gasped, women sobbed. Several men bounced up from their hard benches to help, a couple actually taking hold of his arms. Surry shook them off.

"No," he said, his voice hard with determination. He picked himself up, shoved the crutch under his arm and hobbled forward, the tears flowing down his cheeks. He dragged his lame foot toward the preacher.

Tuck waited, relishing the drama. Times like these made him proud to be a preacher, proud to be a man of God. Surry made it to the platform. Tuck beamed. Now, if only Monk would do as well.

Marshal Gil Hanson crossed his arms and grinned broadly. The cripple was good and Tuck played off of him well. Hanson studied the crowd, the tearful women fanning themselves with paper or silk fans, the men looking stiff and worried in freshly starched collars, the children fidgeting, and an occasional baby crying out.

On the platform, the reverend hugged the cripple. "Your name?"

"Surry Nettles."

"Do you have faith, Surry Nettles, my crippled lamb?"

Surry nodded, then whispered. "I think so."

"Gawd can't hear you! Do you have faith, Surry Nettles?"

"I do," Surry shouted, then sobbed, hanging his head and wiping the tears from his cheeks with the sleeve of his shirt.

The reverend spun around to the crowd. "Does anyone else, have a malady that I can cure through Gawd? You must step forward. You might never get another chance. Do not be afraid. This crippled lamb is not ashamed."

Hanson stared at the homely bearded face

of Monk Partain, who glanced nervously back. The marshal nodded to Partain, who seemed to grow more confused. Partain shook his head, totally befuddled, then stood frozen in fear. Hanson couldn't decide whether the preacher would save Partain for his next sermon or whether he would use him tonight for a dual miracle. By the desperation in the preacher's voice, Hanson figured the plan called for Partain to be cured this very evening. Hanson nodded again at Partain. The stutterer scratched his head.

The Reverend Tuck grew desperate. "Anyone else want Gawd's cure for your life?" he called in a fury.

Finally, Monk Partain seemed to absorb the preacher's words. He jerked his head around toward the platform. "I need," he started, then stopped. "I-I-I n-ne-nee-need h-he-hel-help," he stuttered. "C-ca-can-can't t-ta-tal-talk r-ri-rig-righ-right."

The Reverend Tuck slapped his hand against his Bible. "Come to me, come to Gawd so you can feel His healing touch. He can reclaim your tongue from Satan. You been this way all of your life?"

Monk Partain grimaced. "I-I-I . . ."

The marshal stepped forward and waved at Tuck, who paled visibly. "I can save us all some time."

The Reverend swallowed hard, like a thief caught in the act.

Hanson continued, "This is Monk Partain. He was waylaid riding into town a few days back, took a nasty hit to the head. It addled his brain. He hasn't been able to talk straight since." The marshal stepped back.

Tuck's head bobbed forward. "Thank you, Marshal," the reverend managed. "Come ahead then, my tongue-tied friend."

Monk Partain advanced wordlessly down the center aisle, moving reluctantly toward the platform. Once, he stopped and looked over his shoulder at the marshal.

"Come on," Tuck implored. "You have nothing to fear from anyone, except from Satan."

Suddenly confident, Monk ran forward where the Reverend hugged him, likely whispering instructions into his ear, Hanson thought.

Then Tuck lifted both arms to the crowd. "Are there others who need the help of Gawd's healing touch?" He strode twice across the platform, holding his Bible to the heavens, imploring God to help the sinner who could not walk and the sinner who could not talk. In his holy enthusiasm, he struck the blankets which screened the back half of the platform.

Hanson smiled to himself. Reverend Tuck was out of shills.

Tuck reached for Monk Partain, touching one cheek with his hand and the other with his well-thumbed Bible. "Have faith," he implored Partain, "as you step behind our curtain. We shall pray for your deliverance from the devil." The Reverend parted the blankets and allowed Monk to pass.

Next, Tuck turned to Surry Nettles. "You shall walk, Surry Nettles, if you believe." Tuck placed his hand upon Surry Nettles forehead, then with his Bible brushed away the tears still streaming down the cripple's cheek. "Soon, those will be tears of joy." Tuck took Surry by his free hand and guided him toward the curtain of blankets. Nettles hobbled through. Tuck patted the curtain back into place.

"Now, I must do Gawd's work," Tuck proclaimed. Bending, he placed his Bible on the platform and knelt upon it. Bowing his head, he brought his clasped arms to his chin and prayed. "Gawd Almighty," he shouted, "I humbly beseech you to relieve this crippled lamb and this tongue-tied child of their maladies. I beseech you not with my feet upon this sinful earth, but with my knees upon your Holy Word. May the faith of these two lonely souls grow and release their bodies from the evils that afflict them. Free the shackles of lameness upon the one and untie the devil's tongue upon the other. Hallelujah, your name be praised, Lord Gawd Almighty! Amen."

In unison, the crowd leaned forward together. As if all nature awaited the miracle, not a sound emanated from the audience, not a cough from a bored man, not a sigh from a weary woman, not a whimper from a hungry child.

The Reverend Tuck flung back his hands and lifted his head. "Now, Surry Nettles," the reverend called, "throw away your crutch."

A loud clatter followed, and the quilt curtain quivered.

"Now, Monk Partain, speak to me," implored Tuck.

The world was silent until Monk Partain spoke. "S-Su-Sur-Surr-Surry f-fe-fel-fell d-do-dow-down."

The audience gasped, then howled with laughter. Marshal Hanson snickered with everyone else. The Reverend Tuck, though, never moved, his knees still resting on his Bible, his arms still outstretched in humble supplication, his head still staring toward the dark heavens.

"B-but wa-wait," Monk Partain cried, "h-he's get-getting up. He's getting up. Surry's getting up. He's standing without his crutch. And, I'm talking. I'm talking like I used to," Partain shouted gleefully.

The audience gasped again. Monk Partain had indeed stopped stuttering. Reverend Tuck jumped to his feet, grabbing his Bible and throwing his arms open to his impromptu congregation. "Praise be to Lord Gawd Almighty," he shouted, then lunged for the curtain, parting it.

Monk Partain emerged first, grinning as he spoke. "I can talk. I can talk again," he kept repeating.

"Praise the Lord Gawd Almighty," shouted Tuck.

When Surry Nettles stepped forward, his face was distorted by the emotion, his lips pressed together, his eyes battling the tears, his cheeks drawn in. He advanced toward Tuck on a gimpy leg, then threw his arms around the preacher. "Thank you," he mumbled through his tears. "Thank you all."

The assembled worshipers broke into cheers and applause.

Nettles released Tuck and nodded to the crowd. He stepped off the platform and several hands reached up to congratulate him.

"Now," called the reverend, "while we are basking in the glory of Lord Gawd Almighty, let's pass the hat."

Taking a hat that was offered him, Surry Nettles sent it down the front row. "Thank you, thank you," he cried as each person dropped a coin or a bill in. "I can walk, I can walk."

The lesser miracle Monk Partain stood at the end of the row, taking the hat and licking his lips as he passed it on to the next row.

Not feeling moved to give any of his own monthly pay to the reverend's holy cause, Marshal Hanson stepped away from the crowd and out of the glow of lanterns. He circled among the wagons parked on the perimeter of the meeting ground, thinking he glimpsed Cat Tails slipping among them, probably looking for liquor that some of the men had hidden in the wagons, hoping their wives might not find it.

As the marshal headed back to Fort Griffin, he could hear Tuck's strong voice pleading for the crowd to return next week. "A week from tonight, come back and hear the word of the Lord Gawd Almighty again and witness the many miracles he can perform."

Hanson shook his head. It would take a bigger miracle than was seen tonight to attract another crowd this size.

Derringer in hand, Lop-Eared Annie Lea cracked the door wide enough to see the Reverend G.W. Tuck standing hatless before her. She hid the derringer and pulled the door open, squinting at the bright mid-morning sun. "What do you need, padre?" Annie Lea laughed.

"A miracle."

Annie Lea nodded. "It'll be a miracle if you get in this door without paying. Any man that cures a cripple who ain't a cripple or a tongue-tied loon who ain't tongue-tied ain't no better than my kind."

The reverend nodded. "Like you, I give man what he wants. In my case, it is hope. May I come in?"

Annie Lea shook her head. "No man gets in without paying up front and I don't give discounts, not even to clergy."

The reverend slipped his hand in his pocket and pulled out a twenty-dollar gold piece. "I figure that surpasses your going rate?"

Annie Lea smiled as she grabbed the coin. "Come in, please."

As Tuck entered her modest crib, she

started to shut the door.

"Leave it open," Tuck said, his gaze sweeping the room, taking in the bed, two chairs, two lamps, a washstand, a trunk against the wall, and a dresser beside him with the tintype of an elderly woman atop it. Tuck reached for the tintype but Annie Lea grabbed it and carried it across the room, placing it face down on her unmade bed, leaving the derringer beside it.

Tuck saw the derringer and looked at Annie Lea.

"Nothing personal, padre, but a woman has to be careful. Now, are you ready to look and leave?" she asked, beginning to unbutton her nightgown.

Tuck held up his hand. "I didn't come for that." He looked away, his eyes focusing on a red fox stole hanging over the end of her iron bedstead.

"What did you come for, padre?" Annie Lea asked.

"A business proposition, one that could benefit us both."

Annie Lea fingered the gold piece in her hand. "Go ahead."

"It is a fact, madam, that you have the most talked about bosom in all of West Texas, as I myself witnessed in the Bee Hive."

"So?"

"I'd like to cure them, even them up in front of my next camp meeting."

"Padre, you're about as loco as they come. Even if you could do it, that would knock me out of business."

"Just for one night, which I'd pay you two hundred dollars for. You'd never have to unbutton your blouse."

Annie Lea scratched her chin, then studied the twenty-dollar gold piece. "Two hundred dollars? That's a good week's work. How do you plan to go about this?"

Tuck laughed. "I don't have it all figured out yet." Now, Tuck scratched his chin. "I'd have to have you in front of the crowd so they can see your small side blossom like your big side."

"I don't know, padre. It could cost me business."

Tuck shook his head. "Not at all. It would help business. I'd put word out you were considering giving up your old ways. Men'd flock to see you one last time. Then, after the miracle, they'd want to see if it really took. Seems like business would be more boom than bust, if you'll pardon the expression."

"Two hundred dollars?"

The reverend nodded. "Half before the

279

service, half after."

"Nope. It's all in advance."

Tuck shrugged. "A hundred today, the rest after the service."

Annie Lea held up the twenty-dollar gold piece. "This got you in the door, padre, but it's not part of the two hundred."

"Agreed, madam, but you're a hard one to bargain with."

Marshal Gil Hanson had never seen anything like it, the men lined up at Lop-Eared Annie Lea's crib. The line snaked from her front door, twenty-five yards to the Clear Fork. Ever since word had gotten about town that the Reverend Tuck was going to make Annie Lee right with God and her blouse, men had been anxious to have one final look, something they could remember for the rest of their lives. In fact, Annie Lea's pending conversion had taken folk's minds off the baron and his satchel full of money. Maybe Hide Town was safer with a fraudulent preacher than with a wealthy baron.

Consequently, Marshal Gil Hanson was disappointed the day he saw a ribbon of dust to the west of town. He knew the cavalry had returned and, like it or not, the baron and One-Eyed Charlie Gatliff as well. Hanson walked to the west side of town and

280

past the remaining camps of buffalo hunters who were still convinced they could get
Jake Ellis to offer them the same price he
had given Ike Mann. Most hunters had
given up, either too bored or too hungry or
too sober to outlast Jake Ellis.

Mann and the baron came into view, a
third man riding beside them. Hanson
squinted, then shook his head. Colonel John
Paul Jenkins rode with them instead of with
his cavalry. Beyond the baron, Hanson saw
a solitary rider, his head and shoulders sagging. Hanson laughed at Gatliff.

The baron grinned widely as he neared
the marshal. "Constable, I've seen the wild
country."

Hanson crossed his arms over his chest
and cocked his head. "You find your buffalo
ranch?"

The baron nodded, then patted his carpetbag tied to the saddle horn. "Indeed, this
will purchase it and start the fencing."

Ike Mann twisted his face and grunted.
"That money won't fence far."

"Constable," asked the baron, ignoring
Mann's comments, "is the wealthy Flora
Belmont still about town?"

At the question, the colonel's face con-
torted, and he stared with granite eyes at
the baron.

Hanson nodded. "Saw her just today."

"Excellent, constable," nodded the baron, "because I plan to marry that woman."

"More money for fencing once he weds her," laughed Ike Mann.

The colonel cut an ugly eye toward the buffalo hunter, grunted something indecipherable, touched his spur to his horse's flank and turned toward Government Hill.

Hanson tipped his hat. "Welcome home, Colonel," he offered, but the officer ignored him. "What's the matter with him?"

Ike Mann cleared his throat and leaned over his saddle, resting his arms on the saddle horn. "He's had a bur under his saddle ever since his troops tried to kill him."

The baron shrugged as another rider approached, spooking the pack mule that Mann had tied to his saddle.

"Whoa, boy, whoa!" Mann turned in his saddle and laughed as Charlie Gatliff drew even with him. "Damn, Gatliff, you don't know how to keep from scaring my dumb mule, do you? I guess about all you know is how to stay out of range of my buffalo gun."

Without slowing his horse, Gatliff scowled at Mann and rode on by. "The baron won't always have you and your buffalo gun around, Mann." Gatliff spat at the hooves of the baron's horse.

The Englishman tittered. "First time he's been within spitting distance since we left Fort Griffin."

Watching Gatliff ride away, Hanson knew he should alert the gambler Joe Loper. "Baron, you watch Gatliff awfully close the next few days. I figure he'll try to take your satchel."

The Englishman patted the peashooter beneath his left arm. "Let him try. Just let him try."

Sammy Collins was taking out a bowl of potato peels and scraps when he saw the baron riding down the street. Collins whooped with joy and flung the scraps closer to the hotel than Aunt Moses would have preferred. From behind a nearby woodpile, a grunting and snorting hog scurried out and attacked the scraps. Collins raced back to the hotel, leaving the bowl on the back steps and dashing toward the baron. Behind him, he heard Aunt Moses calling his name, but he ignored her. "You made it," Collins shouted.

The baron smiled. "Greetings, lad. I've found a good spot of land, land that will forever raise buffalo. Good grass, good water. All I need now is a good fence."

"And a good valet," Collins grinned.

"Indeed, lad! Now heat me water so I can take a hot bath. I've more layers of dirt and grit on me than I can count."

"Yes, sir," Sammy shouted, running back to the hotel, charging up the front porch, bursting through the front door and darting into the kitchen, out of breath. "The baron's back. Wants a bath. I gotta draw it for him."

"I need help with supper," Aunt Moses said.

"Not until I tend him."

Aunt Moses' ruddy complexion turned redder.

Sammy ignored her, dipping a pot of water from the water barrel and putting it on the stove to boil. He retrieved the tub from the closet and pulled it to the baron's room. In half an hour, he was pouring water as the baron undressed and got in the tub.

"Now, lad," he said, "have you cared for my rooster?"

"Yes, sir," Sammy replied. "I've got him and his cage outside my door."

"Good, lad, any excitement in my absence?"

"A preacher's in town. You won't believe it, but I saw him cure a cripple and a stutterer the other night at the camp meeting."

"You sure about that?"

284

"Absolutely. I saw it myself."

"Lad, don't be gullible. There's a lot of deceit in the world. It's a fraud."

Sammy shrugged. "It looked real to me and now he's promising to cure Lop-Eared Annie Lea."

The baron shook his head. "The woman that airs her dairy?"

"Yep," Sammy answered. "The preacher says she's due for a cure."

Again the baron shook his head. "This preacher's a fraud, lad, like all the other newcomers in town."

"You're a newcomer," Sammy challenged. "Are you a fraud, too?"

"What do you think, lad?" The baron grinned.

Sammy Collins snickered. "You're the only person in these parts that I can trust."

CHAPTER 12

At the dinner table, Flora Belmont felt breathless. Her heart fluttered and her stomach churned. For the first time since The Night, she was with the colonel, but now he seemed sullen and withdrawn. She sat between the baron and the colonel, one man she wanted to take, the other she just wanted. Despite all her efforts to converse with the colonel, he ignored her. Certainly he must be tired, just back from patrol, but then so was the baron and he talked enthusiastically about the trip and about his crazy buffalo ranch.

Across the dinner table sat the Reverend Tuck, a pompous fool who talked religion, sin, and hell straight from the Old Testament and kept interrupting the baron with his theological meanderings.

"Mr. Paget, you seem to be building quite a kingdom on earth," Tuck started, pointing his fork at the Englishman's nose. "Have you ever thought about your heavenly king-dom?"

"It's Baron, not Mr. Paget," corrected Beulah Fenster. "He has met with the queen, you know."

The baron nodded his thanks at Beulah, then turned his head toward Tuck. "Gover-nor, I . . ."

"It's not governor," shot back the rever-end, "because I refuse to be called by the title of an office of this earth, just as I refuse to use titles of royalty — like baron. Only the Lord Gawd Almighty has a lasting king-dom."

"He's right, the reverend is," interjected Aunt Moses.

The baron looked at Aunt Moses. "Might I continue? Or would you care to entertain us with your insight into the Protestant Reformation, Aunt Moses?"

"The what, Mr. Paget?" replied Tuck.

"Baron, not Mr. Paget!" corrected Beulah Fenster.

The baron touched his lips with his nap-kin, then stared at the reverend. "I have heard that you performed miracles, making the lame walk and the mute speak. Is that true?"

Tuck nodded proudly.

"Were these people from around here,

governor, or did they arrive with you?"

Tuck coughed. "They were here when I arrived. What's the difference?"

Sammy Collins interrupted. "They're newcomers." Aunt Moses cast him a sour look, and Sammy shrank back in his seat.

"The difference, governor . . ."

Tuck hit his fork against the table. "I asked you not to call me 'governor.'"

"And I," cried Beulah Fenster, "told you to call him 'Baron,' not 'Mr. Paget.'"

The baron continued, "The difference, governor, is we can't gainsay the legitimacy of their maladies, now can we?"

"Do you doubt the integrity of a man of Gawd?," Tuck harrumphed.

"Indeed, governor, I do."

Tuck hit his fork against the table again. "This is outrageous, coming from a foreign infidel like yourself."

"Jesus had disciples did he not, governor? Do you have disciples? Or, are they shills?"

"Outrageous!" Tuck exploded. "You blasphemer, you foreigner."

"A blasphemer whose money you gladly would take, if offered." The baron pushed back his chair and retrieved his money satchel, then held it over the table. "Five thousand pounds. That foreign money, governor, is equal to 25,000 of your Yankee

288

dollars."

Tuck licked his lips and rubbed his fingers. His breath came heavy. "You should tithe, baron, one tenth of your money, that's what the Bible says."

The baron placed the satchel in his lap. "I'll not tithe with you, governor, but I may need your services."

Tuck gazed vacantly ahead.

The baron looked from the reverend to Flora and smiled.

Flora felt his gaze hot upon her.

"I plan to wed, if a certain woman says 'yes.' "

Colonel Jenkins hit his balled fist against the table. Beulah Fenster caught her breath.

Flora Belmont felt her face flush, and she glanced toward the colonel. His eyes were livid, his lips tight, his jaw clenched, his fists knotted white. Her sorrow for the colonel was made even worse when she felt the baron's hand slip over hers on the table.

Why was this happening to her? Why now?

The baron patted her hand. "You were all I thought about while I was away."

Flora's heart was pounding. She must stall, must buy time so she could have the baron for his money and title and the colonel for herself. She fanned her napkin at her face. "This is so sudden," she said, grimacing at the colonel's hard expression, "and so public. Perhaps we should talk alone."

Smiling, the baron released her hand. "How foolish of me."

Flora nodded. "There's much to discuss."

"We can meet under the pecan tree shortly," the baron offered.

"No," Flora shot back, "not the pecan tree. The porch will be fine, if the other gentlemen in this room will give us a few moments privacy before they come outside for their smokes."

Each man nodded, except Colonel John Paul Jenkins.

The baron arose, holding the satchel with one hand and patting Flora Belmont on the shoulder with the other. She flinched at his touch. Across the table she saw Beulah Fenster glowering at her.

"Good evening," the baron said, striding from the room.

Flora felt her face grow hotter. Her mind was awhirl. As she pushed herself away from the table, the colonel arose to help her with her chair. As she stood, flustered, her napkin slid to the floor. Both she and the colonel bent for it. "Meet me under the pecan tree later," she whispered. She saw the trace of a smile on his lips and a slight nod of acknowledgment as they stood up.

In a daze, she left the dining room and moved to the porch, pausing at the door to stare at the baron. His satchel of money sat in a rocker by his side. Flora took a deep breath, then moved to the porch, her footfall as heavy as her heart.

The baron turned around, his face masked by the twilight shadows. "I should not have been so forward, madam." He reached for her hands. She acquiesced, quivering at his touch. Reverently, he proposed. "I would like to ask for your hand for the ages, Mrs. Belmont. Would you marry me?"

Flora gulped. She felt tears in her eyes, not for the baron, but for the colonel and what he might think. She glanced away and caught a glimpse of the colonel ducking behind the curtains at the window nearby. Flora could not answer.

Sighing at the awkward silence, the baron spoke again. "You are a monied woman. I am a titled gentleman. I have money but need more, I will be honest. For a share of your money, I shall share my title with you. Perhaps one day, we can come to love each other in the sense you Yankees value. If not, we English are a practical race, and we tolerate dalliances with others, though it muddles the progeny."

Flora bit her lip as the baron pulled her closer to him. Her muscles did not resist, but her spirit flamed against this man.

"Will you become Lady Paget?" he asked softly.

"Yes," she whispered, "yes." She anticipated a kiss, but the baron gently eased back from her.

"It is customary in an arranged marriage that the woman betrothed to royalty provide a sum of money, a dowry I believe you Yankees would call it."

Still dazed by the sudden turn of events, Flora nodded. "A dowry?" All these years she had sought men whose bank accounts she could deplete. Now she had agreed to marry a man who had asked for her money. At least he was straightforward about it.

The baron explained, "It would be a written agreement between us, an agreement you would keep, proving your claim to my title, my estates, and my holdings in England. That in exchange for $2,000."

The mention of money sharpened Flora Belmont's senses for a fleeting moment, then she caught a glimpse of the colonel peeking through the curtain. "I could go $1,500."

"Agreed," he said, instantly releasing his hold upon her. "Please come to my room in

292

the morning after eleven o'clock. I will have the Collins lad there so that no one can question your morality or your integrity in the matter. And, I will commit to writing the arrangement and give you the papers when you provide me the dowry."

"Fine," Flora said.

The baron picked up his satchel. "Good night, then," he said, pausing for an instant, ". . . darling."

She expected him to wrap his arms around her, but he walked by without another word. Her head spun and her eyes brimmed with tears as she bolted from the porch, running down the street toward the pecan tree to await the colonel. She dabbed at her eyes with her sleeve and tried to control her heaving breath.

Suddenly, the colonel stood beside her in the darkness, tall and lean and dangerous. He grabbed her and pulled her to him and pressed his lips against hers until she thought she would faint.

"Did you tell him yes?" he demanded the instant he lifted his lips from hers.

She nodded meekly. "Yes, yes," she sobbed, "but I plan to kill him after the marriage."

The colonel squeezed her tightly. "So do I."

Sammy Collins knocked on the baron's door at eleven o'clock as the baron had requested the night before. Sammy, though, felt sullen and abandoned, the baron choosing Flora Belmont over him.

"Enter," came the baron's voice.

Pushing the door open, Sammy sighed and went in, his lips pursed, his brow furrowed.

"Something's the matter, lad, isn't it?"

Running his fingers through his brown hair, Sammy couldn't deny that. With his foot, he nudged the door shut. "You're not really taking me away, are you?"

The baron slipped his pen in its ink well and stood up. "Now, lad, what makes you ask that?"

"You plan to marry that Flora Belmont, don't you?"

"Sure, lad, but that has nothing to do with you."

"She won't like me going with you."

"Lad, marriage is different in England, much more a business proposition, especially among royalty. Here," the baron said, holding up a piece of paper, "read this."

Sammy walked across the room, setting

the rooster to cackling in its window cage. Taking the missive from the baron, Sammy plopped down on the corner of the as yet unmade bed. He studied the baron's handwriting and mouthed the words as he read. "To all let it be known that in exchange for $1,500 as dowry, the Baron Jerome Manchester Paget promises to take Flora Belmont as his wife and that both shall share and share alike their mutual assets, including titles, money, land, and other possessions." It was signed by the baron. Sighing, Sammy shrugged.

The baron took the note. "You worry too much, lad. I have given you my word I will take you when I leave."

Sammy wished he could believe the baron, but things no longer added up. He pushed himself up from the bed and began to make it.

The baron moved to the wall mirror over the washstand and used a pair of scissors to trim his beard.

Just as Sammy finished the bed, someone knocked on the door. The baron turned to Sammy. "Please stay," he said softly, then called loudly to the door. "Enter." He placed the scissors beside the washstand.

As the door swung open, Flora Belmont waltzed in, carrying a purse.

"Darling," said the baron matter-of-factly, "leave the door open so there's no vicious gossip to sully your reputation."

Flora nodded to the baron and acknowledged Sammy with a scowl. Sammy wanted to run from the room, run from the baron who had betrayed him for this evil woman. Sammy had not felt this low since his parents died.

Flora approached the baron, taking his hand and squeezing it, but displaying no emotion. "I have the money," she said.

"And I the papers, darling," replied the baron, offering the missive to her.

Flora Belmont took the paper rather haughtily from his hand and read over it a couple times. "I suppose you want me to sign?"

"Of course, darling, after you count the money."

Flora dropped her purse on the writing stand, unhooked the catch and pulled out a stack of bills.

Sammy watched wide-eyed, never having seen so much American money. He much preferred the look of American money to the odd-sized bills that the baron carried in his satchel. When she had dropped $1,500 onto the writing stand, she had cut into her stack of bills by less than a fifth at most.

Then, she dropped the remainder back in her purse, which she quickly latched.

The baron took the money and counted it himself, then smiled at his betrothed. He dipped his pen in ink and offered it to her. With a flourish and a scowl, Flora Belmont signed her name to the marriage proposal, then shoved the pen at the baron. He dropped it in the ink well, blew on the ink to dry it, then sandwiched the signed document between two sheets of paper to avoid smudging the contract. He folded the sheets in thirds, then sat them on the corner of the writing stand. He next lit a candle and reached for an envelope at the back of the writing stand. As he retrieved the envelope, he knocked the folded sheets onto the floor. "How clumsy of me," he said, bending over and picking up the document.

Sammy watched, thinking something odd about the baron's movements, but not really caring.

As the baron straightened in his chair, he slid the folded paper into his envelope, then held the candle over the flap. As the wax dripped on the flap, the baron smiled. "Take good care of this, darling." He offered her the contract and a smile.

Flora Belmont snatched the envelope from his hand. "I will."

"Shall we set a date next week for our wedding, darling?" he asked.

Flora's face flushed with embarrassment. "So much has happened so quickly, let me think upon it." She spun around and strode away without closing the door.

"I shall be anxious to introduce you to the Queen of England, darling," the baron called after her.

The baron's fawning over Flora Belmont made Sammy sick to his stomach. He couldn't face the baron so he stared at the floor beneath the writing stand. When the baron popped up from the chair to close the door, Sammy blinked at something that had been hidden beneath his shoe. A sheet of paper folded in thirds! Sammy scrambled off the bed and fell to his hands and knees beside the chair. Picking up the paper, he unfolded it and furrowed his brow. It was the marriage contract Sammy had seen before. Only now, it had Flora's signature beneath the baron's as well.

Sammy looked up at the baron, who stood over him, his arms crossed and a smile on his face. "I don't understand," Sammy said.

"It's our little secret, lad," the baron said as he took the note from Sammy. The baron picked up Flora's stack of bills and slipped it inside his coat pocket. Then, he grabbed the candle he had used to seal the envelope and touched a corner of the marriage agreement. The flame grew, spreading across the paper, blackening it. As the flame reached his fingers, the baron dropped the paper on the writing stand. The paper curled and disintegrated until there was little but the flakes and the memory that it had ever existed. "Lad, if anyone ever asks you about this, you say you didn't see anything, either the note or her money."

"But that's lying. Aunt Moses says not to lie."

The baron cuffed Sammy's head. "She's right, lad, but you've got to remember everything's not always what it seems. If you want to leave with me, you will need to do what I say, lad."

Sammy shrugged. Now he was more confused than ever about the baron. "When will you be leaving?"

The baron turned and faced Sammy squarely, placing his hands upon the boy's shoulders. "I want to stay until after the Reverend Tuck performs his miracle on the woman that airs her dairy."

Sammy snickered. "You mean Lop-Eared Annie Lea?"

The baron nodded.

"That'll be Saturday night. Next stage

won't leave until Tuesday morning, seven o'clock. That's Shorty DeLong's return run."

"Lad, do not tell a soul. That is what this marriage proposal is all about. People won't think I'm leaving on Tuesday if they know I'm getting married on Wednesday."

Now, it began to make a little more sense. Sammy sighed, glad that he understood the baron's motives.

"After I take lunch, lad, and you finish the dishes for Aunt Moses, I'll meet you in your room and we'll take a walk, maybe buy some candy at Zach Fenster's store."

"Aunt Moses may have other chores for me. She doesn't like it that I've done so much for you, and you haven't yet paid your hotel bill."

The baron laughed, tapping his coat pocket where he had slipped Flora Belmont's bills. "Flora Belmont'll pay for my stay through next Wednesday and she'll throw in a little extra for your services."

"He paid through next Wednesday, when he plans to marry, and then threw in fifty dollars to boot for Sammy's services," Uncle Moses told his wife. "And, it's American dollars not that funny money he carries around all the time."

Sammy washed the last dish and placed it on the table, then carried the pail of dishwater outside and dumped it near the privy. As he walked back to the kitchen, he glanced across the street and saw a man standing in the shade of a live oak tree. At first glance, he feared it was Charlie Gatliff, but a closer look revealed the gambler Joe Loper. Sammy breathed easier. Loper appeared harmless, eating an apple and enjoying the shade.

Sammy shrugged and entered the kitchen, Uncle and Aunt Moses both lowering their voices. They were likely planning how to spend the extra fifty dollars, money they would not have had without his work. He moved to the table and grabbed a dish towel to finish up the lunch dishes.

"You can just let them air dry this afternoon, Sammy," Aunt Moses offered.

Sammy grinned, anxious to meet the baron for their planned walk. He tossed his towel down on the table and removed his apron. "Thanks." Sammy ran out the door, catching a glimpse of Joe Loper finishing up his apple across the street, then barged into his lean-to. No sooner had he opened the door and stepped inside than someone grabbed him from behind and covered his mouth so he couldn't scream. The door snapped shut by someone else's hand.

"Be quiet, boy," came a surly voice. "It's time to go calling on the Englishman," Charlie Gatliff snarled.

Sammy shook his head, resisting feebly.

As Gatliff's grip tightened, Sammy knew it had been a mistake to challenge the gunman. Then Sammy felt the cold tip of a gun barrel pressed against his temple.

"I've followed that son of a bitch all over Texas, and I'm tired of waiting to catch him alone, boy. Go to his room and tell him somebody's waiting for him on the porch. Tell him you'll watch his satchel. When he steps out, you remove that damn chicken of his and toss me his bag out the window. If you don't, I'll slit your gut tonight."

Sammy gulped. "I can't."

"Sure you can, if you want to see sunrise tomorrow."

Before Sammy could answer, he heard a rapping at the door. "Lad, you in there? You ready to go?"

The door swung open and the baron entered, carrying his satchel.

Gatliff shoved Sammy to the floor and waved his gun at the Englishman. "Howdy, Baron, come on in. I've been looking to meet you and your satchel," laughed Gatliff.

■ ■ ■ ■

Marshal Gil Hanson patted his bloated stomach after taking lunch at the Bee Hive. The food was greasy and plentiful and free, the perfect combination for a man who only made twenty dollars a month. He yawned and covered his mouth, figuring to walk a little of his meal off before heading back to his office for an afternoon nap.

As the marshal approached the Planter's House, he saw a man with his gun drawn standing under a live oak tree. Hanson recognized Joe Loper, who stared at something behind the hotel, then glanced quickly up the street, catching sight of the marshal. Loper waved his gun, motioning for Hanson. The marshal drew his pistol and sprinted for Loper, his lunch sloshing around in his belly.

"What is it?" Hanson huffed as he drew up beside the gambler.

"Trouble," Loper said.

"Gatliff?"

"Yep. He's in the shed with that kid and the baron."

"The baron? Did he have his carpetbag?"

"Afraid so," Loper acknowledged, stepping out from under the shade of the tree and starting for the hotel.

"What are we going to do?" Hanson whispered as he trailed Loper.

Loper slipped to the corner of the lean-to, peered cautiously around the side, then ducked back when he heard the door squeak open. He motioned to Hanson that Gatliff had emerged. Loper peeked around the corner, then stepped forward, motioning for Hanson to follow. As the marshal cleared the corner, he saw Gatliff sneaking away the opposite direction, the baron's satchel in his hand.

"Hold it right there," commanded Loper.

Gatliff froze. "Loper, you son of a bitch," he growled.

"I ought to return the favor, Gatliff, and shoot you in the back. Now move your hands away from your sides and drop the satchel."

Gatliff failed to respond.

Loper cocked the hammer on his revolver.

The deadly click had a persuasive quality about it. Gatliff let go of the satchel and lifted his hands.

"Now turn around slowly," Loper commanded.

"Remember there's two of us, Gatliff, and we're the law," said Marshal Hanson.

"I make my own law," Gatliff snarled.

"Not this time," Hanson shot back.

Gatliff twisted cautiously about, eyeing both men. "Holster your guns and I'll take you both on."

"Shut up," Hanson ordered, "and keep your hands in the air."

"Keep him covered, Marshal, and I'll take his weapons," Loper said, then moved warily toward the gunman. He jerked Gatliff's Colt from his holster and then pulled a small caliber weapon from the gunman's belt. Loper held it up for the marshal.

Hanson nodded. "That's the baron's pea-shooter."

Loper shoved each weapon into his belt, picked up the baron's satchel and retreated to the marshal's side. "You better check inside, Marshal."

Hanson grunted and shoved the door open, then entered to find both the baron and the boy bound and gagged in chairs. Shoving his gun in his holster, Hanson bent down over the Englishman and untied the cloth gag.

"My club bag, did you get my club bag?"

Hanson nodded, twisting about to the boy and taking the gag out of his mouth. Sammy Collins took a deep breath.

"Undo the lad first, constable," said the baron.

The marshal dug into his pants for a pocket knife and cut the leather strips that bound them. When the boy was free, he rubbed his wrists and stretched his arms. As soon as Hanson cut him loose, the baron shot up from his chair and darted for the door. Hanson followed and saw the baron walk up to Loper, who held his satchel and money.

"We're headed for jail, Gatliff, for attempted robbery," Hanson announced.

Paget shook his head. "Jail the brigand, if you like, constable, but I'll not press charges against him as I do not want to be detained by legal delays before I can get to Austin and purchase my land."

Hanson shook his head. "I saw the robbery, that's reason enough to put him in jail."

Loper grabbed Hanson's arm. "Jail will only delay the inevitable, Marshal."

"But it's the law."

"Sometimes you've got to break the law to uphold it," Loper countered, then stepped to Gatliff. "I oughta shoot you now."

Gatliff sneered. "You'll never get a better chance than this."

Loper spat at Gatliff's feet. "Be out of town tomorrow by noon. If you're still around, I'll kill you, Gatliff."

"I'll be in town, Loper, because I ain't running from you or anybody else."

"Then you'll be dead by one o'clock." Loper shoved his gun in his holster and pulled Gatliff's Colt from his belt. He released the cylinder and held the gun by the barrel until six bullets tumbled from the cylinder to the ground. He tossed the gun in the dirt at Gatliff's feet. "Be ready to use that, the next time I see you. Now scat."

Gatliff squatted for his gun, never taking his eyes off Loper. He jerked the weapon from the ground and shook loose the grit. "You heard him threaten me, Marshal. Next time I see him, whatever I do will be in self defense."

Hanson nodded. "Get out of here before I arrest you."

Gatliff darted around the side of the hotel, Loper following him to the corner of the building, just to make sure the gunman didn't try any tricks.

Quickly, the baron strode to Loper. "Thank you, governor, for assisting me and the lad."

Loper gave the baron his satchel, then pulled Paget's puny revolver from his belt. "Here's your peashooter."

"Thank you, governor, what can I ever do

to repay you?"

Loper shrugged. "Save your thanks until tomorrow. If Gatliff leaves town or I kill him, then you can join me and some friends in a card game. If he kills me, you can buy me a coffin and a stone."

"Certainly, governor, certainly," the baron replied.

Marshal Hanson could only shrug. Maybe it would have been more honest just to let Gatliff steal the baron's money than to let Loper cheat him out of it in a card game.

The baron retreated to Sammy. "Quite an adventure, was it not, lad?"

Jake Ellis sat at the dinner table, simmering over the baron's failure to pay up or even mention his indebtedness on the sale of Ike Mann's buffalo hides. If the baron hadn't owed him money, Ellis would have been glad for Gatliff to have taken the baron's money and his life.

Aunt Moses kept shaking her head. "If only I'd have made you dry the dishes, Sammy Collins, this would never have happened."

Jake Ellis was bored with the baron's tale of the Gatliff encounter but highly amused at Flora Belmont's reaction to her betrothed. She seemed much more interested in the colonel to her left than her future husband on the right. "When's the marriage, Baron?" Jake Ellis asked, just to watch the Englishman and his wife-to-be squirm.

The baron cocked his head at Ellis and grinned "Wednesday, provided the Reverend Tuck is available to do us the honors."

Out of the corner of his eye, Jake Ellis saw Beulah Fenster grimace and the Reverend Tuck shrug.

The baron reached for Flora Belmont's hand and patted it, as he turned to the preacher. "Perhaps we can convince the lame man you cured to dance and the tongue-tied man to sing at our wedding."

"Don't mock the work or the word of Gawd," Tuck shot back.

Jake Ellis cleared his throat and stared straight at the baron. "I'm more concerned about the word of man, Baron, any man that I do business with, any man that owes me money."

The baron smiled. "If you are doubting my word on a debt, governor, perhaps we should adjourn to the next room and settle our business."

Jake Ellis nodded. "That would be a load off my mind, perhaps restore my faith in my fellow man."

The baron pulled his satchel from beneath

his chair and then stood up. His nose in the air, he strutted to the next room and dropped his satchel on the registration desk.

Jake Ellis followed in his wake, patting the coat pocket where he carried the baron's promissory note. The baron swung around to face Ellis, slipping his hand inside his coat and pulling out a stack of bills. He flashed it before the hide buyer's face. "That enough for you?"

Jake Ellis felt a smile warming his face. "For a while, Baron, I wondered if you might be taking me for a fool."

"By her majesty's crown, governor, I am as honest as the next Englishman. It's you Yankees I worry about. You stole this country from us and who knows what else."

"The money?" Ellis said, extending his hand.

"The note?" the baron replied.

Ellis felt a smirk wash over his face as he pulled the note from his side pocket. Ellis waved the envelope at the baron's nose. "Here, Baron. The money?"

"Certainly, governor, once you give me the note."

Jake Ellis ripped the end off the envelope, slid his fingers inside, and pulled out the folded papers. A grin on his face, he crumpled the envelope and tossed it at the

baron's feet. Staring at the baron, he unfolded the sheets.

"Read it, governor," the baron said.

Jake Ellis smiled as he straightened the
papers. The top sheet was blank. His smile
evaporated. He looked at the baron. He
separated the top sheet from the bottom
sheet. It was blank. There was no third
sheet. He looked at the baron. He turned
both sheets over. Both sides of each were
blank. He stared hard at the baron. "You
son of a bitch."

"No note, no money, governor," the baron
said, slipping his wad of bills back inside his
pocket.

"I'll take it to the marshal."

"Do that, governor. See if he believes I'd
pay you a price like that for Ike Mann's
hides just so he could escort me on a land
tour."

Of all his years in the hide business, Jake
Ellis had never been skinned. Until now!
"I'll get you for this!" he shouted, pounding
his fist on the desk.

CHAPTER 13

The Reverend Tuck knelt bedside, praying for a miracle like he had never prayed before. Folks would be coming from miles around to see him cure Lop-Eared Annie Lea. If he failed, he would be laughed out of Fort Griffin and that damned Englishman would ride him even harder. Much as he wanted to pray, praying wasn't the same without the crowd's ear. God's ear just wasn't enough! Tuck stood up, deciding he had wasted enough time, especially if he wanted to get a good position on the street for the rumored gunfight between a gambler and a one-eyed gunman. Tuck figured a death or two, particularly among this breed of man, would be good for business. There was nothing like a good funeral to make folks ponder their mortality. The reverend lifted the Bible to his heart and strode outside where the air was stiff with the smell of the buffalo hides and the sky was empty of everything save the sun.

Marching down the street, the reverend greeted every man and woman he met, introducing himself, announcing his upcoming sermon and proclaiming salvation for this sinful city. Most ignored him, some crossed the street to avoid him, a few scowled at him, and one drunk actually thanked him.

Crossing Griffin Avenue, he sensed the excitement as men clumped together in the limited shade, betting one another whether a gunfight would take place and who would win if it did. If someone were to die, Tuck thought, let his death have a purpose that would serve God through him, the Reverend G.W. "God Willing" Tuck.

At the end of the street, the reverend felt the call of nature much more strongly than the call of God. He stepped between two buildings and headed for the nearest outhouse. Beyond his chosen privy he saw a herd of youths playing some infernal game with a blackened kickball. As he grabbed the door, the ball got past one boy and with a lopsided bounce rolled toward the street before curving right up to the reverend's shoes. The blackened ball was splotched with dirt and sadly warped and misshaped. This was no store-bought ball and its odd appearance touched something in Tuck's memory. Then it struck him. This was the miracle for which he had prayed so diligently. He recalled his days as a kid when his father had killed hogs and given him the bladder. By tying the ends and using a turkey quill to blow it up, the bladder made a passable kickball.

This was indeed a miracle, Tuck thought as he bent down and picked up the ball. Tossing it in the air a couple times, he gave a silent word of thanks as a youth trotted up. Tuck recognized Sammy Collins.

"You won't tell Aunt Moses you saw me, will you?" Sammy asked.

"If she asks I must tell the truth."

Sammy grinned and cocked his head. "Some folks don't think you're telling the truth about Annie Lea."

The reverend tossed the ball from hand to hand, then pitched it to Sammy. "She will be cured."

Catching the ball, Sammy shook his head. "You telling Aunt Moses on me?"

Tuck shook his head. "No, I'm in a benevolent mood."

Sammy scratched his head, then flung the ball over his shoulder toward the impatient cries of the others. "Thanks," Sammy nodded and ran to join his friends.

With the help of a pig's bladder, Tuck could heal Lop-Eared Annie Lea after all! Monk Partain and Surry Nettles would have to steal a pig and slaughter it before the sermon.

Remembering his own bladder, Tuck opened the door of the outhouse, shaking his head that even the call of nature could lead to a miracle. God did, indeed, work in mysterious ways.

When the boys grew bored of playing kick-ball, they ambled in a group toward Griffin Avenue to watch the gunfight. Sammy Collins was surprised to see so many men already lining the walks, leisurely awaiting the showdown between Loper and Gatliff.

Some of the boys drifted away, but Sammy and a few others gathered around an abandoned water trough. Usually, several horses would have been tied nearby, but men who prized their mounts had hitched them off the street or stabled them out of the way of a stray bullet. Alonzo Giddings, pest that he was, kept picking up clods and horse apples from the street and tossing them in the water trough, splashing the others. Sammy grew quickly tired of the mischief and walked away, looking to find a good seat and a little shade. As he meandered down the street, he spotted the baron, carpetbag in one hand, cane in the other, glancing curiously at the crowd. Sammy angled for the baron.

"Morning, lad," the baron greeted him. "Circus come to town?"

"Don't you remember? Loper told Gatliff to leave town by noon."

"That I recollect, but it doesn't explain the crowd."

Sammy shook his head. "They've come to see the shooting, maybe even a killing. Don't you see?"

"Like a duel, is it? Something out of Sir Walter Scott?"

Sammy shrugged. "I guess."

"I must thank our gambler friend for looking out for us, lad, if he does triumph over the one-eyed chap. Or, buy him a gravestone if he doesn't."

Sammy shaded his eyes with his hands and glanced skyward, judging the sun. "It's close to noon."

"This is highly uncivilized, lad, this dueling." The baron studied the gathering crowd. "People must take to it, though."

Pointing to a patch of vacant shade beneath the overhang at the Bee Hive, Sammy grabbed the baron's hand and tugged him across the street. "We can watch from there."

The baron moved that direction, though not nearly as quickly as Sammy would have preferred since patches of shade were harder and harder to come by as the crowd grew.

"Have you ever seen a man die?" Sammy asked.

"No, lad. Had I wanted to see men die, I would've joined her majesty's army. No, lad, it's barbaric, these duels."

"So you wouldn't fight a duel?"

"I'd protect myself and my money."

"Gatliff came close enough to stealing it yesterday."

The baron stopped in the middle of the street and looked around for anyone that might be following. "He'd gotten my satchel, not my money, lad."

"What?"

"As long as everyone thinks I've got my money in my bag, they won't ransack my room, lad." The baron tapped his cane against the hard-packed road. "I'm not the buffoon they take me for, lad. As I've told you before, things aren't always what they seem."

Sammy scratched his head and looked the baron square in the eye. "When you leave town, you're taking me with you, right?"

The baron spoke with exasperation. "When I leave here for good, you shall leave too, but remember 'London Bridge is falling down.' "

"I know," Sammy replied. "I know."

"Fine, lad, now let's claim our shade."

As the baron marched across the street, Sammy noticed several people pointing at his money satchel. Had the baron left his fortune in his room or did he actually carry it? Just how shrewd was the baron? Sammy reached the spot of shade by the Bee Hive and plopped down on the plank walk beside a pole support. The baron leaned against the other side of the pole and dropped his satchel in front of Sammy's legs.

"Keep up with that, will you, lad?"

"Yes, sir," Sammy answered proudly, not caring whether or not the bag held money. Everyone else thought so, which was just as good. Sammy grabbed the red leather handle, pulling the satchel between his legs and looking all around at the festive atmosphere, men talking, joking, betting, a few even drinking. And then, they grew suddenly quiet, several men pointing toward the Clear Fork.

A lone rider approached at the creek crossing. It was One-Eyed Charlie Gatliff. The baron realized something was amiss, but didn't spot the gunman until Sammy pointed down the street. "Here comes Gatliff."

Gatliff advanced as slow and certain as the plague. The town turned strangely silent. Riding down the middle of the street, Gatliff passed people clumped together as quiet as prickly pears. His good eye burned with anger. He spat, then turned toward the Bee Hive, aiming his yellow dun toward the baron.

Sammy felt his mouth go dry. His heart pounding, he pulled the satchel from between his legs and placed it on his lap, an additional barrier between him and the gunman.

The baron stepped away from the pole and out into the sunshine, drawing Gatliff's sneer. "Once I take care of Joe Loper," Gatliff taunted, "there's nothing between me and your money."

"Indeed there is, governor," answered the baron, handing Sammy his cane and unbuttoning his cutaway coat. Pulling the coat back, the baron revealed his .22-caliber revolver in a shoulder holster. "I can fend for myself."

Gatliff laughed like a mad man, then went suddenly silent, his gun hand twitching. "I ought to plug you right now, but I promised a taste of lead to Joe Loper. I'll catch up with you later." Gatliff nudged his horse with his knee and the animal moved slowly ahead.

The baron turned around and grabbed his cane from Sammy.

Sammy glanced up at him. "I don't reckon you are afraid of dueling after all?"

The baron grinned. "Sometimes you've got to bluff, lad."

Midway down the street, Gatliff reined up. "It's noon, Joe Loper," he yelled, "and Charlie Gatliff's still in town. Where are you, you yellow-bellied son of a bitch?" Only the gasps of proper women broke the silence. Gatliff laughed sinisterly, then stood up in his stirrups. "Loper, Joe Loper? You afraid to come out?" Gatliff looked around then sank back into his saddle. "It's past noon and I'm still here. Where are you, coward? You were born a coward, you've lived as a coward, and you'll die a coward." Gatliff taunted.

Sammy felt ashamed that the gambler had turned yellow, ashamed and afraid for himself and the baron.

Then Joe Loper stepped from between two buildings and strode to the middle of the street. The crowd gasped with anticipation as Loper faced Gatliff. Sammy smiled.

320

Suddenly, the taunting caught in Gatliff's throat and he went silent.

Marshal Gil Hanson watched from outside his office, his fingers twitching as if he had to take on both Loper and Gatliff.

Now it was Loper's turn to taunt. "I figured you'd been in New Mexico Territory by now."

"You figured wrong, Loper, like always."

Loper spat out his answer. "Good thing you rode your horse, Gatliff, because this is your last chance to keep riding."

Gatliff sneered. "I'm tired of talking, Loper. Let's get this dance over with."

Loper nodded. It was the only thing they could agree upon. "Marshal," Loper called, "all I want out of this is a fair fight. You be the judge."

Hanson stepped forward. "Loper, you march toward Government Hill. Gatliff, you take your horse toward the Clear Fork, dismount, and tie him. When I fire my pistol, start walking toward each other. Stop when you're ready. I'll count to three. Draw on three. If you clear leather before I reach three, I'll arrest you. Understood?"

"Understood," answered Loper.

"Sure, Marshal," replied Gatliff. "Let's get on with it."

Hanson nodded. "Get going, then." The marshal pulled his revolver. "If either of you tries anything early, I'll shoot you."

Warily, Loper and Gatliff turned their backs on one another and began their retreat.

Gatliff nudged his horse into a trot and stopped at the last hitching post before the Clear Fork. He dismounted calmly, wrapping his mount's reins around the hitching rail. He patted the gun at his hip.

At the other end of the street, Loper slid his gun out of the holster and checked the load. He dropped his revolver back in place, tugged on his britches, and then adjusted the brim of his hat.

The two adversaries stood two hundred yards apart. All the men and women of Fort Griffin seemed wedged between them. The marshal looked at Gatliff, who waved, then at Loper, who nodded his readiness.

Hanson raised his revolver in the air and squeezed the trigger. The gun exploded the silence. Both men started forward, easy and relaxed, each unperturbed that this could be his last walk on Earth. The marshal lowered his gun, holding it at his side in case he might yet need it. Up and down the street, the spectators watched intently, their heads bobbing from side to side as they eyed both men. The air was as silent as impending death.

Both combatants walked slowly, their gait as measured as their gaze, their eyes never leaving one another, their gun hands steady. When sixty feet separated them, Gatliff stopped, his lips twisting into a sinister snarl.

Loper, his steady expression never wavering, kept walking. Fifty feet separated the two men, and still he advanced. When Loper stopped, forty feet or less separated them. Without their gazes ever leaving one another, the two men widened their stances, wriggling their fingers confidently.

Marshal Hanson began the count. "One." Hanson took his time. He didn't want to give a detectable cadence that either man could anticipate.

Gatliff licked his lips as the fingers of his gun hand curled into deadly arcs.

Loper leaned forward, his eyes narrowing in anticipation.

"Two," shouted Hanson.

Gatliff's hand inched closer to his revolver. His nostrils flared and his eyes widened.

Loper's lips went tight and his knees bent slightly.

Hanson delayed the final number, glancing quickly from Loper to Gatliff, neither making an unwarranted move. With his own throat tight from nervousness that Gatliff would win, Hanson yelled, "Three."

In an instant, the two men went for their guns. Loper was snake-quick, his hand sliding effortlessly to his revolver. Gatliff's movement was jerky. Both men yanked their guns from their well-oiled holsters.

Hanson gritted his teeth waiting for the explosions. The crowd shrank back from the street in case their aim was off. A woman screamed.

Loper's gun cleared leather but a fraction ahead of Gatliff's revolver. In one smooth motion, Loper cocked his weapon and fired, just as Gatliff was beginning the same motion.

The street exploded with the retort of Loper's gun. The air was filled with smoke and another scream. A man's scream!

The revolver flew from Gatliff's hand, flying ten yards behind him, then skittering through the dust of the street. The gunman cursed, grabbed his hand, and fell forward to his knees, his eyes widening as Loper advanced.

"No, Loper, don't," he pleaded.

"Now who's the coward, Gatliff?"

Before Marshal Hanson could stop him, Loper fired. Over Gatliff's head!

Gatliff slumped forward, begging for

mercy. "Please, Loper, don't shoot me."

Loper laughed. "I'll end this here." He cocked his revolver and aimed it at Gatliff's head. "Stand up and die like a man, Gatliff, not begging like a woman."

"No, please, no," Gatliff groveled.

Marshal Hanson stepped toward the two men, his own gun level with his waist. Though his emotions wanted Gatliff dead, Hanson had taken an oath to uphold the law. "Don't shoot, Loper," Hanson commanded.

The gambler cursed.

"Kill him now and it's murder, Loper."

"Dammit, Marshal, I intend to repay him for past differences."

"Not today, not in my town," answered Hanson, his voice determined.

Gatliff stared in welcome disbelief, shaking his head and biting his lip.

The marshal turned to Gatliff. "Get out of town and don't ever come back. If you do, Loper can shoot you on sight as far as I am concerned. You understand that?"

Gatliff nodded vigorously and pushed himself up from the ground.

Loper cursed. "He'll be back, Marshal."

Hanson nodded. "Then you can kill him."

Loper shoved his pistol back into his holster, standing with his feet apart, his arms crossed over his chest and his eyes glaring at the marshal.

Gatliff stumbled up, still holding his right hand and started toward his pistol.

"Leave it there, Gatliff," commanded Hanson. "Just get on your horse and ride out of Fort Griffin. Forever."

Gatliff bolted away, charging for his horse, the crowd laughing and jeering at his departure. Without looking back at Hide Town, Gatliff untied his mount, clambered into the saddle and bolted for the distance.

Hanson watched him splash across the Clear Fork before he shoved his own revolver back in his holster.

"That was a mistake, Marshal," said Loper, his voice seething.

Hanson ignored him and walked over to Gatliff's gun. He squatted down in the street and studied the revolver. Shaking his head, he picked it up gingerly. "Damn fine shooting, Loper," he offered.

The gambler scoffed. "I was aiming for his gut. I wanted him to die slow and painful."

"You hit his gun right in front of the cylinder." Hanson studied where the barrel met the body. There the weapon was bent and misshaped, but the cylinder was still fully loaded. Hanson pulled the cylinder release, but it was jammed and the gun wouldn't open for reloading. Hanson offered the weapon to Loper as several spectators approached, including the baron and Sammy Collins. "Care to look for yourself, Loper?"

"Nope. Only thing I wanted to see was Gatliff's body."

The marshal shoved the damaged gun in his britches as the baron extended his hand to Joe Loper.

"Excellent marksmanship," the baron announced. "Better even than the Prince of Wales, who's the best I've seen until now."

Loper nodded. "Maybe Gatliff won't bother you anymore. Then again, you can't be certain about that, him leaving on horseback rather than in a pine box."

"I like my chances better now, governor. How can I repay you?"

"How about visiting me at the Bee Hive for a friendly game of poker some night, like you agreed?"

The baron scratched his chin. "I must warn you, I've beaten the Prince of Wales at cards."

Loper shrugged. "You yourself said I was a better shot than the Prince of Wales, so I figure I'm better at cards."

"Maybe," the baron laughed, "but the

Prince of Wales cheats."

"So do I," replied Loper.

The baron laughed. "Can't do it Saturday night. I want to see the preacher cure the woman who airs her dairy. Sunday I intend to spend courting Flora Belmont. We're getting married on Wednesday, you know. How about Monday night?"

"I'll be ready. Mind if I invite a few others to play with us?"

"Not at all, governor, not at all. The Prince of Wales always had a crowd for his card games."

"I'll look forward to it, Baron. And one more thing," Loper said with a sly grin.

"Yes, governor?"

"Don't forget to bring your satchel!"

The telegram that Colonel John Paul Jenkins had been fearing finally arrived, demanding an explanation for the demise of the late Private Burns. Army regulations had, of course, been violated in the impetuous decisions leading to the cook's execution. Instead of an explanation, the colonel had sent by Army courier his resignation, effective immediately. Since returning from the patrol, the colonel had taken to sleeping in the kitchen rather than his bedroom, fearing another assassination attempt by his hungry, bloodthirsty men. It was a shame that Jenkins could find no cook, but at least he had found a woman he could marry.

In his quarters, the colonel had hung an army blanket over his window and unlocked his army trunk, taking out his meager belongings from a lifetime in the military. Those possessions didn't add up to much — a tin ship his father had given him as a kid, a faded tintype of his mother and another of his father in the uniform of a rear admiral, a scarf with the indelible stain of his own blood spilled at Fredericksburg, and his U.S. Military Academy class ring. In a cigar box, beneath his dress uniform, he kept his life savings, not quite $1,900. He stuffed his belongings in a canvas bag.

Then, without telling even his adjutant, he picked up his canvas bag and strolled casually away from the fort. By the time the courier got the letter to the division command, Jenkins would be beyond Hide Town and the reach of the military authorities. The colonel walked down the hill toward town, never once looking over his shoulder, as if all those years in the army amounted to nothing. He had no place to go, except to the Planter's House and Flora Belmont.

At the edge of town, the colonel turned off Griffin Avenue and cut behind a livery stable, passing the giant pecan tree where he had first kissed her. He thought fondly of Flora Belmont and that moment, a moment that had changed his life. The colonel was relieved to step unseen into the hotel and then slip down the hall to her door. He rapped softly on the door. "Flora," he whispered, "I need to talk to you."

The door jerked open and there stood Flora Belmont, her eyes smiling like her lips. "Come in, quick, before someone sees you."

Jenkins jumped inside and she shut the door behind him. Instantly, she flung her arms around him. He dropped his canvas bag on the floor and kissed her wildly, then broke free.

"I've resigned from the Army," he announced. "When you leave, I'll go with you."

Flora kissed him again.

He broke free from her lips. "I've got close to $1,900 in savings with me. It's not much, not enough to support a refined woman like you, Flora, but I can find work."

"Why?" Flora replied. "Each time I buried a husband, I made sure I didn't bury his money. I've got one more husband to bury. We'll be as rich as the captains of industry. Then you and I can spend our lives together, enjoying the money of your predecessors." Breaking free from the colonel, she marched to her dresser and picked up her purse, pulling out an envelope, its flap sealed with wax. She brandished it before the colonel.

"What's that?"

"The baron's word I'll share in everything. I gave him a dowry of $1,500, cash, and he gave me this signed promise in return."

"I can't believe he was such a fool."

"Then open it. See for yourself," she challenged.

The colonel scraped the wax off with his thumbnail, then opened the flap and pulled out the contents. He unfolded two sheets of paper, looking first at one, then the other. Each was blank, front and back. "There's nothing here."

"What?" Flora Belmont yanked the papers from the colonel's hand. "I know he signed one because I signed my name beneath his."

The colonel scratched his chin. "Maybe he's not as big a fool as we think."

Flora Belmont's eyes flashed. "Makes me want to marry him all the more. I'll enjoy poisoning him even better."

"We must be careful and not let on that you know what he's done."

"I've lied to men before," she responded.

"I just hope I'm not one of those, Flora."

Flora flung her arms around his neck and planted another kiss upon his lips. She pulled away. "Does that answer your question?"

"It'll do." He winked. "For now."

"Forever," she answered.

"Right now, though . . . I've got to find a place to stay."

With a sweep of her arm, Flora offered her room and her bed. "How about here? Until I'm married, of course."

Both giggled until they collapsed on the bed.

Much to Flora Belmont's surprise, the baron was accompanied by the Reverend G.W. "God Willing" Tuck when he joined her on the front porch to discuss wedding plans. If she despised one man more than the baron, it would be the Reverend Tuck, a pompous fool who sold religion like a commodity. With the unfortunate demises of her previous husbands, Flora figured she had sent more men to heaven than had the preacher.

"Evening, darling," said the baron, taking her hand in his and kissing it. "I brought along the Reverend Tuck to plan our wedding." The baron looked to the opposite end of the porch where Jake Ellis, Uncle Moses, and Colonel John Paul Jenkins sat, puffing on cigars. "Perhaps we should retire inside," suggested the baron. "It's not polite for men to smoke in front of a lady."

Flora killed that idea. "No," she said sharply, desiring to stay where she could watch John Paul Jenkins. Later, they would be together, but until then she could at least feast on his rugged profile. "All I need to know is the time and place."

"Madam," offered the reverend, "matrimony requires much more than knowing the time and place. It requires knowing one another, and sharing your lives for eternity with the Lord Gawd Almighty's blessing."

"Tell me, Reverend, are you married?"

"No," he answered.

"You ever been married, Reverend?"

"No."

"Then what the hell do you know about marriage? I've been married five times so maybe I should be giving you advice instead of the other way around."

The reverend gasped. "Five times married, five times divorced?"

Flora scowled. "What kind of woman do you think I am? I would never get a divorce! Five times widowed."

"My condolences, ma'am," Tuck replied.

Flora laughed. "I don't need your condolences, Reverend, because they left me their money."

Aghast, the reverend stammered a moment. "You, you, they, they, you married for money?"

"Indeed, Reverend, and am about to do it again." Flora Belmont grabbed the baron's arm and pulled him to her. "Isn't that right?"

"Reverend, some marriages are for love, some are for money. In England many marriages, especially among royalty, are strictly arrangements of convenience."

"But love," the reverend countered, "is the Lord Gawd Almighty's noblest gift to man and to woman. A marriage should be built upon a foundation of love."

"Will you marry us or not, Reverend?" demanded the baron.

"I don't know, especially when you say this whole marriage is an arrangement."

Flora Belmont clucked her tongue. "Will a hundred dollars help you overcome your reservations, Reverend?"

"In advance?" the reverend asked, extending his hand.

"If you wish, Reverend," replied Flora.

"I'll do it," he answered without hesitation.

Flora Belmont fumbled for her purse until

she felt the baron's hand upon her shoulder. "Darling," he said, "I insist that you let me pay for that."

"Thank you, dear," she said demurely, feeling the anger within her. He was paying with money from her dowry, money that she had given him in exchange for a blank piece of paper. She was glad she had the colonel to keep her company until her wedding. She looked so forward to marrying the baron, then killing him.

The baron pulled a stack of bills from his pocket and peeled off a hundred dollars. He handed payment to the reverend. "Now, no more morality lessons, Reverend. We are both mature adults who know what we are doing."

"Whatever you say, Mr. Paget."

"I say the wedding shall be Wednesday at two o'clock in the afternoon, beneath the giant pecan tree."

"No!" shouted Flora Belmont. She would not blaspheme that ground where she had first kissed the colonel. "Let it be here, at the hotel."

"As you wish, darling," answered the baron.

"If my services are no longer needed," said Tuck, "I must leave and pray for success at tomorrow's camp meeting." The reverend stood up and walked inside the hotel.

"Would you care to walk beneath the stars, darling?" asked the baron.

"I've such a headache, I really should go rest, dear," she answered.

"I shall hope for a quick recovery and shall walk alone tonight in expectation of the many nights to come when we can stroll together, husband and wife, baron and baroness."

"Me, too," she said brusquely, marching away from her fiancée and to her room, hoping that John Paul Jenkins would not wait too long on the porch before joining her.

CHAPTER 14

"You want me to do what?" Lop-Eared Annie Lea shoved her fists onto her hips and glared at Reverend Tuck as he held that disgusting thing on the towel in his hand.

Tuck cleared his throat. "A pig's bladder. Keep it moist until tonight." He folded the wet towel he had stolen from the Planter's House back over the bladder.

"Who says you can order me around, padre?"

"I've paid you a hundred dollars already. Here's the rest," he said shoving a wad of bills at her and placing the towel on her washstand.

She snapped the money from his hand and counted it herself before tucking the greenbacks into her blouse.

"Wear a high-topped dress. Put the bladder over your small bosom after you prick it with this," he ordered, pulling out a turkey quill that had been stripped of its feathers.

The quill was sharpened on one end. "Put the quill under your blouse so you can slip it between buttons. When I ask you to pray, I want you to bow your head and slip the quill out where you can hold it between your hands, like you are praying. Bow your head and blow through the quill until little round top becomes the size of big round top."

Annie Lea shook her head. "Somebody'll see the quill."

Tuck pointed to her iron bedstead and the red fox stole hanging there. "Wear that around your neck. It'll screen the quill from others."

"You sure this will work?"

"Don't you believe in miracles? This one will be talked about for years in these parts."

"How you gonna explain to folks when my bosom shrinks back?"

"Your sincere faith in Gawd, despite my holy and noble efforts, was merely temporary. A shame, isn't it, but you'll still have your profession to fall back on."

"There's more integrity in my line of work than in yours, padre. At least men get what they pay for from me."

Tuck rubbed his hands together. "Madam, my work is done in the name of the Lord Gawd Almighty. That'll always separate my job from yours, no matter how low they both may be. See you tonight."

They started arriving at noon, the wagons and buggies filled with ranching families and farmers' broods. By mid-afternoon, the cowhands from ranches as far as forty miles away began to show up. Marshal Gil Hanson watched in amazement as the meadow was covered with conveyances and horses and, most of all, people. He had never seen so many people in Fort Griffin. They were an orderly group, except for the kids who ran wild among the parked wagons, screaming like Comanche warriors. Around their wagons, women sat up camp and brought out pots and Dutch ovens for cooking. They sent their men with axes down to the bank of the Clear Fork to bring back firewood.

After strolling around the crowded meadow, the marshal headed back for town and a free meal at the Bee Hive.

Burley Sims greeted the marshal. "Big doings, huh?"

Hanson picked up a plate and began to gather well-salted victuals from the food table. What Sims gave away in free food, he more than made up from drinks bought to quench salty thirsts. "We'll have more than a thousand folks, I figure, before the preaching starts and the healing begins."

Sims wiped his hands on a clean towel. "How's he gonna do it, Marshal? We know Lop-Eared Annie Lea ain't one of his shills like those other two jackasses."

The marshal shrugged as he ambled for a table. "I can't figure it."

"Well, everybody's been talking about Annie Lea, that and the baron's poker game, Monday night."

"A cold beer, Burley, and what about the baron's poker game?"

"Joe Loper's been putting the word out for fellas that want to take on the baron. Seems nobody alone's got enough money to match the baron's $25,000. First time I ever heard of fellas grubstaking a poker game."

"Loper doesn't want to risk any of his money."

Sims pursed his lips and nodded as he filled a mug with beer. "There's a meeting here tomorrow afternoon."

The marshal attacked a plate of cold potatoes, warm pickles, and greasy beef. "If the preacher does cure Annie Lea tonight, I figure he might take up an overflowing collection plate that won't leave enough money in Hide Town to buy a bucket of warm spit, much less for Loper to raise $25,000."

Sims plopped a mug of beer on the table by the marshal. "You know as well as I do if the baron sits down with Loper, the baron won't have enough money left to buy a free meal. The day Loper arrived, he gave me two bottles of whiskey and a pair of marked decks of cards for his shot at the baron's money."

Hanson shrugged. "Don't sell the Englishman short. He's held onto his money longer than most folks thought he would."

Zach Fenster with Beulah Fenster by his side carried his wallet and a simmering anger to the camp meeting. Maybe this supposed miracle might take Beulah's mind off the baron. When the baron arrived, Beulah had been taken with the idea of knowing royalty. That was all she had talked about, the baron this, the baron that until it made Zach Fenster loathe the Englishman. And since the baron had announced his impending marriage to that noisome Flora Belmont, Beulah Fenster had been silent and morose, ignoring his every effort to revive her mood and maybe even rekindle their marriage. Fenster knew his wallet could buy him a good pair of seats up front, but he wasn't sure what it would take for Beulah Fenster to regain her old form. Sour as it had been, it was better than her current depressed state.

The benches were filled as Zach Fenster knew they would be, but that presented no problem for the richest merchant in Fort Griffin. Fenster pulled his wallet from his coat pocket and marched up to the front row. He eyed a farmer in clean overalls and his wife in a cotton print dress. Marching up to the old couple, he tugged on his lapels. "Ten dollars apiece for your seats," he offered.

The man and wife glanced at each other, nodded simultaneously and stood up, taking two bills from the merchant. Zach helped his wife into her seat. Then he slid beside her on the bench, taking her hand in his. Her hand was as limp and lifeless as her spirit. It had never been easy being married to Beulah, but this made it even worse. Zach Fenster had a score to settle with the baron for ruining his wife's spirit, foul though it may have been.

Fenster gritted his teeth when he spotted the baron standing at the edge of the crowd, holding his money-filled satchel in one hand and his cane in the other. Zach Fenster watched the baron, loathing him even more as he stood with his nose held arrogantly in the air. The hide buyer Jake Ellis had spoken poorly of a dealing with the baron, though Ellis was leery of giving many details. And something odd had happened between the baron and the Sikes couple, Amanda and Wallace.

Zach Fenster watched the baron with disgust until he heard a murmur run through the crowd. Turning, he saw the spectators staring and pointing at a new arrival. There was no mistaking Lop-Eared Annie Lea, for neither the high-neck black blouse nor the red fox stole wrapped around her neck could disguise her disproportionate bosom. A man near the front offered Annie Lea his seat.

It wouldn't be long now, thought Fenster as men began to light lanterns and hang them in the trees around the overturned wagon bed the preacher would use for a platform.

Marshal Gil Hanson shook his head at the virtually abandoned town. The Bee Hive, the town's most popular establishment, was open and lit and empty. Most of the Bee Hive's competitors were locked up. Most everybody had deserted town for the miracle on the Clear Fork. And like all the others, Hanson was curious.

At the sound of singing, the marshal

started for the creek, where dozens of lanterns formed a halo of light around the assembled multitude of a thousand or more people. With a crowd this size, there was likely to be mischief out back around the wagons, where many men hid jugs of liquor from wives. Hanson figured the heavy male attendance was testimony to the drawing power of Lop-Eared Annie Lea and her peculiar breastworks. Most every man would have preferred that Tuck keep his hands off such a treasure.

As he worked his way among the wagons, Hanson thought he caught a glimpse of a shadow crouching beside a buggy. He recognized Cat Tails, who was likely trying to steal whiskey. Hanson went on, taking in the pale sliver of moon overhead and its ghostly haze of illumination upon the land. When the singing stopped suddenly, the quiet was eerie as a grave yard. Then, Hanson heard the snap of a twig behind him. He spun around. The marshal felt his hand tremble. Was he imagining things or had he seen One-Eyed Charlie Gatliff? He swallowed hard. Surely not? Though he could pick out nothing through squinted eyes, his blood ran cold in his veins.

The marshal retreated from the wagons and elbowed his way through the throng of

344

men stamping their boots, impatient for the miracle to begin. A few men grumbled as the marshal squeezed by, but they quieted when they saw the badge on his vest.

The Reverend Tuck flew into his sermon with the enthusiasm of a man who anticipated a large collection plate. He ranted and raved and pranced and jumped and gesticulated wildly from side to side of the platform, threatening hell to non-believers, hell to sinners, hell to selfish men and women. He preached redemption and everlasting life upon heaven's golden streets. Whatever appeal heaven might have, to Hanson's way of thinking, was offset by having to share eternity with the likes of the Reverend G.W. "God Willing" Tuck.

Soon the preacher was frothing and holding his open Bible to the heavens. "You've got to have faith," he yelled. "Faith can cure the ill. Faith can make the blind see. Faith can make the lame walk. Faith can heal deformities. Faith can move mountains. But to prove your faith, you must confess of your sins before man. And you do that by stepping forward before us all. We Baptists call it an invitation because it comes straight from the Lord Gawd Almighty. If you feel him calling, come forward. If you want your sins forgiven, come forward. If you feel him calling to heal your deformities, come forward. Now is the time, the Lord Gawd Almighty is calling." The Reverend Tuck dropped his hands and his head in prayer.

Every other head in the crowd turned toward Lop-Eared Annie Lea. She bowed her head a moment, then stood up. Those on the benches sat up straight and those standing on the perimeter stepped forward or rose on their tip-toes for a better view. This was the show everyone had been waiting for.

Annie Lea walked to the platform, her face calm, her head proud and erect, her manner sincere. There was about her a softness Hanson had never noticed before. She straightened the red fox stole around her neck as she advanced, then stepped upon the platform.

Tuck looked up from his prayer and smiled. "Lord Gawd Almighty, thank you for bringing this lost sheep to your flock. Your name, my lost one?"

"Annie Lea," she said meekly.

"And you come to be saved, to walk with the Lord Gawd Almighty the rest of your life?"

"Yes," Annie Lea answered, "and to be cured."

"Cured? You look too healthy from any

maladies, my precious lamb."

Annie Lea flung back the fox stole and thrust out her chest. The right side of her blouse was full and tight, while the left side was loose and atrophied.

"I see," said Tuck. "Do you believe the Lord Gawd Almighty can heal you?"

"I do," she answered adjusting the fox stole to cover her deformity.

"Then," intoned the preacher, "I must lay my hand upon you."

Women throughout the audience gasped as he extended his hand toward her bosom. Just as the reverend's hand was about to touch her blouse, Tuck jerked it skyward and placed it against her forehead, bringing the sighs of a dozen women. "Believe and you shall be cured, believe with all your heart, with all you mind, with all your soul and you shall be cured, Annie Lea."

Women held their breath, men craned their necks, and every eye in the crowd focused on the left side of Annie Lea's chest. There was movement, but only from her excited breathing.

"There is resistance, Annie Lea. Your faith must grow for your bosom to expand." Tuck jerked his hand away from her forehead and squared her to face the audience. "Lift your hands to your chin, Annie Lea, and pray as hard as you can, to show the Lord Gawd Almighty your growing faith."

Annie Lea bowed tightly, her chin resting on the fox stole, her jittery fingers seeming to linger at her blouse a moment before she pressed them together at her lips.

"Pray, Annie Lea, pray," yelled the reverend. "Show the Lord Gawd Almighty your growing faith." Tuck stomped his boot against the wooden platform. "Help her, all of you," Tuck continued with a sweep of his arm. "Pray, everybody, pray."

Several men and women began to pray, but not one with closed eyes. They stared wide-eyed and gap-jawed.

The miracle started as a quiver in her blouse, only noticed by those on the front rows. It drew gasps and finger pointing. Men and women craned their necks and forgot their prayers. The left side of the blouse budged again as Annie Lea, her eyes tight, her cheeks bloated, prayed for the miracle of a balanced chest.

"Lord Gawd Almighty's will be done," shouted the preacher, who bent over to look at the left side of her blouse, then backed out of the way for the crowd to see. "Hallelujah," he shouted, "her faith is working miracles."

Then, her blouse began to rise noticeably

so that even the men standing beyond the benches began to point and murmur. Marshal Hanson couldn't believe it. He shook his head and rubbed his eyes, but the impossible was happening right before him. Lop-Eared Annie Lea's bosom was growing.

"Hallelujah!" shouted Tuck again.

It was a miracle indeed.

Hanson stared dumbfounded. It was a trick sure, but how? No matter what the trick, it was impressive.

When Annie Lea stopped praying, she fiddled briefly with her fingers and the opening of her blouse, then dropped her hands to her side.

Indeed her bosom had grown, though her left side was lumpy and nowhere as shapely as her right.

"Give us a look!" yelled a man from the crowd.

Women gasped and screamed. Men shouted. The reverend lifted his hands for silence. "She has given up that way of life," he answered, but his words were lost in the noise.

"Show us!" came a male chant.

More women screamed and gasped.

Annie Lea stepped off the platform, starting for her seat, the fox-skin wrap bouncing on her inflated breast as she moved.

Then, above the noise, came a shrill, blood curdling scream. Marshal Hanson twisted around in time to see Cat Tails burst through the crowd. Holding a knife above his head, the Tonkawa charged down the aisle, straight for Annie Lea.

These were strange rituals that the white man conducted. Cat Tails couldn't make sense of the music or the white-haired chief who screamed so. Stealthily, Cat Tails slipped among the wagons, crouching as he moved. Passing a couple of staked horses, he froze as the animals lifted their heads, nickering softly. Cat Tails then sneaked toward a wagon and climbed inside. He fumbled among the bedding and belongings, groping for something to drink. Finding nothing, he climbed out of the wagon and moved to a buggy. A dog growled as he reached the buggy, but he climbed inside, patting the seat, then exiting on the other side within reach of another wagon.

At this wagon he slid through the open tailgate. He patted the bedding and the cooking utensils and then he found what he was after — a corked jug. Cat Tails uncorked the jug and held the cork to his nose. Yes, this was what he was after. Whiskey!

Cat Tails slid out of the wagon and slipped toward the Clear Fork, settling down next to a tree to kiss the jug. He took a long draw on the liquid, then let out a deep breath. This was good whiskey, whiskey that burned all the way down into his belly. Whiskey that singed the entrails like this was good, strong drink, drink that made a man see strange things. It was like a vision.

The white men continued their strange cavorting, sometimes sitting silently on their benches or occasionally yelling out "Amen!" The deeper Cat Tails got into the jug, and it was near full when he appropriated it, the more ridiculous the white man's ceremony became.

Now and then, one of the men around the edge of the gathering would slip down by the river to heed nature's call, then amble by a wagon to take a nip on his own jug. It was a strange religious rite these white men conducted. Why didn't they share the jugs of whiskey rather than hide them in their wagons? That bottled fire would make everyone happier.

When the white men and women began to sing again, Cat Tails began to chant with them, but their beat was off and it was too confusing for him to continue. He stood up, his steady feet wobbly now, and leaned against the tree, then took another hard swallow. He howled like a coyote, drawing the growls of a dozen dogs these people had brought with them. His eyes still worked, but he saw double images. He did not like that, but he liked the whiskey.

Cat Tails tried to focus on the ritual and was appalled at what he saw. A woman stood before the great talking chief. Cat Tails stood on his tiptoes to get a better view, then dropped his jug. He fell to his knees, slapping at the ground, moaning when his hand felt a puddle of whiskey. He righted the jug on the ground. Realizing all was silent, he stood up.

Had they discovered his presence?

Trying not to wobble too much on his feet, Cat Tails heard loud gasps and many words spoken in great excitement. There was screaming and crying now.

Cat Tails held his hand to his eyebrows and stared, finally spotting the reason for the terror. A red fox had attacked a white woman and wrapped itself around her neck. And while many white men were much closer, not a one had lifted a hand to save the woman. Cat Tails had an idea! Maybe he could snip the fox's tail before the animal escaped. A fox's tail would make a great addition to his necklace, if only Cat Tails could get to it before a white man came to the rescue or the fox darted away under the cover of darkness.

His hand jerked his knife free. Circumnavigating the wagons, Cat Tails found himself at the back of the clump of white men, all of them standing and watching the fox and yet doing nothing about it. If he advanced quietly, he might be able to slip up on the fox. He started to yell, then realized it might scare the fox away, then yelled anyway. He took a step, then a second, then a third, gradually building momentum until he darted through the clump of men and down the aisle between benches. He lifted his knife in the air and screamed once more.

It had worked. It was another miracle, one that would be talked about for years, thought Reverend Tuck. Granted her left breast beneath her blouse was more lump than shape, but it nonetheless was bigger and the approximate size of its mate.

There would be a great collection tonight in the offering plates. He looked out over the crowd and estimated more than a thousand souls. The former "Lop-Eared" Annie Lea stepped off the platform and started back down the aisle. Women applauded, men stared in disbelief. Once she reached her seat, Tuck would start the collection plate.

At that moment, Tuck heard an ungodly screech as a half-naked heathen brandishing a knife burst from the crowd, racing down the aisle toward Annie Lea.

Everyone seemed to freeze and the Indian raced untouched toward her, shrieking all the way. Women screamed and grabbed their children, covering their eyes so that they might not see the terrible crime that was about to take place.

"Stop," yelled the Reverend Tuck, "in the name of the Lord Gawd Almighty!"

The Indian charged ahead. With his empty hand, he lunged for Annie Lea's neck, grabbing the red fox stole.

Annie Lea screamed as the Indian sliced the knife toward her.

Men stumbled over one another to assist Annie Lea, but none could reach her in time.

Tuck threw down his Bible, flung back his frock coat and jerked his six-shooter from his holster. He aimed but could not get a clear shot for fear of hitting Annie Lea or another worshiper.

Annie Lea's knees sagged. The knife flashed and sliced into the tail of the fox stole, then slit the left side of Annie Lea's blouse.

The bladder popped, then hissed as the air escaped. Beulah Fenster fainted and other women throughout the crowd collapsed.

Brandishing the knife in one hand and twirling the fox tail over his head in the other, Cat Tails dashed past Annie Lea and up onto the platform. Tuck lifted his revolver to fire, but Cat Tails slapped him across the nose with the fox tail, then darted around the blanket backdrop and into the darkness that shrouded the Clear Fork.

Now everyone stared at Annie Lea, the shock on her face, the slit in her blouse. As they watched, something brown and black began to slide out. More women fainted and men with weak stomachs wretched as the bladder fell out of the slit and splattered on the ground.

Annie Lea looked from her blouse to the ground to her fox stole, now missing a tail. Then she gazed at the eyes staring intently at her. She began to giggle, then laugh uproariously.

Things had turned bad, Tuck thought, jumping to Annie Lea's side and grabbing for the bladder, wondering where he would hide it. Just as he touched the bladder, someone stepped on it. Tuck tugged at the bladder, but the polished shoe would not move. Slowly, Tuck lifted his head and looked up at the baron.

"Your religion is a fraud, Reverend," challenged the baron.

Annie Lea laughed. "It was a trick," she cried to everyone. "The reverend paid me to fool you."

The crowd turned surly.

"But fellas!" she yelled again, "I want you to know that Lop-Eared Annie Lea's back in business!"

The single men broke out with spontaneous cheers, while the married men shook their heads for benefit of their wives. A few men, Zach Fenster, among them, tried to revive their unconscious wives.

The Reverend Tuck stood up, shaking his head in disbelief at the baron.

Now the baron scooped up the bladder with the tip of his cane and lifted it in the air. "Here's the reverend's trick," the baron triumphed.

"You've ruined me," Tuck muttered.

The baron shook his head. "You ruined yourself."

"Then find you another preacher for your wedding," he shot back. "There's not another one for miles."

■ ■ ■ ■

"Best Sunday I ever had," Burley Sims told the gambler Joe Loper as he arrived five minutes after six Sunday evening. "I owe it to one man and he's sitting right over there."

Joe Loper followed the saloon owner's pointing finger. At a corner table sat the Reverend Tuck, a bottle of whiskey in front of him. "Well, I'll be damned. He ran out of miracles." The gambler turned back to Sims. "Did anybody show up?"

Sims nodded. "They're in the back room."

Loper smiled.

"I want in for a thousand, Joe."

Loper shook his head. "I don't think so, Burley. Our deal was I wouldn't take your regular customers as long as I got a shot at the baron. I don't figure any in back are your regulars."

"Nope," Burley admitted.

"Then it's best we leave things this way."

Burley shrugged. "I hate to miss out on sure money."

"You just remember to bring the bottles out in the order I've told you and the same with the decks."

"Understood, Loper, understood."

The gambler nodded and ambled to the

357

preacher. Leaning over the table, Loper picked up the bottle. It was mostly full. "Thought you Baptists were against bottled sin. Don't tell me you're performing another miracle, turning it to water before you imbibe?"

"It would've worked except for that damn heathen," Tuck muttered, "and that damn foreigner."

"You've a grudge to settle with the baron?"

Tuck nodded.

"Maybe you should join me in the back room with a few others who feel the same way about the baron."

Fire in his eyes, the reverend looked up at Loper. "Anything to get that damn foreigner." Tuck pushed himself up from the table and grabbed the bottle from Loper. The reverend was steady on his feet as he marched with Loper to the back.

Loper pushed open the door and led the reverend inside, smiling at the gathering. The hide buyer Jake Ellis was there. So were Wallace and Amanda Sikes. The former Colonel John Paul Jenkins sat with his arm draped around the baron's betrothed, Flora Belmont. Loper pointed to a seat for the preacher. Loper closed the door.

"Now," said Loper, pulling a chair from

the wall to the table. "I want to strip the baron of his money, every cent of it. With your grubstake, we can do it."

The door rattled with a firm knock. "Loper," called Burley Sims' voice, "there's another one for you."

"Send him in," the gambler answered.

The door opened rather hesitantly and in marched the merchant Zach Fenster. "I'm not accustomed to saloons," he said, his voice squeaking and his pale face blushing red.

"You're in good company, then," answered Loper, "because we've got us a Baptist preacher here, too."

Fenster shook his head. "That so-called preacher almost killed my Beulah from shock yesterday, inflating Annie Lea's bosom like that." He glared at the preacher while he pulled a chair to the table.

Loper continued, "Even if we don't all like each other around this table, we hate the baron even more. I don't know if he's a baron or not, but I suspect he's a swindler."

Jake Ellis hit the table with his fist. "I know he is. He promised me money on a hide buying deal and reneged, switching his promissory note to a blank piece of paper."

Flora Belmont cleared her throat. "He did the same thing to me. I gave him $1,500 for a dowry in exchange for a signed agreement that I would become his wife and heir to his estate, money, and title."

Wallace Sikes exploded. "That's nothing compared to what he did to my wife." He started to say more, but choked up and began to blubber so much that no one could understand him.

His wife comforted him, patting his shoulder. "It's okay, Wally," said Amanda.

Colonel Jenkins scowled. "He thinks he's gonna marry the woman I love."

Zach Fenster coughed nervously. "After he arrived, all I heard about from my Beulah is about the baron this and the baron that until I'm sick of it. Then, the baron announces he's gonna marry Flora Belmont, and she won't even talk to me or let me . . ." He left the rest unsaid, though his down-turned eyes and blushing cheeks told all.

Loper nodded. "I don't know if he's a swindler or just lucky, but his luck is about to change. When I ran One-Eyed Charlie Gatliff out of town to save the baron's tail, he promised me a card game. The luck will be on our side."

Jake Ellis nodded. "How much backing you need?"

Loper nodded. "I've got $1,000 of my own, but that won't last long against his

$25,000. It's like grubstaking a mine. You'll get a cut of the profit equal to the percentage you put in."

Ellis rubbed his hands together. "I want to see that worm crawl out of town. Count me in for $8,000."

Flora Belmont held up her hand, spreading her fingers apart. "I'll go $5,000."

Jenkins nodded. "I'll throw in $1,500 of my savings."

Loper smiled. "That puts us at fifteen-five. Anybody else care to join?"

Wallace Sikes hit the table with his balled fist. "We've about $1,200. We're in with the rest of you." Amanda patted her husband's shoulder, then held his hand.

Reverend Tuck took a long swig from his bottle. "Us Baptists don't drink or gamble, except when we feel called upon by the Lord Gawd Almighty. I feel called. I'll tithe $1,600 to the cause."

"Thank you, Reverend. I think God will be pleased," Loper said. He did a little adding in his head. "That puts us at about $18,000. It's a little short, but we can take him with that."

"Wait a minute," interrupted Zach Fenster. "Am I invited to join in? I am the most successful merchant in Fort Griffin and not without access to sizable monies."

"Say the amount," Loper replied, "and we'll put you down."

Fenster smiled. "Seven thousand dollars."

Everyone grinned. "That," said Loper, "puts us over $25,000."

Ellis nodded confidently at Loper. "How will we break him?"

"Straight poker," Loper replied. "I want to get him in a long game. Some of you will have to lose out as the game progresses. I'll stay in with a little money so I can keep the deal. I figure Ellis here, since he's putting up the most, should stay in the longest. When it's down to me, Ellis, and the baron, I'll ask Burley Sims for a new deck of cards. On the first hand, I'll deal them both good cards. The baron won't suspect a thing."

Flora Belmont tapped her fingers on the table. "Since the baron and I are to be married," she laughed sardonically, "I shouldn't play against him. The colonel can handle my cards."

Ellis nodded. "That'll make six of us, not counting the baron. You sure the baron will fall for this?"

Loper shrugged. "We don't know until we try. I've got another surprise for the baron as well. I've got a couple of bottles of liquor that Sims is holding. To start the game on friendly terms, I'll have him bring one out.

The whiskey's straight in it and everybody can have a jigger or so. When that's gone, I'll request a second bottle. It's drugged so don't take a sip of it. Gradually, the baron will get drowsy enough that he won't be able to keep up with the cards. Any questions?"

"Yeah," swaggered Wallace Sikes, "can we kill him when we're done?"

CHAPTER 15

Baron Jerome Manchester Paget tugged on the lapels of his maroon swallow-tailed coat. "You remember your instructions, lad?"

Sammy Collins nodded, then blew out a heavy breath. "Buy two passages on the morning stage, but not before six in the morning. If anyone asks, the baron and his bride-to-be are taking an excursion."

"Remember, lad, get my trunk to the stage stop during darkness. And, pack your things. I'm taking you with me."

Sammy sighed. "You shouldn't be gambling with Loper."

The baron threw his arm over the youth's shoulder. "You're right, but he did scare off that Gatliff chap for us."

"You don't understand. He'll cheat you out of your money, him and all the others I hear he's taken on. The colonel, Wallace and Amanda Sikes, the reverend, Jake Ellis, Zach Fenster, even Flora Belmont, all team-ing up against you."

The baron smiled. "I'm armed and prepared to defend myself, though it does pain
me about Flora."

Sammy groaned. "You don't stand a
chance."

"Lad, they figured I was a buffoon when I
arrived by stage, but I've still got my satchel,
and I'll still have it when the stage departs.
You worry about your tasks, and I'll watch
out for myself."

Sammy nodded, knowing he could never
change the baron's mind, but at least he
had tried. The Englishman refused to see
Loper and the others as predators. At least
the Englishman would take him away from
the menial chores of the Planter's House,
Sammy hoped, as long as the baron didn't
lose all his money in the Bee Hive.

The Englishman picked up his bowler
from his bed and tapped it into place. Next,
he grabbed his cane, twirled it a moment,
then stuck it under his arm. He grinned as
he picked up his satchel and shook it by its
maroon leather handle. "This is what they
want and now they'll have their chance at
it."

Sammy frowned. "Don't let them cheat
you."

"Cheat me? Why, lad, I'll have all their

money by the time the stage leaves. It will be a long game so don't you wait up. Get a good night's sleep so you can arise and buy stage passages for me."

"For us," Sammy corrected.

"Certainly, lad, for us."

For a moment, Sammy wondered if the baron really meant it.

"Come on, lad, escort me to the Bee Hive. I'm prepared to teach those chaps a lesson."

Together the two walked to the front of the hotel. From the kitchen, they could hear Aunt Moses mumbling to herself about having to do all the dishes since the baron needed Sammy. The pair exited the hotel and ambled toward Griffin Avenue. Sammy saw the Bee Hive, all lit up and waiting.

A crowd of spectators lined the plank walk on both sides of the door, one of them pointing and yelling, "There he comes." A cheer arose.

Though the men taunted and mocked the baron, Paget just smiled, greeting them cordially. Sammy hung his head, embarrassed that the baron didn't recognize the mockery.

Sammy trailed the baron into the smoke-filled room. All the tables, except a large round one, had been pushed to the walls. At the round table beneath a smoky kerosene lamp, sat Joe Loper with the others, all smiling broadly as the baron stepped up and dropped his satchel in the empty chair. He looked at the seated men, then the two women standing behind Wallace Sikes and Colonel John Paul Jenkins.

"Evening, madam," he said to Amanda Sikes, then turned to Flora Belmont, tipping his hat to her. "How's my betrothed? I certainly didn't expect to find you here, darling."

Flora Belmont offered him a sickly smile. "I came to bring you luck." She stepped from behind the colonel and walked around the table to the baron, taking his arm in hers.

The baron twisted to kiss her, but she turned her head quickly and his lips brushed against her cheek. "Less than two days until we marry, darling," the baron offered.

"I can't wait for the moment," she answered flatly.

The baron turned from her to the men seated before him. Sammy could see the scowls of each, Joe Loper excepted.

"Baron," Joe Loper said, picking up a deck of cards, "I hope you don't mind me inviting a few of your friends to play with us. I figured it might make things more interesting."

The baron nodded at Wallace Sikes, who responded with a venomous glare. "How do you like the Southern Hotel? You and Amanda doing well, are you?"

Growling his disgust, Sikes pushed back his chair, but Amanda shook her head and placed a soothing hand on his shoulder before he could arise to challenge Paget.

"And Zach Fenster," the baron said, shifting his attention to the next man at the table, "I'm surprised to find you in a place of this low reputation. How's your lovely wife?"

"Rather inattentive," the merchant shot back.

"Unfortunate indeed, governor, a woman of her raw beauty. Maybe you need a miracle. The reverend there can provide you one." The baron patted Flora Belmont's hand as he spoke. "He has, after all, agreed to marry us, come Wednesday."

The Reverend Tuck scowled beside Zach Fenster. "You forget I've withdrawn my offer. Nobody makes a mockery out of Gawd's work. Come Judgment Day, you'll pay."

"Not as much as you will pay for your fraud, Reverend."

"Gentlemen, gentlemen," interjected Joe Loper, "this should be a friendly game."

The baron tipped his bowler to Loper.

"My apologies," he answered, then nodded at Jake Ellis and the colonel.

The colonel answered with a grunt, but Ellis cut straight to the quick.

"Are we gonna play cards or jabber like women at a quilting bee?" Ellis grumbled.

"We ain't doing nothing, 'til the baron takes a seat," interjected Wallace Sikes.

The baron smiled around the table. "Friendly game?" He picked up his satchel and slid into his chair, placing his English club bag in his lap and leaning his cane up against the side of the table. Unlatching the satchel, he pulled out a bundle of British bills. "These are pound notes, worth about five Yankee dollars apiece."

"You got any American money?" challenged the colonel.

Cocking his head, the baron nodded toward Flora Belmont, who stood over his right shoulder. "Thanks to her dowry, I have more than a thousand Yankee dollars."

The colonel's face clouded and he shook his head. "Let's play with that first," he scowled.

As the baron settled into his chair, the crowd began to tighten the circle around the table. Sammy Collins inched toward the baron until he stood over his left shoulder. "Good luck," Sammy whispered.

"Thanks, lad," the baron replied. "Don't linger here. You've a big day tomorrow."

"Yes, sir," Sammy answered, looking from the baron to Flora Belmont beside him. Her scowl would have curdled granite.

Joe Loper began to shuffle a deck of cards, but before he announced the game, the baron picked up his cane and tapped its gold head on the table. The gambler looked up from his cards.

"Governor, I'd feel a lot safer if we started with a new deck, one you hadn't had a chance to work."

For a moment, Joe Loper just stared at the baron, then he licked his lips. "Sims," yelled Loper, "bring me a fresh deck. And when you come, bring me a bottle of your best stuff and jiggers all around."

Burley grunted from behind the bar and in a moment made his way through the crowd, approaching the table with a tray held over his head. He squeezed in beside Loper and placed the tray on the table. He tossed a fresh deck of cards in front of the gambler, then unloaded a new bottle of whiskey and the empty jiggers.

Loper gathered up the used deck and tossed it on the now empty tray. "The baron doesn't trust me, Burley, but to show him there's no hard feelings, I want drinks all around."

Loper reached into his pocket and flipped a twenty-dollar gold piece onto the tray. "That's for the first bottle and any more we need before the night's over." Loper picked up the bottle and turned it so everyone around the table could see the "S.O.B" brand. "In your honor, Baron," Loper said and everyone laughed, including the baron himself. Loper handed the bottle to Sims.

The saloon keeper took it, worked the wax seal off the top, then clamped the cork between his teeth. Pulling on the bottle, Sims jerked the cork loose.

Loper broke the seal on the new deck and pulled the cards free. The baron watched intently, his eyes never leaving the cards as Loper manipulated them between his fingers.

"You care to inspect the deck yourself, Baron?" Loper asked, holding half in each hand and offering the cards to the Englishman.

The baron shook his head. "Not with a fresh deck."

Loper grinned and resumed mixing the cards, his eyes never leaving the baron's, even when Burley Sims began to pour shots of whiskey in the jiggers.

Still standing beside the baron, Sammy

Collins could feel Loper's cold stare and he shifted on his feet uncomfortably. He was scared what might happen to himself and even more scared what might happen to the baron before the night was over. His hand trembled, more so when Flora Belmont pushed her way between him and the baron. Sammy backed away from the table and watched Burley Sims fill the last jigger of whiskey. Sims placed one in front of Joe Loper, then went around the table, leaving another by each player.

Taking his jigger between his nimble fingers, Joe Loper held it up to the kerosene light and admired its amber contents. "Gentlemen," he said as the others lifted their jiggers, "good luck."

The baron hesitated, then raised his glass. "May the best Englishman win."

Reverend Tuck said something unholy. Wallace Sikes grumbled something indecipherable. The colonel snarled. Zach Fenster drank the liquor like bad medicine. Jake Ellis downed the whiskey and glared at the baron.

The baron tossed his drink down his throat, then held the empty jigger up to the lamp. "Ahhhh," he nodded at Loper, "this is better liquor than I've had since England. Another?"

Loper grinned widely. "With pleasure." He picked up the bottle himself and stretched across the table for the baron's proffered glass. With a flick of the gambler's wrist, another shot of whiskey filled the baron's jigger.

Retracting his arm, the baron looked from Loper to the liquor. He smiled and downed this second jigger quickly. "Excellent," he said, plopping the glass down on the table.

"Sims," Loper called, "bring another bottle of 'S.O.B.' for the Englishman so he'll have his own."

"Yes, sir," Sims answered, his lips cracking into a wide smile. "Only the best for the Englishman."

Quickly, Sims returned, uncorking the bottle as he approached the table. The Englishman jerked the bottle from his hand, offering it to the others around the table. Wallace Sikes eased his jigger closer to the Englishman, then pulled it back at the sound of Loper's voice.

"Let the Englishman have his own bottle, Wallace. You can take another shot of mine," the gambler instructed.

"Thank you," the baron said, then put the whiskey bottle to his lips and drew a deep swig from its contents. "Now," he said, "I'm ready to play cards."

Sammy Collins covered his eyes for a moment. This game wouldn't last through the night if the baron kept kissing the bottle like that. Didn't the baron understand what was going on? Sure, Loper would buy the baron a bottle of his own because the more liquor the Englishman swallowed, the more his poker-playing senses would fade. It was an old trick to get a man drunk and then take his money. Sammy could only shake his head. The baron was doomed. Sammy felt helpless to stop Paget's approaching demise.

And Flora Belmont! She stood behind the baron, massaging his shoulders and his neck. Occasionally, she would look away from the table and Sammy could see her profile. There was no affection in her face, not for the baron. She was a rattler ready to strike. How could Sammy make the baron understand? He couldn't! He just prayed the baron would survive the night.

Joe Loper picked up the cards again, mixing them. "Five card draw, jacks or better to open. You understand that, Baron?"

"Indeed," the baron shot back. "The Prince of Wales taught me to play so I've a good eye for the game because the prince cheats."

"None of us cheat," answered the reverend.

"Speak for yourself, Reverend," Loper said, drawing nervous laughs from around the table. Loper instructed everyone to ante five dollars, then began to deal the cards. The baron picked up his hand and Flora Belmont bent closer to him. The baron held his hand to his chest and fanned the cards slightly. Flora Belmont leaned even closer yet, all the time massaging the baron's neck.

Flora Belmont was trying to see the baron's hand. Sammy knew it as sure as he was standing in the Bee Hive. Wasn't anybody other than himself on the baron's side?

The baron, though, shielded his cards from Flora. The pot was upped a modest five dollars and everybody stayed in. They were feeling one another out. Each discarded a pair or a trio of cards except the baron, who discarded a single card. The pot was raised another five dollars and everyone stayed in, then showed their hands. A pair of kings for the colonel. Threes and nines for Jake Ellis. Three sevens for Zach Fenster. Queens and tens for Wallace Sikes. A full house of jacks and aces for the reverend. Twos and kings for Joe Loper. When the baron put down his hand, he exposed a single ace and a bunch of junk, nothing that made sense for a man who had taken but one card on the draw. Sammy gritted his teeth. The Prince of Wales must be a poor teacher at poker.

The pots started small and stayed small for the half hour that Sammy watched. The pace was so slow, the pots so small that Joe Loper, seemingly bored, pulled a silver inlaid pipe from his pocket and lit up, his head soon wreathed in blue smoke. When it was time to go, Sammy slipped by Flora Belmont, who tried to nudge him aside. He watched the baron lose another hand, then said, "Good night and good luck! See you in the morning."

"Thanks, lad, don't you be worrying," the baron said without taking his eyes off Loper as the gambler mixed the cards again. "It's best to start out with bad luck, lad, so when your luck changes, it changes for the better."

It would take more than luck to improve the baron's chances, Sammy feared. Flora Belmont nudged him again. Sammy scowled at her, then turned and retreated through the crowd and out the door.

Outside the air was cool and fresh, a change from the smoke and odors of the Bee Hive. He walked leisurely down the street, which was unusually quiet tonight with so many of the rowdy men at the Bee Hive waiting for the baron to be plucked.

As he neared the Planter's House, he paused to study the porch in case Uncle Moses was out smoking his cigar. He saw no one outside so he plowed ahead confidently, then froze in his tracks. Someone was climbing out of the baron's room, holding a gunnysack. The dark figure hopped to the ground and stood up, looking all around. Sammy stood motionless, though his heart was pounding. The shadowy figure turned away from Sammy, but in that brief instant before the burglar scurried away Sammy thought he recognized his profile. Sammy caught his breath. One-Eyed Charlie Gatliff!

The burglar ran around behind the hotel and Sammy dashed for the porch, wishing Uncle Moses were there. Sammy was terrorized by the thought that Gatliff might be in back, waiting for him in his lean-to. He would have to face that danger in a minute, but for now he had to check the baron's room, see what had been stolen. Sammy bounded up the porch and through the hotel door. He ran past Aunt and Uncle Moses in the front parlor and toward the baron's room.

"Sammy, Sammy Collins," scolded Aunt

Moses, "come back here."

"I got to check on something for the baron," he yelled as he flung open the baron's door. He ran to the lamp and lit it. As the flame took hold and cast a ball of light about the room, Sammy let his eyes adjust. He looked around, first spotting the open trunk with clothes scattered about. Nothing seemed to be missing or out of place except the rooster's cage. Then it struck him. The room was unusually quiet! The cage was empty! And, the rooster was gone!

But why the rooster? What would Gatliff want with a rooster? A reason came to his mind and Sammy grabbed at his throat. Without the rooster to sound an alarm, Gatliff would be able to slip into the room and kill the baron during the night if the gamblers didn't kill him at the saloon first. Sammy blew out the light and retreated back into the hallway, quietly closing the baron's door.

Turning toward the parlor, he realized Aunt Moses was standing at the end of the hall, staring at him with her arms crossed over her abundant chest. As Sammy marched toward her, she shook her head. When he approached her, she sniffed then wrinkled her nose. "You smell like you've

378

been in a saloon with all that cigar smoke."

Sammy shrugged.

Aunt Moses shook her head. "That baron's been a bad influence on you, Sammy Collins. You've grown lazy, but from what I hear, he'll get his due tonight and there won't be anyone sorry when he leaves this town broke."

Sammy lifted a defiant chin. "What'd he do to you, other than help fill this place with folks, make you some money?"

Aunt Moses shook her finger at Sammy. "Don't you sass me like that, boy. You remember that the Good Book says 'Pride goeth before destruction and a haughty spirit before a fall.' The baron's about to fall. I don't want you around him anymore. He's a bad influence on you, Sammy Collins."

Sammy had no answer because he no longer cared. Come morning he would be on the stage away from Fort Griffin and away from Aunt Moses. Forever! He frowned and brushed past Aunt Moses.

"You answer me, boy." Aunt Moses called in disgust.

Sammy burst out the front door and onto the porch, then ran around the side of the hotel to his lean-to. Cautiously, he entered, lighting a candle, holding his breath until

379

he confirmed the room was vacant. He let out his breath slowly, relieved. He smiled to himself with the thought that tomorrow he would leave Fort Griffin. Unless something happened to the baron tonight!

The first time Marshal Gil Hanson saw the card game, he was convinced it was the oddest poker match ever played. Hanson knew it was rigged, but it was taking so long for them to pull the trap on the baron. Hanson couldn't quite figure Loper's plan or why he took on partners. A gambler with Loper's skill didn't need partners. It was evident to everyone but the baron that Loper was cheating. With every deal, he would put his silver-inlaid pipe down on the table near the deck. Then as he dealt cards, he would use the shiny patches on the pipe as reflectors to see what everyone was getting.

Hanson didn't have time, though, to figure it all out. He had rounds to make, and he preferred getting a few minutes of shuteye during the night to help him stay alert. Even so, he checked in on the poker game once an hour until midnight. By then, only the Reverend Tuck had gone broke, though he kept his place at the table. In most games, losers left mad, yet there sat the reverend watching the game as if he still had money on it. Something was definitely in the wind. By Hanson's third visit, Flora Belmont had given up trying to read the baron's cards and had taken a seat by, of all people, the colonel — or was it the former colonel, the way rumors were flying?

At Hanson's midnight visit, Wallace Sikes made a grab for the Englishman's whiskey bottle, but the baron snatched it from his hand and downed a slug of the liquor himself, then scowled at Sikes. Hanson thought Sikes' move had been made to distract the baron from Loper's dealing so he stood through the next hand, but was surprised that the baron actually won a pot of a hundred dollars. Hanson couldn't figure it, and he gave up trying. He pushed his way back out of the Bee Hive and made the rounds of Fort Griffin. As long as the card game lasted, things would be quiet in Hide Town. Reaching his office, Hanson went inside and found his cot in the darkness as he had a hundred times before. Dropping his hat in the adjacent chair, he collapsed on his bed.

He dozed off quickly and slept peacefully until about three o'clock. Arising by habit, he picked up his hat and ambled out into the dark street, shaking his head of the muddle in his brain. He started for the Bee

Hive, figuring that the game was likely over and that the baron had lost his money by now. Though the crowd had thinned out considerably, the game was still going and not a man who started the game had left the table, though Zach Fenster and Wallace Sikes had been wiped out of cash like the Reverend G.W. Tuck. Hanson walked around the table, drawing worried glances from Amanda Sikes and Flora Belmont.

Between hands, the baron winked at Hanson. Picking up his bottle of S.O.B. whiskey, the baron lifted it in the marshal's direction. "Morning, constable," he mumbled, then took a swig of liquor. He slammed the bottle on the table, drawing glares from every man seated with him. Then he picked up his satchel of money from his lap and held it by its maroon handle over the table. "These ruffians thought they would have my fortune by now. Indeed, they don't." He dropped the satchel on the table.

"Get it off," Loper ordered, nodding at the satchel. "We need to see your cards to make sure you're not culling them."

The baron lifted his chin and nodded slowly at the marshal. "They fear I might outsmart them, constable."

Hanson shrugged. He didn't figure the baron would last much longer. His speech was spotty and his movements exaggerated from too much liquor.

The baron picked up his satchel and dropped it in his lap.

Hanson moved on around the table as Loper began to deal.

"Shouldn't you stay, constable," the baron said, "to make sure they don't cheat me? Or, that I don't cheat them?" The baron laughed, drawing more scowls from around the table.

Hanson could only shake his head. He didn't like the baron's chances of finishing this game ahead or alive. "Good luck, Baron." Hanson strode past the remaining observers.

Walking back to his office, Hanson couldn't figure why Loper was carrying the baron so long. It was a crooked card game, a swindle from the beginning, but why so long to consummate? Something was definitely odd, though, and when Hanson returned to his cot, he couldn't doze off for trying to figure out the swindle at the Bee Hive.

A little before six o'clock, when the eastern horizon was pushing away the blanket of darkness, Hanson got up and stretched his aching muscles, then grabbed his hat and pushed his way outside. He headed down

Griffin Avenue for the Bee Hive, passing the Bain and Company stage office, which would be opening shortly for any passengers catching the seven o'clock stage for Jacksboro. Hearing a scraping noise on the plank walk, Hanson glanced that direction and made out someone hunched over a trunk, shoving it onto the roughhewn planks. The marshal walked that direction to check things out.

"Morning," Hanson said, and the figure froze wordlessly. "Who is it? This is Marshal Hanson."

Meekly the figure answered. "Sammy Collins."

The marshal walked toward Sammy. "Who's leaving town? It wouldn't be the baron, would it?"

Sammy lowered his head. "I promised not to tell anyone."

Hanson nodded. "It is the baron, then, isn't it?"

Sammy stood mute.

Now it began to fit in place for Hanson. "Okay, Sammy, no names, but answer me one question. Will you?"

Collins nodded.

"How many are leaving on the stage?"

For most of a minute, Sammy stood shuffling his feet on the plank walk.

384

"No names, Sammy, just the number of passages you are buying."

"Two," Sammy whispered.

Hanson nodded. "And you're buying them so no one will know they are leaving, right, Sammy?"

"Yes, sir," Collins whispered.

"I won't tell a soul, Sammy. The baron is paid up at the hotel, isn't he?"

"Yes, sir," Sammy replied.

"Then your secret's good with me."

"Thanks, sir," Sammy replied, then finished dragging the trunk to the door of the stage office. Sammy climbed on the trunk, propping his elbows on his knees and resting his head in his hands.

Hanson moved on down the street, fighting the temptation to go into the Bee Hive, just yet. He wanted to wait until a quarter of seven when he expected the scam to be pulled. Hanson marched to the end of the street, then back around the Bee Hive and past the Planter's House all the way to the foot of Government Hill. As he started back for the Bee Hive, the sun was just peeking over the horizon, a bank of eastern clouds appearing blood red in its fresh light.

Taking deep breaths of fresh morning air outside the saloon, Hanson patted the revolver on his hip, then strode inside. The crowd was gone now except for a half dozen bleary-eyed men watching from adjacent tables. All the original poker players still sat at the table, but the only ones with money before them were Loper, the baron, and Jake Ellis, the hide buyer.

Ellis licked his lips like a wolf smelling blood. Loper sat clear-eyed and calculating across the table from the baron. Behind the table, the saloon owner Burley Sims was seated on the bar, satisfied with a great night of business and with knowledge of what was about to happen.

Everyone seemed to know except the baron. His head kept bobbing like he was about to pass out or fall asleep and his speech was slurred. Still, he had been holding his own, his winnings freely mixed with the pound notes scattered in front of him. His bowler hat was askance on his head and his hair poked out from under it like straw from a scarecrow. His swallow-tailed coat was unbuttoned, revealing the butt of the peashooter he kept under his arm. He and Jake Ellis contested a pot, which the baron won with a full house over the hide buyer's two pair. The baron laughed and reached for the money, his hands trembling as he pulled his winnings from the middle of the table. As he did, he saw the marshal.

"Un-til nowww," he slurred, "theeese fellas haven't beat-ten me, con-sta-consta-bull. Us English-mens can poke player, err, play poker." The baron blinked his watery eyes and stared at the cards as Loper began to mix them for another hand. "May-may-be I shou-should be quit-quitting," he mumbled. "You-you can't bea-beat me."

"Whatever you think," answered Loper and every gambler around the table turned with gaping mouths to the dealer. Loper winked. "Maybe one more hand, Baron? Think you can last one more hand?"

The baron shook his head vigorously, then nodded slowly, confidently. "I ca-can bea-beat you-you onct mo-more."

"Okay, then, Baron. You mind if I call for a fresh deck, these being awfully dog-eared and somebody might know their markings?"

The baron shrugged. "The-the Prin-prince of Wal-whales-wales doesn't ca-call fo-for a ne-new dec-deck." The baron began to stack his winnings and determine his ante.

"Burley Sims," yelled Loper, "bring me fresh cards."

"Yes, sir," yelled Sims exuberantly as he hopped off the bar and scurried around behind it for Loper's marked deck.

The baron picked up his liquor bottle and

tipped it to his lips, his head falling back until the bottle was perpendicular and empty. Putting the bottle down on the table, he knocked it over as he wiped his lips. He grinned sheepishly at his clumsiness and was greeted by wolf-like stares from around the table.

Sims tossed the fresh deck to Loper and grabbed the loose cards at Loper's elbow.

Hanson could only shake his head. Here came the swindle! When Loper began to mix the cards, the marshal studied the gambler's hands, certain Loper was doing false cuts and shuffles. The deck was rigged and when Loper was through mixing the cards, they would be in exactly the order they had been in when he had opened the pack. The winner of this hand was already determined.

Loper pushed the cards to the baron. "Care to cut?"

The Englishman responded with an exaggerated nod, then broke the deck in half. Loper picked up the two halves and put them back in the same order.

"What do you say we ante a $1,000 this time, Baron?" Loper asked.

The baron shrugged, then answered with another exaggerated nod. He tried to count out the money, mixing American dollars with English pounds, but the overturned liquor bottle kept getting in his way.

Hanson stepped beside the Englishman and picked up the baron's empty bottle. Joe Loper's eyes went wide, the first time the gambler had revealed any emotion to the marshal. Hanson lifted the lip of the bottle to his nose.

Loper's face seemed to pale.

Hanson sniffed. Just as he had expected. Like the deck of cards, the bottle of liquor the baron had been suckling all night was a ringer. Instead of whiskey, it smelled like weak coffee. Hanson smiled knowingly at Loper.

"A thousand dollars," Loper repeated, staring at Hanson.

The baron grew exasperated with trying to count his money and just put a handful in the middle of the table. Ellis added his money in a neat stack, then Loper put in a thousand of his own.

Hanson sat the bottle up on the table and backed away from the baron, nodding at Loper. "Smells like good whiskey."

The color seemed to return to Loper's cheeks. Quickly, he dealt five cards to Ellis, the baron, and himself.

Outside, Hanson heard the rattle and creak of the morning stage down the street.

Shorty DeLong was handling the reins today so the stage wouldn't tarry past seven. Hanson pulled his pocket watch out of his pants and unsnapped the cover. It was seven until seven. He held the watch in his palm while Ellis, the baron, and Loper, picked up their hands and studied their cards.

Ellis grinned broadly. "I'll up the pot $5,000," he announced.

The baron hesitated, folding his cards together like he was going to throw in. His head bobbed with indecision before he pushed out another pile of money that seemed to be well over $5,000.

Loper matched the ante, but virtually depleted his winnings. The room was so quiet that Hanson could hear the tick of his watch. Six minutes to seven.

"I'll take two," Ellis said and Loper passed him a pair.

Hanson figured Ellis was holding three of a kind and would draw into four of a kind.

The baron paused a moment, then discarded three cards and held up three fingers for their replacements.

Loper tossed three cards over the pot to the baron, then announced he was taking three cards for himself.

Hanson looked at his watch. Five minutes to seven.

Ellis studied his cards, but could not conceal his excitement, though the baron seemed not to notice. "I'll raise $15,000," he said, his voice quivering with anticipation.

The baron shook his head from side to side, studying his cards. "I-I'm in and raising," he stuttered, pushing all his money to the center of the table, then jerking his satchel from his lap and putting it atop the pot like a crown.

Loper threw his cards down. "You boys are too rich for me."

Ellis shoved all his winnings in the middle of the table. "That should cover everything you bet."

Four minutes to seven read Hanson's watch.

Ellis laughed, then slapped his cards down on the table. "Four kings with an ace," he announced triumphantly. Laughing, he reached for the baron's satchel and all the money.

The baron seemed befuddled for a moment, then slowly turned over his cards. "Not so fast, governor" he said, his enunciation suddenly perfect. The baron revealed a jack-high straight flush. "A straight flush beats four of a kind, you jackass."

The laughter caught like a boulder in

Ellis's throat. "What the hell? We've been double-crossed." Ellis looked from the baron to Loper. "You son of a bitch," he yelled. Wallace Sikes shoved his wife from his lap and reached for his pistol until he saw the revolver in the hand of the baron at his side.

"You sons a bitches," yelled the Reverend Tuck.

Zach Fenster turned pale. "They cheated us, Marshal?"

Hanson shrugged. "I saw the baron win a big pot. I didn't see any cheating."

Three minutes to seven.

The colonel clenched his teeth and tightened his grip on Flora Belmont's hand.

Flora nodded in admiration. "Well done, you bastards."

"Thank you, ma'am," answered the baron, "I guess you realize we won't be getting married tomorrow after all."

She nodded again. "We wouldn't have stayed married long."

"I thought not," answered the baron, who turned to Loper. "If you'll gather our money, brother, we've a stage to catch."

"Brother?" gasped Ellis. "You two were in this all along?"

Loper reached over the table and snapped open the satchel, then began to rake the money quickly inside. "Yep, we're kin."

From down the street, Hanson heard the call for passengers for the imminent departure of the Jacksboro stage.

Two minutes to seven.

Loper finished scooping up the money and rounded the table. He nodded at the marshal as he ran past. "You need to protect Fort Griffin from folks like us." Loper laughed, then drew his gun. "Just in case anyone tries to stop us."

Hanson shook his head. "These folks got what they deserved."

"So long, governors," said the baron as he backed out the saloon door with his brother. "The luckiest Englishman won after all."

Hanson checked his watch. One minute to seven.

CHAPTER 16

Shorty DeLong climbed into the driver's seat. Sammy Collins looked down the street at the Bee Hive. No sign of the baron. Shorty tugged on his gloves and unwrapped the reins from the brake lever.

"Wait a minute, you've got two more passengers," Sammy pleaded.

"Not unless they get here by seven o'clock!" Shorty spat a muddy stream of tobacco juice at Sammy's feet and released the brake lever.

His heart pounding, Sammy ran to the front of the team and grabbed the halter of the lead horse. The animal shied away, rising on his hind legs as far as the harness would allow.

"Leave the team alone, kid," Shorty yelled angrily.

Sammy held on for a moment, then heard a commotion at the Bee Hive. Releasing the leather strap, Sammy spun around to see the baron running from the saloon. Sammy caught his breath. Something had gone wrong because Joe Loper was chasing the baron. And, the gambler held the baron's carpetbag!

"Hurry, hurry," yelled Sammy Collins, then turned to Shorty DeLong. "The baron and me, we're the passengers."

Shorty shook his head. "Who's that other fellow?"

The baron raced up, gasping for breath. "The passages, lad, were for me and my brother." The baron looked up at DeLong. "We're paid," the baron said as Loper flung open the coach door and jumped inside. The baron threw himself inside and pulled the door shut as Shorty DeLong snapped the reins. The stage lurched forward.

Stunned, Sammy watched the coach start rolling. The baron stuck his head out the coach window. "Sorry, lad!" he called.

"You lied to me!" Sammy cried as the coach rumbled down the street, the baron disappearing inside. Sammy felt bitter tears streaming down his cheeks. "You lied to me! You lied to me!" Sammy repeated as the stage neared the Bee Hive.

At the saloon, several men piled out onto the street, pelting the stage with stones and dry dung. Sammy could hear the men's curses. He shared their anger. He didn't understand what had happened, just that he had been betrayed. Damn the baron!

As Sammy watched the stage splash through the Clear Fork, he remembered he had packed his belongings and stowed them in the baron's trunk. Not only had the baron double-crossed him, the baron was stealing his few clothes and possessions. Sammy kicked at the dusty street, then turned around. He didn't think it could get any worse until he saw Alonzo Giddings leaning over the nearest hitching rack.

Alonzo laughed.

Sammy Collins swiped at his tears, embarrassed that Alonzo had seen them.

Alonzo approached Sammy. "Seems like the baron was a crook and a liar," he taunted. "And, you, Sammy Collins, were a fool."

Sammy jerked back his balled fist and clobbered Alonzo's nose.

Staggering backward, Alonzo grabbed his face and screamed.

Before Alonzo could protect himself from another blow, Sammy landed a hard punch to his gut. Alonzo doubled over. Sammy caught the bully's shoulders and shoved him down into Sammy's uplifted knee. The breath and fight went out of Alonzo as he tumbled to the ground.

Sammy dove atop him, his arms flailing at his tormentor, pummeling him with punches that matched his frustration, his disappointment. Alonzo was helpless before the onslaught. Sammy was driven by a fury unlike any he had ever known.

He didn't stop until Marshal Gil Hanson pulled him off. "Give it up, Sammy, and go home. Alonzo's needed a good beating for years, but I figure you better stop short of killing him."

Sammy rubbed his sore knuckles and marched wordlessly away, his shoulders slumped, his head hung low, his spirit even lower. Now, more than ever, he had to get out of Fort Griffin.

Ten miles out of Fort Griffin, Shorty De-Long pulled back on the reins and eased the team up. Just ahead, the trail crossed a stream he called "Cuss Word Creek" because he cursed it every time he reached it. The creek was tree-lined and rock strewn, making it impossible for the coach to take at Shorty's regular pace. Bordered by cottonwoods and big boulders, the crossing dipped to a swale where the footing was rocky and rough, but solid. While the creek offered more level sites for crossing, those places had quicksand bottoms that which could not support a stage.

Shorty DeLong approached the crest and put his foot on the brake as he started down. It was steep and the stage wheels slid into pitted ruts, then bounced over stones buried like corpses in the corrugated ground. As he descended the slope, he came under the cool shade of the huge cotton-wood trees. He bounced about on the seat, holding back on the reins and braking with his foot. As the stage reached the bottom of the slope and leveled out into the knee high stream, Shorty shook the reins and released the brake, catching a glimpse of three horses tied fifty yards downstream around a flaming campfire. As the stage started up the facing slope, the tired horses struggling, a man appeared on the trail, a bandanna covering his face and a rifle pointing at Shorty DeLong.

"Stop the stage. This is a holdup," commanded the robber.

Were it level land, Shorty would have run the man down, but this was incline and he couldn't do much but obey. He jerked back on the reins. "I ain't got a strong box."

"I'll take your passengers."

"Just two of them," Shorty replied, studying the robber. Even the bandanna could not hide the patch over the bandit's left eye.

"Have 'em get out," the robber commanded, "and no tricks. I've men in the rocks with rifles."

Warily, Shorty looked to his side and saw a rifle pointed between two rocks at him. The boulders screened all but the gunman's rifle and large sombrero.

The robber noted DeLong's gaze at the sombrero. "I've another friend with a shotgun in the trees. You best unload the passengers."

"Passengers," Shorty shouted, "get out. I've a schedule to keep."

The door swung open slowly.

"Hands up or you're dead," cried the robber.

"Do as he says, boys," Shorty warned.

The baron slid out first, satchel in hand, then Joe Loper.

"Well, I'll be damned if it ain't Joe Loper and that damned Englishman," laughed the robber. "Driver, your passengers are staying with me. Do they have a trunk in the boot?"

"Yep," nodded DeLong.

"Then unload it, and you can be on your way."

Shorty pointed at Loper and the baron. "What about them?"

The robber laughed again. "Unless you're

taking this stage to hell, they'll be following a different road away from here." The robber shook the gun at Shorty's face.

Shorty gulped. "Sorry, boys." Quickly he tied the reins over the brake lever, scrambled from the driver's seat and scurried to the rear of the stage, unfastening the tarp over the boot.

"Help the driver, Loper," the robber commanded, waving the gun at the gambler. "I won't shoot you in the back. For now!" He laughed.

Shorty jerked the trunk from the boot and dropped it on the trail. Loper and the baron grabbed a handle at the end of the trunk and moved it away from the stage.

"And Baron, don't let go of the carpetbag because I need the money."

Shorty inched back toward the front of the stage.

The robber waved his pistol at Shorty. "Get up there and get going unless you want to join them on their trip to hell."

Shorty scrambled atop the stage, unwrapped the reins from the brake lever and nodded at the masked man. Shorty looked downstream at the three tethered horses, a yellow dun catching his eye because of the live rooster bound and hanging from its saddle horn.

"Boys," said the robber, waving his pistol at his victims, "carry your trunk to my fire. There's a shovel there you can use to start digging your graves. This is where we bury the baron." The robber laughed.

Shorty DeLong released the brake lever and slapped the reins. "Giddyup," he yelled, then whistled. The team struggled forward, then cleared the top of the incline. No sooner was he out of sight of the creek bed than Shorty heard two shots explode in the draw. Shorty let out a slow breath. He sure hated to lose a couple passengers like that, but at least he hadn't lost more time than could be made up with an empty coach. Shorty hollered and urged the team on. If he met someone heading for Fort Griffin, he'd send word back of the holdup and the unfortunate demise of the baron.

Marshal Gil Hanson felt a gnawing in his gut that told him it was about time for lunch at the Bee Hive. If he could've eaten curses, the marshal would have had a full stomach for all the epithets Flora Belmont, Zach Fenster, Jake Ellis, Wallace and Amanda Sikes, and even the Reverend Tuck himself had called him for not stopping Loper and the baron this morning. Maybe he should have, but Hanson figured they had gotten tangled in their own trap.

Hanson picked up his hat and strode outside. Maybe Fort Griffin would settle down now that the baron was gone. All the other swindlers would be leaving soon, though Jake Ellis and Zach Fenster would remain, of course. Even they deserved what they got, Ellis for not paying fair prices on buffalo hides and Fenster for overcharging on everything from soap to gunpowder. As Hanson turned down the street toward the Bee Hive, he heard a commotion at the creek.

A solitary rider splashed water at the crossing, flailing the end of his reins against the horse's lunging neck. "Where's the law, where's the law?" shouted the rider. A half dozen men pointed toward the marshal's office and the rider spurred his mount in Hanson's direction. The gelding was lathered and wild-eyed like the out-of-breath rider reining him up in front of Hanson.

"You the law?" he gasped.

Hanson pointed to the badge on his chest.

"I met the stage on the Jacksboro road," the cowboy gasped, then caught his breath while a crowd gathered around him. "The stage was held up. Two men taken off and killed. Driver said a one-eyed fellow and two more did it."

"Where?" Hanson asked.

"A rocky bottom creek. I came by there a couple hours later, and three men shot at me. I rode like the devil to find you."

"Obliged," Hanson answered, "I'll check it out." Hanson ran to the livery stable and saddled his mount. Damned if Gatliff didn't get the baron and Loper like he said he would. Hanson didn't have to investigate the robbery as it was out of his jurisdiction as town marshal, but he was likely the closest lawman. And, he was curious!

As he was cinching down his saddle, several men rushed into the stable. "You need a posse to go with you?"

"Nope," Hanson answered, shoving his foot in the stirrup and mounting up quickly. He didn't want to answer questions, just to get a head start on the trail before a lot of others decided to have a look for themselves. Hanson nudged his horse through the crowd and out the livery door. He turned the gelding toward Jacksboro and put the animal into a trot until he crossed the Clear Fork, then pushed his gelding into a gallop. Though he made good time, it seemed to take forever before he reached the rocky crossing. He eased up on the gelding and pulled his pistol from his holster as he started down the slope toward the creek.

About fifty yards downstream from the crossing itself, he saw the smoldering remains of a fire and two freshly turned mounds of earth in a sandy curve of the river. The breeze beneath the shade of the cottonwood trees felt cool against the marshal's sweat-drenched shirt. Hanson dismounted and tied his gelding near the water so it could drink and blow.

Hanson skirted the creek's edge looking for signs of life, but he was alone with the smoldering embers of what had been a large campfire. He toed at the embers with his boot and kicked loose a scorched leather handle. One patch of leather undamaged by the fire was maroon, the color of the handle on the baron's satchel. Digging a little deeper in the embers, the marshal uncovered a dozen or more bundles of burned paper. The paper crumbled at the touch of his boot and some of it was picked up by the breeze and carried further downstream. A couple of partially burned paper fragments reminded Hanson of the English money he had seen the baron flashing around Fort Griffin. One-Eyed Charlie Gatliff must not have wanted to steal the English notes for fear they would connect him to the baron's murder.

Hanson squatted to pick up the scorched

handle, then stood up and moved farther downstream toward the two mounds of freshly turned earth. He stepped over a dark crimson splotch upon the ground where someone had likely died. At the graves, he toed around in the newly turned dirt until he exposed the brim of a hat. Pulling the hat from the freshly turned soil, he recognized the baron's bowler, now defaced by a hole in the crown and a large, unmistakable bloodstain. He beat the hat against his thigh, shaking the caked dirt loose.

He shook his head as he studied the bowler, still sticky with blood. He could uncover the bodies, but what would be the point? A grave here would be as good as a grave back in Hide Town. Hanson looked for horse tracks and saw that Gatliff and his two compatriots had ridden into the stream to mask their escape. Hanson could have found their trail, but this was out of his jurisdiction.

"*Adios,* Baron," Hanson said. "It's a shame you and Loper didn't figure on meeting up with Charlie Gatliff again."

The marshal considered tossing the hat in the creek, but figured he ought to take it back to Fort Griffin should anyone doubt his word. He returned to his gelding and headed back for town.

His hunger was burning by the time he dismounted in front of the Bee Hive. A crowd poured out of the saloon, Burley Sims leading the charge toward him. "What about it, Marshal?" asked Sims. "You find Loper and the baron?"

Hanson tied his reins around the hitching post, then held up the baron's bowler. "Dead and buried. Both of them."

Several men in the crowd laughed, then cheered.

Jake Ellis stepped forward. "I'll give you a dollar for that hat, Marshal."

Hanson shrugged and handed it to Ellis. "Take it. I guess you already bought it with what the baron took you for."

"He lost more than I did, Marshal," Ellis replied, his face bursting with a grin. Ellis grabbed the macabre souvenir.

All day Sammy Collins had hated the baron for betraying him. With every chore he was assigned, Sammy worked out his hatred, scrubbing the dishes until he might erase the patterns baked into them, chopping wood with a vengeance, flinging the contents of the chamber pots behind the hotel rather than dumping them into the privy. He hated the baron more than Alonzo Giddings, even. The baron, or whoever he was, had pretended to be his friend and had betrayed him. That was the worst thing anybody had ever done to him.

The rage and the hate simmered until just before supper when he was washing the bread pans. That was when he heard Aunt Moses and Uncle Moses talking, then laughing.

"Serves him right," said Aunt Moses as she marched into the kitchen, wearing a smile as wide as her ample hips. "Your friend, the baron," she announced, "was killed in a stage robbery this morning. Him and that gambler fellow."

All the hate evaporated. Sammy's head, like his spirit and his anger, fell lower than a grave.

"They were common crooks, Sammy," lectured Aunt Moses, "and you shouldn't have taken to him. He was nothing more than a swindler who defrauded some fine people of their money."

Now Sammy didn't know what to think. It was harder to hate the baron now that he was no more. Maybe that was the baron's ultimate sense of betrayal. By letting himself get killed, the baron had robbed Sammy of his only recourse, his hatred.

"Let that be a lesson to you, Sammy, about the wages of sin being death," Aunt

Moses continued.

Sammy sighed and kept washing the bread pans. He couldn't take much more of this. He must run away tonight!

By supper time, the dining room was full with Sammy watching from the kitchen. Now that the baron was gone, he was relegated once again to serving the diners and foraging on leftovers for himself.

He despised the laughter of the others, all the talk about the baron getting what he had deserved. Yet, the baron was the only man who had ever insisted that Sammy sit at the table like regular folk.

The colonel and Flora Belmont were there, hanging on to one another like moss on a rock. Wallace and Amanda Sikes had joined the table this evening, Wallace Sikes smiling for the first time since his wife had slipped into the baron's room to swindle him. Everyone seemed to forgive the Reverend G.W. Tuck for his camp meeting frauds as he offered thanks. Zach Fenster and his wife sat side by side. And, Aunt Moses and Uncle Moses sat at their respective ends of the table, enjoying the conversation that no longer centered on the baron and royalty.

Jake Ellis had the biggest smile of all and after he finished downing his supper, he stood up. "Ladies and gentlemen," he said,

"I have a surprise to show you, if you'll excuse me a moment."

The diners tittered as he moved quickly to the parlor and returned, carrying a bottle of whiskey in his left hand and hiding his right hand behind his back.

"I know," Ellis announced, "that some of you aren't drinkers, but this is a good whiskey, the kind that is sipped by the finest royalty of England."

Everyone laughed, except Sammy.

"But Reverend and Uncle and Aunt Moses, I think you will find in my right hand the reason for celebration." Ellis gave the bottle of wine to Uncle Moses, then he pulled his hand from behind his back.

Sammy felt his lips tremble as he recognized the baron's bowler.

"The hat," announced Ellis, "of the late Baron Jerome Manchester Paget, the blood still fresh upon it." Ellis poked his finger through the bullet hole in the crown and wriggled it at the table. "Let's toast the baron, may he burn in hell, and let's toast Charlie Gatliff for sending him there, even if the one-eyed bastard got all our money from the baron."

Everyone laughed as Jake Ellis passed the hat to Zach Fenster. Sammy stared blankly at the blood-stained bowler, then turned away as if he might vomit.

"Glasses, Sammy, bring us glasses for whiskey," called Aunt Moses."

Sammy gritted his teeth and fetched glasses all around. Damn them all. His stomach churned when he passed the baron's derby in the colonel's hand.

He placed the final glass before Uncle Moses then scurried into the kitchen. He had lost his appetite. To keep his mind off the hat, he heated water to do dishes and banged pots and pans to drown out the celebration in the next room. That worked until Aunt Moses called him down for making too much noise. Then he worked in dejected silence, wishing there were someone in the world he could trust.

It seemed to take all night before everyone cleared out of the dining room and to the porch where the men smoked their cigars and the women enjoyed the cool night air. Sammy was glad Aunt Moses went with them. He had a stack of dishes to do, but he also had the dining room and the kitchen to himself now. There was too little food left to make a meal, but that was okay. His appetite had disappeared since he saw the baron's bloody bowler. After an hour of dishes, he carried the scraps out behind the outhouse and dumped them, knowing one of the stray pigs would eat them during the night. He was glad for the darkness because it could hide his emotions. He ran back into the kitchen and washed the scrap pan. That done, he had only to dump the dishwater outside, but he was tired and figured he would leave something for Aunt Moses to complain about.

He walked outside, stretched, and headed for his lean-to. He eased open the door and slipped inside. Just as he started to grab a candle and match, he heard a noise. He froze, then realized he was not alone. Before he could move, he felt an arm wrap around his chest. Before he could scream, he felt a gloved hand cover his mouth.

"Listen to me, kid, and listen good," came a familiar whisper.

It was One-Eyed Charlie Gatliff. Sammy felt his knees go weak. The man who had killed the baron had now come for him.

"London Bridge is falling down," Gatliff whispered. "Do you understand?"

It was the baron's message! Sammy didn't know what to think.

"London Bridge is falling down," Gatliff repeated. "Do you understand?"

Sammy nodded.

"I've a horse outside for you," Gatliff said. "We're going for a ride. You will be safe as long as we can get away from here without being seen. I'm gonna let go, Sammy, but don't you call for help or run away."

Sammy nodded again.

Gatliff released his hold.

Sammy took a deep breath.

"Let's get out of here, quick," Gatliff whispered. He stepped to the door, opened it slowly. He poked his head out and looked around. "Okay," he instructed, "follow me."

Sammy did as he was told, feeling like a prisoner breaking out of jail. They ran around the hotel and then toward the giant pecan tree, jumping a mongrel dog that took to barking, then howling. Up ahead, Sammy heard two horses nickering and stamping.

Gatliff boosted Sammy in the saddle, then untied the reins and handed them to him. After unknotting his own reins, Gatliff climbed in the saddle. "Go at an easy pace around town," he whispered. "Don't talk until Fort Griffin is out of sight, you hear?"

"Yes, sir," Sammy managed as he tried to sort things out. How did the man who killed the baron know the baron's coded message. "Is the baron okay?"

"No talking, just ride, kid," Gatliff answered.

As they rode away, Sammy could hear Aunt Moses calling out the kitchen door.

"Sammy, Sammy Collins, you forgot to dump the dishwater."

Gatliff rode in silence and Sammy kept looking over his back until the lights of Fort Griffin disappeared. The night was still and sound seemed to carry forever. When Sammy could wait no longer, he spoke. "Is the baron okay?"

"Let's ride," Gatliff said, pushing his mount into a lope.

They rode wordlessly for maybe two hours, then approached a camp where Sammy could see a flickering fire. Drawing nearer, Sammy saw two men reclining on bedrolls. One Sammy recognized as Joe Loper, but the other's face was covered with a sombrero. In camp, Gatliff took Sammy's reins as the youth jumped out of the saddle.

"Is that you, Baron?" he said to the sombrero.

The hat lifted slowly and Sammy was disappointed. Whoever this was, he lacked the baron's close-trimmed beard. Then the man spoke. "Lad, I told you I wouldn't leave Fort Griffin without you."

It was the baron! He had shaved.

Sammy was stunned. He didn't know what to say. His dreams had been answered, but he didn't know how. He was so excited he ran and hugged the baron, then felt embarrassed by what he had done. "But how? I don't understand? Who are these people?" He pointed to Loper and Gatliff.

The baron patted a place on his bedroll. "Take a seat and I'll explain. Loper here is my brother and Gatliff is our father. Of course that's not their real names. And I'm not a baron, never was."

"But your hat, the blood."

"Easy, lad, easy. Pa stopped the stage and sent it on without us. We fired two shots to make the driver think Pa had killed us. During the poker game last night, Pa stole the rooster from my room and that's where the blood came from. We left the hat in hopes someone would find it and assume our bodies were in the graves by the creek."

Sammy could only shake his head. "And the two men that stopped the stage with your pa?"

"There was no one else. Pa wedged a rifle between two rocks and placed this sombrero over it. The driver bought it."

Sammy shook his head.

"Lad, I told you all along that things weren't always what they seemed. Even the British money I came to town with, it was counterfeit and worthless. Now, though, we've got more than $25,000 for sure."

Sammy looked from Loper to Gatliff, then

realized the older man was no longer wearing an eye patch. "Your eye?"

Gatliff laughed. "Had 'em both all along. Any posse that looks for a one-eyed outlaw will have a hard time finding him now."

Still in disbelief, Sammy kept asking questions. "What about the gunfight between you and Loper? Loper shot the gun out of your hand. Didn't he?"

Loper laughed. "I fired over Pa's head."

"But I saw where the bullet struck his pistol."

Gatliff nodded. "The gun was that way before we ever came to Fort Griffin. I kept it in my saddlebags until the day of the gunfight."

"And the fistfight in front of the hotel?"

The baron rubbed his nose. "My nose still aches. Nothing was faked about it. We had to put on a good show."

Gatliff laughed. "Yeah, I just had to make sure he never knocked my eye patch askew so people wouldn't find out I had as many eyes as the rest of them."

Sammy shook his head at the baron. "But I thought you deserted me, and then I thought you were dead."

The baron put his arm around Sammy's shoulder. "I hated to do that to you, lad, but there was no other way. I kept my promise. I took a liking to you and your plight when I saw they wouldn't let you eat at the table with the other folks. That's the way it was in England with my kind."

"Then you've been to England?"

"Yes, lad," the baron said. "I spent ten years in England with my mother, who was English. She and my pa split up, me going with her and my brother with Pa. When Mother died, I returned to America and rejoined the rest of the family."

"I can't believe you're still alive."

"It's true, lad, it's true. Now, you must make a decision. You're welcome to stay with us or you can ride back to Fort Griffin."

"That's easy. I'm riding with you three. Where are we going?"

The baron leaned back on his bedroll. "We've got more than $25,000. I think the best place to put it to use is in Nevada, say, Virginia City? Nobody knows us around there."

He smiled at Sammy. "Yet."

Historical records, land-case photography and color photographs of the Old West, and the Civil War.

ABOUT THE AUTHOR

Preston Lewis is the author of more than two dozen historical, western and children's novels. A former president of Western Writers of America, Lewis has received Spur Awards from the organization for best western novel and best nonfiction article.

Now retired, Lewis began his professional career working for four Texas newspapers before moving into higher education communications and marketing at Texas Tech University and Angelo State University. He holds a B.A. in journalism from Baylor University and an M.A. in journalism from Ohio State University, where he was a Kiplinger Fellow. He subsequently earned a second M.A., this one in history, from Angelo State.

A native West Texan, Lewis lives in San Angelo with his wife, Harriet, with whom he shares a son and daughter and five grandchildren. For hobbies, he enjoys historical research, landscape photography and visits to historic sites of the Old West and the Civil War.